# REINVENTING MONA

## Jennifer Coburn

D0167688

Strapless

KENSINGTON BOOKS
www.kensingtonbooks.com

KENSINGTON BOOKS are published by

Kensington Publishing Corp.
850 Third Avenue
New York, NY 10022

ISBN 0-7582-0627-5

First Kensington Trade Paperback Printing: January 2005
10  9  8  7  6  5  4  3  2  1

Printed in the United States of America

"Hilarious! Jennifer Coburn keeps you laughing until you cry along with Prudence, a character you'll want to hang with long after this book ends. *The Wife of Reilly* is comedy at its best—a walloping, cosmopolitan chick adventure with a huge heart. Can't wait to see more from this gem of an author."

—Roz Bailey, author of *Retail Therapy*

"An outrageously entertaining novel . . . fresh, funny and wonderfully nutty, it's a promising debut from a very savvy, sensationally chic author."

—*Heartstrings*

"Move over Bridget Jones! You have just been replaced as the most neurotic woman on the planet by none other than Prudence Malone, the outrageous heroine of Jennifer Coburn's *The Wife of Reilly*. Despite her flaws (and there are many . . . many many many), it's through the writing magic and comic genius of Coburn that Prudence remains so damn likable. The premise of this book is one of the most creative and original I've ever encountered (a warped . . . *very* warped version of *The Bachelor),* and Coburn delivers it with wit, humor (lots of humor!), and style. I loved, loved, loved this book!"

—Patrick Sanchez, author of *Girlfriends* and *The Way It Is*

"From beginning to surprising end, you will find yourself laughing along with Prudence . . . most of all, you will find yourself completely and thoroughly entertained."

—*Girlposse.com*

"In her sparkling debut novel, Jennifer Coburn introduces an irresistible heroine—the ironically named Prudence—who's sure to engage both discerning chick lit fans and newcomers to the genre. Populated by a charmingly campy cast of characters and driven by a hoot of a premise, the tale unfolds in a series of laugh-out-loud scenes and a page-turner of a flashback during which we get to see just how our hapless heroine landed in her hilarious predicament in the first place. Coburn's nimble first person narrative is sprinkled with cleverly amusing similes and dead-on observations delivered in a voice so real and contemporary that reading the novel is the next best thing to a gossipy girls' night out.

—Wendy Markham, author of *Slightly Single* and *Slightly Settled*

"Catty, witty and creative, *The Wife of Reilly* is surprising and entertaining."

—*Divatribe.com*

"A totally delightful book that will have you laughing out loud."
—*The Romance Reader's Connection*

"Wonderfully malicious fun. I enjoyed every catty, conniving page."
—Robert Rodi, author of *Bitch Goddess*

# Acknowledgments

I am so fortunate to have a wonderful group of people in my life who are always willing to help me get these books into shape. First is my sharp and hilarious agent, Christopher Schelling. Kensington editorial director John Scognamiglio always has keen insights and direction that I always appreciate immensely. The keen eye of Lisa A. Davis corrected my myriad of blunders throughout the manuscript.

Reading early drafts and giving me excellent feedback (yet again!) were Deborah Shaul, Bonni Graham, Joan Isaacson and Audrey Jacobs. With Audrey and Joan, Belen Poltorak hosted a fabulous launch party for *The Wife of Reilly*. The behind-the-scenes guys at the party who helped make everything run smoothly were Greg Tate, Mark and Ray at Hummingbird Confections, Mike Poltorak, Karl Jacobs, Bob Slavik and Steve Isaacson. Thank you for the wonderful event.

During the process of writing a book, I always send out e-mails asking for insider language and possible scenarios. My friend (and Web master) Milo Shapiro consistently comes through with fun stuff. Luke Coburn provided a great passport to Missoula, Montana. Vince DeFelice gave me good sports lingo and general guy stuff, as did Matt Levy and Vince Hall (along with three cowardly guys who would rather not be mentioned as vital contributors to the Dog House columns). Vince Hall and Bob Mackey offered unthinkable amounts of tech support to promote the last book; I am eternally grateful.

Jacqueline Lowell, who I never thank enough (but am always grateful to), never fails to promote my books and take photos. Her greatest gift to me, though, was introducing me to my husband, William. Jim McElroy made the process of reviewing film option contracts a pleasure; then again, I have no doubt that were we together in a salt mine, it'd be a blast.

Thanks to the readers who wrote to me and said *The Wife of Reilly* made them laugh. (Those e-mails are more appreciated than you know!) And all of the wonderful staff people I met at bookstore signings. So many went the extra mile and personally recommended my first novel to their chick-lit readers. That made such a huge difference, and was enormously appreciated.

Most of all, my husband William was there every day, encouraging me to write—and making it possible by doing more than his fair share at home.

# Chapter 1

It was the first truly impulsive decision I'd ever made. I'm not sure I can even call it a decision because it would imply that thought or deliberation went into making this choice. It might not even qualify as a choice. It was an instinctive blurt.

Last December when Larry Fontaine told our department that the company was offering elective buyouts for engineers, my hand shot up involuntarily, epileptically. There was only one answer to this question, and it escaped from my lips without a moment of consultation with my brain. Without thought. Like a gunshot signaling the start of a race, I fired the words that changed my identity from mechanical engineer to tabula rasa.

"Would you care to hear the details of the buyout package?" Larry asked with an eyebrow pointing upward like an accent mark. I couldn't tell if he was amused or annoyed that I so quickly embraced the idea of early retirement. Not exactly a scene from the company recruitment videos, but then again, with the recession layoffs in San Diego, hiring new engineers was not going to be a priority for Larry for quite some time. Still, no one likes to think of his workplace as one an employee would leave for what may have been a compensation package of an economy-size bag of Doritos.

*It's not you, it's me,* I said silently. I've always wanted to say that in a breakup, and thought I might as soon as everyone stopped laughing at Larry's inquiry.

Larry continued. "Our goal is to identify five engineers in this department who are interested in taking a generous voluntary buyout package so we can avoid layoffs. Ms. Warren's response leads me to believe this may not be as great a challenge as some of our consultants had suggested." His use of my last name let me know without question that he was irritated with me.

He handed everyone in the department a thirty-page proposal which outlined a pay schedule, retirement bonus and an eighteen-month continuation of health and dental benefits. I flipped through the pages pretending to review every section. I didn't want to insult Larry any more than I already had, but my mind was already made up. Regardless of the offer, I would take it. Early retirement sounded a little ridiculous at my age. With just three weeks before my thirty-first birthday, it seemed more appropriate to call this buyout option a late-bloomer's second chance. Or my last chance at blooming at all.

It's funny how the timing on this worked. Just that morning, I was looking in the mirror lamenting the fact that I had absolutely no life whatsoever. I realize when people say this, they're often being dramatic. Perhaps they're having a bad day. Maybe they're a year or so behind schedule in reaching their lofty goals. Sometimes it's just a case of PMS. Not the case with me. I really and truly had no life. I would've welcomed a bad day because it would mean something happened in this otherwise currentless puddle known as the existence of Mona Warren. I would've even welcomed failure because it would mean that I actually tried something.

Last December, I really and truly had no life. No family. No boyfriend. No friends. No hobbies. No passion. No clubs. No style. No look. No skeletons in my closet. No regrets. Just a good car, a huge house, TiVo, and an unmaxable charge card—all fine trappings in Southern California, but no actual signs of life.

I'd been buying my coffee at the same place for the past six months and every morning the guy behind the counter looked at me and asked for my order as though he'd never seen me before. Every morning, I'd tell him the same thing. Iced chai latte with nonfat milk. Then he'd ask my name. I'd tell him it's Mona. And every morning it was the same routine. Even if there was absolutely no one else in the shop, he'd announce my name and look around, wondering who the iced tea could possibly be for. After all, the store was empty in his eyes. "Mona?" he'd shout. "Chai nonfat latte for Mona?" Sometimes I'd make up fake names to see if he'd notice the difference, but he never did. Even when I gave myself outrageous names like Cleopatra or Spartacus, I never seemed to register.

This is not, as one might suspect, the downside of life in the big city. I live on an island that prides itself on being a tight community. An oasis south of downtown San Diego and north of Mexico. Coronado is a posh version of Bedford Falls. Coronado people are always very sure to mention that when something bad—or even unfriendly—occurs it is "over the bridge." A puppy was abandoned—over the bridge. A homeless person begged for change—over the bridge. A sales clerk was discourteous—over the bridge. Because things like that just don't happen in Coronado. The bay and bucks act as a filter, protecting us from any disturbing realities of life.

The freckled clerk at Starbucks always shot off everyone else's name and regular coffee orders, too. Even tourists staying at the Hotel Del Coronado for a long weekend registered with him. Yet every single day, he stared blankly and asked what I wanted. Like he's never seen me before, he asked the same question: "What would you like this morning, ma'am?"

What would I like? To be seen. To be known. To matter. That, a nonfat chai latte, and a life. "Skinny iced chai for Beyoncé," he'd shout five minutes later.

So anyway, I was looking in the gold rococo bathroom mirror that morning in December, impressed only by the fact that I was a perfect sample of extraordinary plainness posing a stark contrast to the ornate frame. Quietly, I reminded myself that in three weeks I would be thirty-one years old, and I hadn't achieved a single goal that I never set for myself.

I looked at my shoulder-length brown hair, neither curly nor straight. My body was not fat, but certainly not thin. It was doughy. I checked out my face, neither strikingly ugly nor pretty. My coloring could only be described as mashed potato with sunspots littered around the edges. I sighed with disgust at the sight of my eyes, puffy with exhaustion far beyond my years. Of course, a little makeup and a hairstyle wouldn't have hurt, but primping always seemed futile. I've seen unattractive women with a face full of makeup and it looks a bit silly to me. Silly and sad, like someone trying too hard to be what she's not.

"Mona Warren," I said to myself in the ridiculously ornate mirror. "You are a mustard stain on a Sears tweed couch." Not even fancy mustard, I silently added. Though my economic status would clearly cast me as Grey Poupon, the rest of me screamed French's picnic-style mustard in the squeeze-top dispenser.

I read every piece of spam I receive because it's the only time the e-mail guy tells me I've got mail. I stared into a mirror that was purchased forty years ago by my dead grandmother, who decorated every square inch of this colossal home. She died nearly a year ago, and I've done absolutely nothing to make this house my home because these two words mean nothing to me. My. Home. If you have no idea who you really are, how do you create a home?

I always envied women in films, especially the classics. Their roles seemed so clear to them and the rest of the world. You can immediately tell what type of people they were by the way they dressed, the way they spoke, and how they carried themselves. They always seemed to have a cohesive presence, whereas I am a thousand scattered pieces that no one has bothered to put together.

Silently, I looked in the mirror and realized, at nearly thirty-one, Mona Warren was never going to be a supermodel. I wasn't even going to be asked to pose with an oven mitt for the Bed Bath & Beyond insert in the Sunday paper. The transformation from duckling to swan was never going to happen. I was never going to be the uber-babe orthopedic surgeon for our pro football team. I was never going to speak seven languages and turn down marriage proposals across the globe. I was never going to capriciously refuse roses sent to my hotel room by a bullfighter named Enrique—or even Harvey. I was never going to stand on a foggy runway deciding whether I should get in an airplane with my Nazi-fighting husband or stay with Humphrey Bogart. I would never tell a man that we'd always have Paris.

What I wasn't going to be, or wasn't going to do wouldn't have bothered me quite so much if I had any idea whatsoever who I *was* or what I *would* do.

When I elected for the early buyout in December, I still wasn't exactly sure who I was or what I would do with myself. One thing was for sure, though. I was no longer a mechanical engineer for a military defense contractor, and the world was wide open before me in a way I'd never felt before. I could do anything with my life. I could dye my hair an angry shade of green and write poetry. I live across the street from the Pacific Ocean; I could learn to swim. I could take a trip around the world. The trouble was my poetic license had been suspended long ago, I have no desire to swim, and I have already been to every continent on earth with Grammy. Abroad, I learned that I am invisible on foreign soil, too. I am universally not compelling— even in Italy where I was warned that men would pinch my butt. They pinched Grammy, who cursed at them in Italian, but never once did they go for her nubile companion with the brand-new boobs and orthodontically enhanced teeth.

The truth is that my dreams were as pedestrian as I was back then. What I wanted most was to marry the love of my life, Adam Ziegler, have his children, and spend my free time volunteering at elementary school, cheering for their Little League teams, baking for fund-raisers, hand-sewing Halloween costumes, and learning how to make ceramics. Even as I silently uttered these words, my heart sped up at the thought. I was terrified that someone might hear my terribly unrealistic fantasy and lock me away in a home for the terminally out-of-touch. I know it's not as though I wanted to redesign the space shuttle or cure cancer, but the picket fence fantasy felt that out of reach to me. Because it was.

"So what are you going to do with yourself now, Mona?" Larry asked as we sat in his sterile office. He handed me papers upon papers and asked me if I wanted to have my attorney review them. Larry persisted in his inquiry. "Do you have another job lined up?"

"Kind of," I stammered. "Not really," I corrected. "Not a job job, like this. I'm just going to, I don't know, work on myself, I guess."

Larry's phone rang and he asked if I could wait a moment. *That's my specialty,* I muttered inaudibly. I leaned back in Larry's mushy leather chair and stared out the window at the ships docked at the bay. I mentally left Larry's office and dared to imagine my life as I hoped it would look by the next Christmas season.

I am wearing a Donna Reed holiday party dress, hanging Christmas tree ornaments with twenty-some-odd friends and neighbors. My hair is rolled into neat retro styled sections, and I am softly backlit at all times, creating a dreamy halo effect. We joyfully sing "Hark! the Herald Angels Sing" in a living room crowded with community, charity, and warm mugs of eggnog. Adam, frantically elated with the spirit of the holidays, looks at everyone as though he's seeing them through new eyes, wishes them a merry Christmas, and kisses me passionately.

It's a wonderful life. Okay, it's recycled, but the point is we're happy. Jimmy Stewart, Hollywood, Christmastime happy. And that's a wonderful kind of happy.

"Sorry about the interruption." Larry's voice snapped me back to reality. "I'll tell you, this is a tough time for us." He sighed. "You're fortunate that you don't have to work, Mona. What I'd give to be forty again and have the money to retire."

*Forty?! Did he just say he thinks I'm forty?!*

"I'm thirty," slipped out defensively.

"Of course, of course," he backpedaled, though it was clear that he really did think I was ten full years my senior. "You *look* like a college kid, Mona. You seem more mature than other people your age. There's a seriousness about you."

*Lack of panache,* I silently corrected him.

"I don't know how you'd describe it, but there's earnestness about you, Mona. There's nothing frivolous about you."

*They call it boring. Insipid. Vacuous. Dry. Dull. Plain. Vanilla minus the vanilla flavor. But thanks for trying to make it sound like an attribute. Now I feel as though I should schedule an appointment with a cosmetic surgeon for both a facelift and a personality implant.*

"I meant no offense, Mona. You seem older than thirty, that's all. You were probably one of those kids they skipped in school for being so precocious. Born older, you know the type?" Larry scrambled to change the topic. "I'll tell you, the things I'd do if I were in your position. I'd grab my wife and go to Maui, open up a bar on the beach and have pig roasts and limbo contests for tourists." He laughed. "Maybe I'd go without her and really live it up."

That's what I love about my Adam. He would never laugh about leaving me on the mainland while he "lives it up." He knows what we have at home is special, and that he doesn't need to jet off without me to experience life. Plus, I think he's Jewish so pig roasts are probably out of the question.

There was so much I needed to learn about Adam before our wedding. I needed to show him how perfect we could be together. I had to win over his friends and family, possibly convert to Judaism, then get him to propose. I needed a serious action plan.

I needed a first date.

# Chapter 2

"You will absolutely, positively never believe what I just did!" I shouted into my cell phone as I pulled out of my office garage. Sunlight flooded my car as I reached the street, and the cool December air wrapped itself around my skin.

"I have a patient due to arrive in two minutes. May I call you then?" Greta asked. The first truly huge announcement I've ever had was superceded by the needs of the mentally ill.

"When are you going to call me back? I did something so unbelievably not me, I still can't believe it!" I shouted. I glanced at myself in the reflection of a convex mirror in the back of a Shell oil truck. I didn't even look like myself anymore, but this car has always given me a little zip. When Grammy died, I had no reason to get rid of her sky blue Mercedes two-seater convertible. When we used to drive together, she looked like something out of a movie from the era that boasted Technicolor. She wore a silk Kandinsky print scarf over her head and tremendous tortoise shell sunglasses as we drove up the Pacific Coast. "We are two single gals in Southern California in a hot sports car!" she'd exclaim. Every time. Without fail. This is who we were in Grammy's eyes. Two chicks on the open road. A car can do that for a person. Even I felt different in this car. If a car could transform a person, imagine what I could do with a well-engineered plan and no budget? I could completely reinvent myself. If my eighty-one-year-old grandmother with psoriasis and a heart condition could see herself as a babe simply by pulling down her convertible top, why couldn't I accessorize my life and make myself over into the ultimate after girl? Why couldn't I become the woman of Adam Ziegler's dreams? Why couldn't I shift gears and change to the wonderful life lane?

"I'd love to chat, but I've only got two minutes," Greta clipped. "Give me the abridged version."

"I quit my job," I shouted. "Meet me for lunch when you're done with your session? I have much to tell. I'm giving myself an early birthday present—a life."

Greta said, "I'm having trouble hearing you. Can you meet me for an early lunch? You sound distraught."

Distraught? Forty? I am misunderstood by the only people who bother to listen. The only one who sees me as who I really am—who I'm going to become—is the ass of a Shell oil truck. It's a start. A meager one, but a start.

I wasn't lying when I said I had no friends. There's Greta, but she only moved back to San Diego a month earlier. Greta and I met a few weeks after I moved in with Grammy, which was my junior year in high school. We were inseparable nerds, which earned us the nickname Mona and Groana. We were charged with the high crime of being "lezzies."

Grammy used her many social and political connections to enroll me in one of San Diego's most elite private schools. Most were rich kids who had either been on the wait list since gestation, or had parents who were surgeons, attorneys, and CEOs. There was one lottery kid, a fact that, once discovered, sent her social status on a downward spiral from which there was no recovery. I certainly did not let anyone know that a month earlier I was living on a commune in Montana with four other families. Or that I'd never been to a school with chandeliers and mounted animal heads on the walls. In fact, our home school desk was a kitchen table made out of an old barn door, and my parents, along with the others, taught us about calculus, chemistry, and the history of the labor movement in the United States.

As it was, my brown corduroy pants and embroidered peasant shirts made the other girls maintain a four-foot distance from me for fear my dated style might be contagious. I wasn't about to add to this misery by letting these privileged snots know where I was from, and why I suddenly showed up at their school in the middle of the year. I didn't even tell Greta until our senior year. Not that she didn't ask. Even then, her career as a therapist was taking shape.

After a few weeks at the Coronado Academy for Girls, the rumors about me started. Popular student culture cast me as a drug addict who had to live with Grammy after being kicked out of multiple rehab centers for a love affair with crystal meth.

"Hey, new girl," Greta said to me in the lunch arbor. *Great,* I thought. Now even the loser girls are going to taunt me. I shuddered. I begged Grammy to let me finish high school through correspondence courses or tutors, but she refused. Consequently, I decided that if I was forced to attend a real school, I'd try to be as invisible as possible. I never raised my hand in class. I wasn't part of any clique. Only accidentally did I ever make eye contact with my classmates. If there was an eraser for human flesh, I would've paid any price for it.

"What?" I folded my arms at Greta's call to me at eleventh grade lunch period.

"My, my, aren't we defensive?" she shot back. I couldn't tell she was trying to be friendly. "I was just gonna ask if I could sit with you, but if you're gonna have an attitude, forget it." She turned to walk away and I realized Greta was my only chance at having a friend at school.

"Greta," I shouted after her. She turned around and scrunched her mouth to one side with snide skepticism. "I'm sorry. I just thought you were going to, I don't know. I didn't think you were going to ask to have lunch. I thought you were going to say something mean."

She sat down and leaned toward me conspiratorially. "It's so easy to think that way in a hellhole like this. I mean, have you ever met a bigger group of bitches than these girls?"

I could honestly answer that I had not. The reality was that I hadn't met that many people in my sixteen years. We lived in a farmhouse with nine adults and ten kids, but other than them, I had little interaction with the outside world. We knew the folks who worked at the food co-op, and everyone who shopped at the Missoula Farmer's Market where we sold produce, hemp macramé, beaded jewelry, and wool sweaters and hats that my mother made. When I say she made them, I mean she really made them—from shearing the wool, spinning it to yarn, and knitting it as she softly sang her favorite Cyndi Lauper songs. We were eighties hippies, after all.

So, in all honesty, I could tell Greta emphatically that no, I *had* never met a bigger group of bitches than the girls at the Academy. Greta was beautiful in a natural, not-trying-at-all sort of way. Other girls in our school spent a tremendous amount of time making sure their irreverently individual appearance received high marks from our peer fashion critics. It absolutely amazed me that many girls were allowed to highlight their hair, don leather pants, and have their weak chins reconstructed. Greta threw herself togather like a girl who didn't give much thought to her looks, and yet was still stunning. She has her Japanese mother's straight black hair and thick lips, and also moss green eyes compliments of her American father, the chief of staff at Scripps Memorial Hospital. Greta always wore a blue hoodie with "La Jolla County Day Soccer" in chipped white print on the back. Her hair was always combed and tied in a low pony tail. No one could see that she was pretty because she had an unfinished, tomboy look. But there was no doubt about it, Greta was the best-looking girl at our school. Today, she maintains the same low-maintenance style with a uniform of starched white button-down tops, simple black pants, and patent leather "roach stompers," accenting the look with one of her dozens of artistic necklaces from her travels.

"So, new girl. You got a name?" shot young Greta.

"Mona." I wasn't sure if Greta was really being friendly, or if she was just taking inventory of the new, lowest level of the social totem pole. She was so blunt in her delivery. "So, what's your story, Mona? Where'd you come from? What are you in for?" Greta was the first to confront me with the rumor of my drug addiction. I kind of liked the cache of being the exiled tweeker, but then again, anything was better than the real story of my journey to Coronado, so I decided I'd be evasive with Greta and let her draw her own conclusions.

"You know, sometimes a girl needs a change of atmosphere to clear her head," I said.

"Clear her head of what?" Greta shot.

"You know, stuff."

"No, I don't know. That's why I'm asking," Greta persisted.

"I don't really want to get into it. I just thought I needed a change in scenery, and what better place than sunny Southern California?"

"You know what they're saying about you, don't you?" Greta asked. I shook my head and knit my brows, coaxing her to continue. "They say your parents kicked you out. Couldn't deal with you anymore." My heart took a five-story plunge. I hated this group of over privileged nitwits. I had heard about my supposed drug problems. I was even amused by the ludicrous rumors. But my parents kicked me out? Not amusing in the least.

I saw my mother sweeping a spider up with a sheet of newspaper and gently escorting it out the door. Once she even argued that a grape juice stain had every right to permanently reside on the blouse she spilled it on. She said there was no point in trying to wash out grape juice, so she may as well think of it as a new design. She used watercolor paints and placed petals around the misshapen purple center of her makeshift flower. Fully functional clothing would never be discarded on our Utopian commune. Ants were "redirected" to the outdoors through strategically placed slices of lemon rind. But according to the know-it-alls at the Academy, my parents kicked their own daughter out of the house.

I remembered how my father looked the last time I saw him, closing the door of the school bus and giving me a thumbs-up as if their road trip to the capitol for a nuclear disarmament rally would actually make a bit of difference. As if a few thousand hippies were going to change Ronald Reagan's mind and get him to think, "Well, what do you know, this peace-through-strength thing really *is* a bad idea. Now that you mention it, why *don't* we just give peace a chance?" Laughably, the girls at the Academy cast my father as a pinstriped CEO of an electronics company who sent me to the finest rehab programs for teens.

"My parents didn't kick me out," I told Greta through my gritted teeth. "I had to leave Montana, but it's not what you think."

"Then educate me." Greta smirked. "Are you running from the law? Shady past? Ex-boyfriend with a vendetta? And what's the deal with the freaky hair?"

"I don't know what it is that makes you think that just sitting down next to me and asking rude questions entitles you to hear my life story, but I can tell you right now, you are sorely mistaken," I stood up with my tray and no particular exit strategy. "I think you're a very nosy person and I don't like you one bit."

I really don't remember how we came together after that, but I do recall that by spring we were best friends. By senior year, we were inseparable, doing homework together by telephone and spending weekends pretending to be tourists at the Hotel Del Coronado. I loved looking at the photographs of Marilyn Monroe and Jack Lemmon from when they filmed *Some Like It Hot* there. I'd run my feet across every inch of the hotel's deep red-patterned carpet hoping to soak up some sex appeal Marilyn left behind.

Greta convinced me to join the girls' soccer team at the Academy and tried desperately to get me to apply to colleges out of state. A therapist-in-the-making, Greta considered me her personal project, always trying to get me to explore what was best for my personal development. At that age, however, she lacked the maturity to help me truly discover what was best for me, and simply imposed her agenda of what she thought I should do. Her heart was in the right place, but the reality was that she had the wisdom of a teenager. Within three days of hearing about how I came to live with Grammy, she had my entire future mapped out, including what issues I needed to work through and how I was to do it. I never needed to figure out who I was. Greta was always there to do it for me. Perhaps that was a cheap shot. Greta is a truly decent person, but it was tough being the source of her frustration when I dared to disagree with her often hurried analysis of my life.

When Greta left for Texas to attend college, I was free to continue my quiet pursuit of nothing at UCSD. I received an engineering degree, but otherwise camouflaged myself into the wooded seaside campus. I remember the first day of class when I noticed how many kids attended the school. It wasn't like the Academy, where we graduated sixty-one girls; at the university, students bustled about everywhere. No one seemed to notice me, or the intoxicating scent of eucalyptus leaves drooping from countless branches overhead. This was the perfect place for me, I thought. My momentary sense of peace in having discovered my personal Valhalla was interrupted by guilt over the fact that I was both relieved and saddened to have lost my best friend to the Lone Star State.

# Chapter 3

I found a parking spot across the street from the Big Kitchen, a three-room breakfast joint in Golden Hill. Greta said that on weekends there was an hour wait for a table, but on a Wednesday morning at eleven-thirty, the wooden screen door was motionless and the bench outside sat empty. The crisp December air was still and dry. Most purple blossoms clung to their homes on the branches of the street's jacaranda trees while others speckled the sidewalk. Directly outside the door was a three-foot wooden coffee cup, brightly painted, reading, SMALL WORLD; BIG KITCHEN.

The dining room was cluttered with thousands of snapshots stapled to the walls. Beside them hung handmade posters, postcards from around the world, and autographed pictures of comediennes with a woman with a tie-dyed dress and salt-and-pepper wavy hair. A large cutout of Jerry Garcia stood in the corner beside a framed newspaper article about a group that burned sage to ward off evil spirits at the San Diego Convention Center the day after the 1996 Republican National Convention ended. On the menu, house specials were crammed together like commuters on a New York City subway.

The woman from the pictures emerged from the kitchen

like smoke. She introduced herself as Judy the Beauty in a pack-a-day gravelly voice that was an inviting combination of boldness and warmth. "You're Mona, *oui*?" I nodded my head. She had a New York Jewish way about her, but I imagined Judy took on snippets of foreign languages in her everyday speech depending on what type of mood she was in. Some days, it very well may have been Yiddish; others French. "Greta is running late so get that little tushie in here and grab a seat while I pour us a fresh cup of coffee," Judy offered. "Welcome to the Big Kitchen where everyone's a friend," Judy said, motioning to a bearded man at the counter. "Ain't that right? If you don't act right at the door, we don't let you in."

The beard smiled. "Good eggs this morning, Judy."

"What are you talking about?! I've got the best cook in the world. Buenos huevos every morning, *oui*?" Judy turned her attention back to me as she led me out to the patio through the kitchen.

Rather than hiding from the world like I did, Judy was constantly seeking a connection with people. Silence that was the soundtrack of my life was as intolerable to Judy as an empty coffee cup. She scurried about refilling sturdy mugs with coffee and dead air with chatter. I was amazed at how comfortable she seemed at having all eyes on her while I could barely keep from blushing from just her attention.

"Do you want to see where Whoopi signed my wall?" Judy asked.

The Big Kitchen was like a huge game of connect the dots, from the people in the photos, to the celebrity graffiti, feminist posters, to the bizarre painting of the restaurant without its roof and children playing with it as a dollhouse. Trying to piece together what it all meant seemed futile, compelling, and oddly comforting. The smell of sizzling bacon, coffee, and something buttery sweet was beyond compelling.

"Um, okay," I said, game.

None of the cooks seemed especially surprised to see Judy taking a customer through the kitchen. High on a dingy yellow wall, Whoopi Goldberg demanded in black Sharpie pen, "Don't paint over my spot, goddamn it!"

"Why did Whoopi Goldberg write that on your wall?" I asked.

Judy smiled, raised her eyebrows, and peered at me over her down-tilted wire-rim glasses. "She didn't want me to paint over her spot," she said slowly, as though I should have read more into her answer than I could. "And she felt pretty strongly about it."

When Greta arrived, she gave me a bit of background on the Big Kitchen. Not only did she swear the place had the best biscuits and gravy she'd ever tasted, but that Judy was something of a political entertainment muse. Whoopi Goldberg worked there as a dishwasher while she was homeless in San Diego. Sheri Glaser, another performance artist, also did time as a waitress at the Big Kitchen. Lily Tomlin and Pat Schroeder came to the phone personally when Judy Forman called. She led the sage burners to the convention center after the GOP convention, then called the media for film at eleven.

"What has you distraught?" Greta finally inquired after our meals had been delivered.

"I'm not. I'm thrilled, actually. I quit my job," I said, recharged and remembering my impulsive move.

Greta took a deep breath, signaling that she was trying to not react. She placed her fingers against the edge of the table gently, as though she were about to play piano. She leaned in and smiled. "Tell me everything. How did this come about? Do you have a plan for what you're going to do next?"

"I'm not entirely sure what I'm going to do," I began.

"This happened so suddenly. Larry started talking about a buyout option, and two hours later I'm here taking a few vacation days, and Monday I start my two-week transition out the door and on to I don't know what. I do know one thing for sure, though." I paused for dramatic effect. It was so rare I had news to report, much less a life-altering announcement.

Grandiose announcements were made every Monday morning at our office break room. Nancy once went to a weekend workshop to reprogram her attraction to abusive men. Fred announced he was an alcoholic and attended his first AA meeting after he woke up on a bench in Balboa Park one Sunday morning. And most recently, Sandy announced that she got married by Elvis in Vegas. I'd seen plenty of the dramatic pause; I just never had a use for it before.

Pause. "I know one thing and this is it. Are you ready to hear my news?" I asked, straightening my back and leaning in as if I had the biggest news in the world.

"By next Christmas I am going to be blissfully and disgustingly happily married to Adam Ziegler."

The skin on Greta's face dropped two inches. My announcement was like emotional Botox. I had no idea what she was thinking. The look of anticipation was replaced by one of vacancy.

"Surprised?!" I tried to resuscitate the giddiness we shared ten seconds prior to the words Adam Ziegler coming from my mouth.

"Who the hell is Adam Ziegler?" she asked with annoyance and not an ounce of actual curiosity. "Before I moved back to San Diego, I specifically asked you if you were dating anyone and you said you weren't."

Out of sheer stupidity, I tried again to revive the excitement. "We're not officially dating, but we've known each other for seven years, and I pretty much knew the moment I met him that he was *the* one, but I never had the guts to do anything about it. Now, I feel like I've got this second lease at life and I want to start a relationship with him. You know, get out there and take the bull by the horns?"

Greta was silent for a few seconds, then sighed pityingly. "I completely support the idea of taking life by the horns, but that doesn't translate to marrying some man you barely know. Mona, you have an opportunity to discover who you are and what you want from life, and all you could come up with was marrying your puppy crush? You have the time and the money to do absolutely anything, Mona. I hate to say this, but you're a good enough friend that I will. This adolescent fantasy of yours is more than a smidge uninspired. You should be taking painting lessons in Paris, going to therapy, doing social work. Something, *anything* other than attaching your happiness to marriage to some guy you hardly know."

The air left the room, which is difficult to do on an outside patio.

"Oh," was all I could say. "I was—I am—excited about this, to tell you the truth." I hoped she felt guilty for deflating me, but she didn't react. "I've been to Paris, I don't need therapy, and I'm not the most social person in case you haven't noticed. And I do know Adam. I've known him for years."

Greta snorted and rolled her eyes.

"I have known him for years!" I snapped.

"It's not that," Great retreated.

"Then what?"

"Mona, don't take this the wrong way, but if anyone needs therapy, it's you. You've been through a lot. I still can't believe Caroline never sent you to a therapist after you came to Coronado."

We each used the next ten minutes of silence to eat. With each chew, I started to grow more annoyed with Greta's immediate condemnation of my plan. "I know I have a lot of choices, which I think really validates whichever one I make," I began. "I'm not getting married to Adam because I need someone to support me, or because I'm pregnant. I want to marry him because I think being with someone as wonderful as him will make me happy."

Greta dropped her expression and her fork at the same time. "Grow up, Mona," she exasperated. "Why don't you try making yourself happy first, then see if you still feel the need to marry a stranger. I try very hard to refrain from treating my friends like patients, but in cases where I see a friend on a collision course, I need to step in and say something." Greta gasped as she realized her poor choice of words. "Mona, I am so sorry. What a horribly insensitive comment. I am so, so sorry."

"It's okay," I said, insulted that she assumed I was so fragile that the reference would break me. "Stop apologizing, Greta. It's fine."

# Chapter 4

The first sounds I heard were the clattering of kitchen pans and dishes, and the sounds of adults talking. My mother laughed and teasingly scolded my father for something I'll never know. His quick retort earned an uproarious laugh from the rest. "Go wake up the kids, Mr. Hilarious," she ordered. "Come on, Andy, I'm serious. We've got an hour to hit the road, and no one's even out of bed yet."

"S'Mona coming?" asked one of the guys. Freddy, I think.

My mother answered, "Her temp was normal last night, but we'll see how she feels. Andy, wake the rest of the kids and I'll check on Mona. Fran, you still okay with staying behind? I can stay back if you want to go."

Francesca was legally only the grandmother of Leah, Maya, and Karah, but as the only person living in our house who had crossed the sixty-year mark, she was a surrogate grandmother to us all. She was the attending midwife for the six youngest kids in the house, including my two brothers. Francesca was the one we all went to first when we skinned a knee or got sick. So she was the natural choice to stay behind and take care of me that day.

"Don't be silly, Laura," Francesca assured my mother. "We'll be fine here. I think she needs one good day of rest, and with you all gone, she'll kick this thing and be good as new."

The truth was that I had already kicked it two days earlier, but enjoyed the solitude the flu had afforded me. I loved my humongous patchwork family, of course, but in a full house like ours, there was rarely a moment of silence. Never a minute to just sit and think before some little kid would whiz past yammering about who knows what. Hardly a second to just perch myself at the window and daydream about what I wanted to do with my life. Barely time to be one person. There were so many of us under one roof, it was impossible to hear one's own thoughts.

We were peaceful people living in a house of perpetual chaos. It is tempting to try to rewrite history now, and idealize life on the commune. Glorifying the dead and the life I lost seems to be the virtuous thing to do. As virtuous as dishonesty can be, that is. I remember hearing the adults talk about how disingenuous it was when people eulogized the deceased as though they were saints or living sages. How every thought the person had ever uttered suddenly became prophecy. I remember Asia saying that when she died, she wanted to be remembered "true and real," for who and what she was, good and bad. "May my tombstone have many chips," she said, raising her glass of red wine one evening. "A life well-lived is a life filled with mistakes and stupid shit you should've never done." The rest of the family toasted her for this pearl of wisdom, which, in the height of irony, was Asia's final prophecy. I tried to remember life in Montana as it really was, not to reproduce it in my mind as a blissful childhood singing "Kumbaya" with my soul sisters. How I wish they gave me permission for such honesty while they were alive.

Even as a teen  the time of separation from one's par
ents—I felt extremely guilty about not appreciating this
paradise  the adults created for us. My only consolation
was that my best friend Jessica shared my antipathy for
commune life. We rolled our eyes and charaded a finger
down the throat during the Womyn's Forest Walks where
the moms and younger girls sang "Siyahumba" in three-
part harmony. Jess nearly died of embarrassment when her
mother hosted a "Red Party" when she got her first period. All of the women and girls blew some goofy hollow
animal tusk and shouted these crazy guttural chants at the
full moon. The men served us all tea and fruit bars they actually baked, and kept calling us Goddess Jessica, Goddess
Mona, Goddess So and So. When I think of it now, their
baking for us really was kind of sweet. Really. I don't just
want it to be sweet, it really was. At thirty years old, I can
see this with greater ease than I could as a teenager trapped
on a commune.

As Jessica and I churned the compost, we fantasized
about what it would be like to live with normal families.
We'd never met any mainstream families, and we didn't
own a television so the Cosbys were strangers to us, but
somehow we knew they were out there. Our parents acknowledged the people of "Babylon" (which Jessica and I
actually thought was somewhere in Montana) with thinly
masked disdain. They valued things instead of people, my
mother told us. They had become a culture of disposabil-
ity, said Freddy. They were out of touch with their human
capabilities, said Asia. They watched too much television,
Morgan said. Francesca was the only one who'd interrupt
these self-righteous tirades with "Oh, let them be. You
chose your lifestyle, now be happy and live it." I always
took great comfort when Francesca piped in with these
comments, because it showed that our parents weren't al-

ways right. Someone older and wiser could—and did—chide them for judging others. She never knew it, but Francesca always equalized the ever-present, taxing guilt I felt about desperately wanting to take a field trip to Babylon, not to attend a nuclear disarmament rally, but to go to the mall, flirt with boys who watched TV, and drink half of an Orange Julius from a Styrofoam cup.

The night I spiked a fever of 104 degrees, guilt was the furthest thing from my mind, though. I felt only a shivering, painful delirium with spoonfuls of joy about getting to sleep in my very own room. Normally, I slept in a large dorm room shared with other kids from age four-to-Todd, the wavy-haired seventeen-year-old son of Asia and Morgan. The babies slept with their parents until they were weaned, which was just fine by the three of us teenagers. We heard enough sniffling, moaning, and giggling as it was. My father and Freddy built bunk beds for the boys, and for some reason, all of us girls had futons on the floor. On the ceiling was a sky blue, sheet-thin tapestry with cotton clouds that my mother made after our first year in Montana. When she tacked it to the bedroom ceiling, the sheet billowed down, creating a soft illusion of natural sky. My mother said ceilings were oppressive. She even wove threads of gold subtly into the sheet so in the daylight it looked like the thinnest rays of sunshine. For the four days I was sick, I got to stay in my very own room, which was really the sewing room, but I didn't care. It was such a luxury to spend my days in absolute silence that I decided to extend my illness for just a little longer.

"So what are we going to do today, Miss Camille?" Francesca asked after the school bus filled with antinuke protestors had pulled out of our driveway.

I smiled at the reference to the film.

"We have time to braid your hair if you still want,"

Francesca offered. I nodded, went upstairs to grab my brush, and returned with a skip. It was liberating to be able to walk with the energy I felt instead of pretending to drag sluggishly in my attempt to ditch the protest. "Now I can't do it like that Bo Dudley character, mind you, but I'll do what I can."

The thing I remember most about Francesca is her set of reaching and nimble fingers. Her hands were older than she, bony with blue veins pressed through papery skin. But they moved like a pianist, quick and soulful. When her long nails separated sections of my hair and she combed through it with her fingers, I almost curled up like a cat and went back to sleep.

"Will you tickle my arm when you're done?" I begged. Francesca agreed, but we never made it that far. Two hours later, as she was wrapping colored thread around the last of my hundred or so braids, the phone rang with the news.

"Hold on a sec," Francesca said when she heard the phone rang. We had no idea that was the last minute of life as we knew it. "In a second," she reprimanded the phone for ringing a third time. "Hello. Francesca's House of Beauty," she lilted, expecting it to be my parents.

After a moment of silence, she said, "It sure is," equally chipper. Francesca then fell silent as she listened to the caller. She dropped her full weight onto the chair under her and she cupped her forehead with her palm. Tension flooded the room as tangibly as if it were water rushing through a broken dam into our kitchen. Francesca kept glancing at me, then returning her attention to the caller. She sighed a deep, painful exhaust and rushed the caller to the bottom line. When people have to break bad news to someone, the preamble is a futile attempt to pad the fall. She was undoubtedly listening to the details of the crash. Our painted blue school bus slid on a sheet of ice, I later learned. It had a head-on collision with a truck and fell off a cliff. "So tell me," Francesca interrupted. "Was anyone seriously injured?" She paused again and tears fell from her eyes. She was silent for a few seconds, then exploded into tears.

"What happened?" I asked, though I already knew the accident must have been very serious.

Francesca inhaled deeply to regain some composure and wiped her nose with her sleeve. "Mona, I don't know how to tell you this," she started.

"Is everyone okay?" I asked. It was odd. Even though I knew that everyone was definitely not okay, I felt that the question provided a last grasp at not knowing. To the tragedy not being real.

Francesca shook her head, scrunching her face with pain.

"Are they at the hospital?" I begged urgently. With each question, my hopes for a happy ending were skidding downward.

Her head shaking was then accompanied by more sobbing.

"Did someone die?" I asked meekly.

"They all did, Mona." She began sobbing again and held her arms out for me to hug her. I was immobilized by shock and half held on to the notion that if we didn't move, didn't cry or acknowledge the fatal crash, that we could halt the progress of time and perhaps even rewind it.

"Maybe it wasn't them," I offered. "Maybe it was another school bus." Another blue school bus with tie-dyed curtains and peace signs painted on the windows.

I remember trying to hold as still as possible, desperately clinging to the hope that if we just stayed absolutely motionless, we could navigate our way out of this. With every tear that fell from Francesca's eyes, it became clear that the phone call apologizing for the mix-up was never going to come. Still, I stood frozen, feeling a pulse in my ~~ears and nothing else. I know Grammy came to get me be~~ cause she told me so, but for the life of me I can't remember even leaving Montana. In my mind, Francesca is still sitting in that same chair and has been grieving for fifteen years.

# Chapter 5

A week later I stared at a pink lace canopy over my queen-sized bed at Grammy's house. Except I couldn't call it Grammy's house anymore. It was my home, too, now. Just she and I living together in slightly less square footage than the commune, on an island with roads that had never been touched by ice. My new home was on Ocean Drive in a brick estate with seashell pink trim and gold accents. A gate with our family crest and an intercom separated us from the tourists who drove down our block to gawk at homes. Inside, the house was a tribute to royalty with everything overdone in a European golden lacing. Hand-painted vases were the size of my toddler brothers. An oversized chess board held hand-carved ivory pieces. Rugs looked as though they had never been walked on. Everything had a remote and unwelcoming feeling, like a museum of wealth.

Standing in the marble floored foyer for the first time, I must have looked like Julie Andrews walking into the von Trapp home in *The Sound of Music*. "I hope you'll be comfortable here, my dear," Grammy said with a voice that was as icy and unfamiliar to me as the Queen Mum's. "I've asked Patrice to make up the room for a teenage girl. You may put your personal touches on it, of course; my only rule is that I don't allow any Scotch tape on the walls," she explained.

I cannot blame Grammy for having her maid furnish my room, but I did find her timing on the no-tape rule a bit odd. It definitely could have waited until we made it out of the foyer. After losing all but one person in the only family I'd ever known, it wasn't as though decorating the room was my primary focus. It's not as if I spent our plane ride telling her about all the decorating with Scotch tape ideas I had.

Grammy didn't seem as though she reveled at all in the idea of being my legal guardian, much less a grandmother. I got the distinct impression that she had an entirely different vision of her retirement years.

For the first few months after the accident, I used to play a game with myself where I'd imagine how life would be different if I'd been in the bus with the others. I closed my eyes and pictured the morning fog. I tried to imagine which sweater and turtleneck I would've worn to the rally. Which mittens I'd have chosen, which seat I would have taken in the bus. And there I was in my own mind, sitting beside Jessica, talking about how ridiculous these rallies were, and how no one would ever change their hard-bribed political stance on account of some past due hippies in an aqua blue school bus. We hear the deep honk of a truck, feel a moment of sheer terror, slide out of control, crash into the truck, plunge for five seconds, and fall back into each other as our bus nosedives to the ground. I hear the crushing metal and breaking glass, and I am dead. I wonder if it hurts to die or if it's the euphoric freeing sensation Francesca used to tell us it was. No one on our commune ever questioned how this very alive woman knew firsthand what death was like. We all just seemed to accept that since she was the oldest, she somehow knew. I wondered if we died on impact together, or if some of us grasped for life in the last few moments. I wondered who screamed. Who had the presence of mind to exchange a final thought? Who was lucky enough to have slept through the whole thing?

I wondered what—if anything—would be different today if I'd gotten on that bus and died. After pondering this several times, I stopped playing this game. It was too depressing realizing that my life had made no significant impact on anyone.

Patrice told Grammy she had a telephone call from the assistant headmaster at the Academy. It was just two days after Christmas, a holiday we spent having dinner at the Hotel Del Coronado and window-shopping for gifts we'd purchase the next day when the stores reopened. "Hello," she answered, removing her clip-on mother-of-pearl earring. "Yes, Kyle." She waited for him to speak, shifting her weight impatiently. Digging her wide patent leather heel into the plush blue carpet, she occupied her time before it was her turn to speak. "Of course I understand. What you fail to understand is that my granddaughter will start at the Academy next week. I don't care what type of strings you have to pull." She listened for almost a full minute. "This is so crass, Kyle. I just lost my daughter, for God's sake. Just make this happen and of course I'll be generous with the school." She slammed the phone down, and with that I knew that I would be attending whatever academy Grammy wanted me to.

Grammy smiled tightly with her thin coral lips and asked if I'd like an omelet. "Okay," I replied, almost frightened to decline. Patrice brought us two omelets with huge cubes of ham and potatoes and melted cheese resting on sprigs of charred rosemary on white china plates. I smiled as I picked up my gleaming silver fork.

"What?" Grammy asked, not necessarily amused.

"It's just that this is the way she used to cook her eggs, too," I told Grammy. "The ham and potatoes perfectly square, and the burnt rosemary." I smiled. "Just without all of this other fancy stuff," escaped.

"Oh, I don't doubt it," she said sadly. "Laura hated all my fancy stuff."

"You look just like her," I told Grammy.

"I know. She hated that, too."

"No she didn't," I quickly corrected. "She loved that she looked like you, she just didn't like all of your . . ." I trailed off.

"Fancy stuff," Grammy finished.

"No, um, plastic surgery," I said awkwardly, and was hugely relieved when Grammy burst into laughter.

"Laura and I were different people. That is indisputable," Grammy said heavily. "Maybe she was right with her communist thinking. It's not as though any of these things ever really bought me happiness." She sighed. "I always felt as though I failed your mother. If I'd done a better job as a mother, she wouldn't have run off to that crazy ranch."

"That's so untrue," I jumped in. "She didn't run away from anything. They created their version of paradise. They used to talk about it at Berkeley all the time, and finally they all had the guts to quit their boring jobs and make the simple and fulfilling life they'd always dreamed of." This description was almost verbatim from Asia's evening grace. I continued with my own spin. "She couldn't have done any of that if you hadn't done your job well, Grammy. She said that all the time. That her mother had a lot of things to give her, but the best gift of all was the freedom to think for herself and live her own life."

"She said that?" Grammy gasped.

I nodded emphatically. "All the time." She said it once.

"What else did she say?" Grammy asked. "Tell me everything, Mona. I feel as though we were truly strangers these past few years. Tell me about her. Anything you can think of, even if it seems inconsequential."

"Um, okay," I replied. "What does inconsequential mean?"

"Do you like driving, Mona?" Grammy asked. I shook my head. "After breakfast, I'm going to show you around San Diego. We'll start on the island. I'll show you your new school, then we'll head up the coast for the afternoon, and you'll tell me all about Laura. Even the little things that don't seem important. That's what inconsequential means: of no consequence."

We did so much driving that day that when we returned home, my ten-day-old braids degenerated into something frighteningly similar to dreadlocks. I looked at my image in Grammy's gold mirror and began to cry at the sight of myself. I frantically rummaged through the bathroom drawers until I found a pack of loose razor blades. I sliced each braid from my head and watched them fall to the ground like thin sardines wrapped in colored fishing wire.

# Chapter 6

"Please stop apologizing already," I told Greta. "I know what you meant. You're so used to working with lunatics, you expect everyone to go off the deep end over the slightest thing."

Relieved by the reprieve, she laughed. "Mona, I work with people saner than you. My clients mostly tell me that after ten years of marriage they don't know who their husbands are anymore—*not* that they didn't know them before the wedding. I think your time would be wiser spent discovering who you are rather than trying to land a husband you can't possibly know if you're truly compatible with. How can you find a soul mate when you're not sure of your own?"

I adamantly defended myself. "I will use this time to figure out what I want from the rest of my life, but the thing I know for sure is that I want to be Adam's wife. He'd make a great husband and father, and from what I know of him, he's exactly the type of man that can give me what I want."

"Mona, *you* need to give yourself the life you want. How exactly are you going to discover who you are when you're busy trying to find out who this person wants you to be?"

I smiled sheepishly because Greta knew me well. I can't

even count how many times I wondered if Adam was look-ing for a pantsuit-wearing intellectual equal à la Katharine Hepburn in *Adam's Rib,* a tomb-raiding Lara Croft, a small town girl like Mary Bailey, or a flighty Holly Golightly. With-out my even telling her, Greta knew that my life makeover after shot would look a whole heck of a lot like Adam's dream woman.

I decided not to give an inch because she has a tendency to take any concession as an invitation for analysis. Despite her claims to the contrary, Greta is always at work. "Greta, looking for love doesn't mean losing myself."

"I hate to be blunt about this, but you're already quite lost, Mona," she placed her hand on mine condescend-ingly. "You've had a tough road of it."

I withdrew my hand and took a sip of my coffee, which Judy never let go cold. "What's wrong with my wanting to give my life a makeover? Like you said, I've had a tough road of it. What's wrong with my forging ahead full steam to get what I want? It's not like I'm hurting anyone."

"Changing yourself into who you think someone else wants is hurting yourself. It's a rejection of who you are, and that's toxic. You're committing emotional suicide."

I rolled my eyes, wondering if Greta was thinking what I was—that the friendship we once had might not survive our thirties.

Emotional suicide?! "Listen Greta, I know you're trying to help, but your terms are a bit much. It's not like I'm jumping off the Coronado Bridge, or anything."

"I stand behind my theory. Emotional suicide is exactly what you're committing. Suppressing your true self may seem benign, but it slowly kills you."

I wondered if our friendship would survive this lunch.

"How are you so sure that my plan to marry Adam will include morphing myself into Adam's dream woman?" As soon as these words occuped, I regretted asking the question. I knew I'd provided her with at least a half dozen examples of times I became a chameleon for love.

"Kenny Schneider," Greta clipped. "Remember him from the Boys Academy? He loved fishing, so you became Little Miss Bait 'n' Tackle? Exhibit B: Punk Rock Pete from La Jolla Country Day. Remember when you literally emptied the punk section of Tower Records so you would 'understand him through his music'? Of course, this turned out to be a fruitless endeavor since you never uttered a single word to him! Shall I go on?"

I waved my hand and smiled as though her recollections of my teen modus operandi had no bearing on today's pursuit of Adam Ziegler.

"Mona, I don't mean to sound patronizing, but could it be that it's easier to focus on someone other than yourself?"

"Why don't you do all of us a favor and write a self-help book and get all this out of your system? Frankly, it's boring the shit out of me."

I looked through a thick wool blanket hanging over a patio screen and noticed that a man in the apartment building next door was turning on his shower. What do people do that they can take showers at nearly noon? I'd soon find out. I smiled. Perhaps Greta had a point. Maybe I should spend this time trying to figure out who I am, instead of who Adam Ziegler might want me to be. But if who I want to be happens to overlap with who Adam wants me to be, then so be it. That was a good compromise, I figured.

"Listen, maybe you're right," I reluctantly conceded.

"There is a God in heaven!" she rejoiced, dramatically gesturing above.

"If there is, He'll spare me any further analysis from you." I smiled. "I'm not giving up on Adam, but I'll reinvent myself to become somebody you'll like, too."

"I already like you, Mona. Go through with the little makeover if you need to, but be sure the person who loves the new you is the *real* you. For the record, I think you're perfect already. Misguided for sure, but I do love you. You're my oldest friend in the world, do you know that?"

*You're my only friend,* I didn't say.

On the drive back to Coronado, I stopped at a news-stand that sells every glossy from *Good Housekeeping* to barely legal porn. *Good Housekeeping* promised tips on how to keep my husband hooked. A little too soon for this, I decided. I navigated my way around the store until I found the section with fresh faced fifteen-year-old vamps on the covers—the single women's mags. The cover stories barked at me, beckoning like restaurant hosts in Athens and Rome who promise the ultimate culinary satisfaction. If love had a library, this was it.

WIN HIS HEART IN 30 DAYS! leapt off the stand and into my arms.

YOUR GUY, YOUR WAY! GETTING WHAT YOU WANT FROM HIM NOW! seemed a bit aggressive, but I needed to be a student of dating, and these smoky-eyed women seemed to really know their stuff.

BUILD A BETTER MAN TRAP! seemed cute, though I hated the idea of capturing Adam. My plan was to help him see what I already knew—that we were a perfect match. Once he saw this, he'd pursue me. The idea of rigging a contraption of head games was unappealing, but I was curious what the article would advise. After all, knowledge is power and I needed a healthy portion of both.

TEN THINGS THAT FREAK GUYS OUT! I hadn't considered this, but if I was serious about being a scholar of seduction, I had to learn about potential mistakes before I made them.

DRIVE HIM CRAZY IN BED! Okay.

MAKE HIM BEG FOR MORE! Please, please!

REAL GIRL MAKEOVERS! Jackpot!

TURN HIS HEAD WITH YOUR FABULOUS ASS! Surely the editor was fired for that one.

I loved the verve. The exclamation points alone sent me into a wild magazine-hoarding tizzy until I had to set my pile onto the counter while I continued browsing.

SEX IN ONE DATE OR LESS, another cover blurb boasted. Oh, the men's section.

BE THE GUY SHE TELLS HER FRIENDS ABOUT—THEN DO THEM, TOO, chest-thumped *Y Chromosome*.

WHAT I WISH CHICKS KNEW, offered another. These men's magazines intrigued me. They sounded like the raw facts, not some processed, feminized version of the truth. I needed to know what a Neanderthal of a guy really, truly felt about women—and what this guy wished we knew. The kind of stuff he talked about with his buddies after a rugby game, when he's sweat-drenched and pumped with testosterone. I wanted to hear from the worst of the dogs, not some freshly showered pansy in a pastel combed cotton sweater that *Glamour* found nibbling a scone in a coffee shop. I didn't want tips from guys who are being interviewed for a women's magazine because they are most likely completely and thoroughly full of shit. Nonetheless, I would read the women's mags and see what they had to say. These writers certainly knew more than I did, so there was absolutely nothing to be lost reading what the pouty lip brigade had to say about men.

I brought my final selection to the counter. *Maximum for Him*. Translation: minimum for her. Opposition research. I could barely contain my grin at the thought of delving into this colossal pile of information. I felt like a spy about to cross the border of another country. I felt alive.

# Chapter 7

I always drive the same route home. I cross the blue vein of the Coronado Bridge, head straight through town until I hit Alameda Avenue, then drive it all the way down toward the ocean. Every day, I pass the North Island Naval Station and see the same uniformed guys out front, waving in their comrades. For the first two years I lived here, I never understood how the navy guys knew who was military. I assumed that they just had great memories and recognized the faces of all North Island personnel. Grammy laughed when I told her this. "You little goose! They have stickers on their windows. See?" She pointed at the car ahead of us, and sure enough, there was a small navy decal on the corner of the windshield." I never actually wanted to go onto the naval base. If I had, it would have been easy enough to arrange through Grammy. What I longed for was the guy in uniform giving me the official wave. "Come on in, Mona. You're welcome at our private little club. Please, come in. We want you here."

In fact, my fondest sexual fantasies take place behind the walls of the naval base. It wasn't the guys in uniform. I know some women go for that, but I'd just as easily fall for a guy in a suit and tie, which I suppose is a uniform, too. But I could very easily be attracted to a man in a soft black sweater and khaki pants. It wasn't even so much the location. It was, I suppose, getting behind those walls. Some nights, the fantasy would start with the guy at the gate waving in my car; other nights I'd imagine scaling the walls and jumping over the fence until I landed on the other side with scraped knees and twigs in my hair.

When I arrived home with my new magazines, I poured a glass of iced tea and carried it out to the backyard. Our yard is spacious by any standard, but humongous by Southern California's measure. Every year without fail, a housing developer wants to purchase three quarters of my yard to build another home. He always assures me that I'll still have plenty of yard left, tells me how "classy" his projects are, and then leaves me with the tired old line about oceanfront property—"they ain't making any more of it."

Grammy always said that when a developer tells you that he builds elegant homes, it's because he almost always throws together half-baked cookie-cutter models of what twenty-five-year-old trophy brides deem tasteful. "Always consider it a tremendous service when a person tells you how honest he is," she also said. "It's a warning round. When they start talking about how honest they are, run. If you're honest, you don't need to talk about it. When you build elegant homes, you most certainly do not need to tout their elegance. If someone makes a point of telling you who he is, rather than showing you with his actions, you can bank on the truth being quite the opposite." Whenever we shopped together, we spoke a secret language of facial expressions. At the Mercedes dealership, the owner carried on about how he created a "second home" for his employees and how they all loved working there. Grammy gave me a look, which I knew meant "Where is *this* coming from? Did we inquire about the job satisfaction level of his staff?" We left that day without a car, but instead with Grammy's pregnancy-like craving for information about this dealership. After a half hour of pounding away at the computer keyboard, Grammy shouted "I knew it!" from her office. "Get in here, Mona. Are my instincts keen, or are they keen?"

"Well," I stretched the word to tease. "If they're so keen, why do you need to talk about them?"

"Oh pish posh, get your rump over here and see what I've found on the Internet." When I arrived, she continued, "Sexual harassment charges. Hmpf! He sees two women walk into the dealership and immediately starts talking about the big happy family, the low turnover, and how happy, happy, happy everyone is there. Silly fool might have had my money in his pocket today if he would have simply focused on the car. I don't care about what kind of place he's 'created' for his second family of car salesmen."

"Grammy!" I chided. "You don't care if this man sexually harasses his employees?"

"Not in the least," she replied, astounded that I could even consider it. "Why should that matter to me?"

I set down my iced tea and began reading the women's magazines first. "Learn How to Give the Perfect Massage," one suggested. "Learn to Listen." Hmmm. Let's see what the men's mag has to say. I turned to the table of contents and the cover story I was looking for was a guy's monthly column called *The Dog House*. How perfect! Mike Dougherty, the Dog.

### What I Wish Chicks Knew
### —Mike "the Dog" Dougherty

*My ex-girlfriend is pulling out of the driveway in a U-Haul truck. Up until a few minutes ago, I*

*got the feeling she would have stayed if I asked.
She was shuffling, hemming and hawing and talking about our problems like there's still an "our."*

If I didn't want to talk about these so-called
issues when we were together, why would I want
to talk about them now? I could see what she
was doing. She was waiting for me to tell her
what she wanted to hear. Believe me when I tell
you, it wouldn't take a genius to figure out what
that was. One night, during one of our interminable
festivals of feelings (hers) she told me exactly what
I was supposed to say to make her feel "special."
Stop now and grab a bag. It gets worse.

When my latest ex realized that screaming at
me wasn't working, she actually wrote a script
for me. She shouted, "Do I need to write a script
for you?" I said no, but she did it anyway. (And
I have the communication problem?!) I kid you
not, she handed me a piece of paper with things
she'd like me to say. So, you're wondering, my
friends, what did these crib notes say?

"I love you."
"I wish we could spend more time together."
"I think about you all the time."
"I am so lucky to be with you."

In the interest of enhanced male-female relationships (hey, they've got all the pussy, what are
we going to do, guys, right?), I'd like to offer a
little free advice to my female readers. I hope
you both enjoy it.

First, let's start with the obvious. If we're with
you, we're into you. We either like you or we
love you. 'Nuff said.

Second, if I wished we could spend more time

*together, we would. Sorry, ladies, but it's the truth. What we want to do, we do. There are exceptions that keep us from doing things we really enjoy, but as a general rule, if we're not spending a whole heck of a lot of time with you, it's because we don't want to. It's not because we're jerks. It's because everyone—women included—makes time to do what they enjoy. Bottom line, if we're not spending time with you, it's probably because you're a huge pain in the ass, no fun, or look like hell these days.*

*Third, we don't think about you all the time. In order of importance, here's what we think about: sex, sports, sex, food, sex, work, sex, gadgets, sex, going bald, sex, getting fat. Yeah, we think about you, too, but here's a tip: The yapping and scripting is not sexy, and if you're not fitting into our time for thinking about sex, you're slipping down to the "work" slot. You should not be work. You should be sex.*

*There are a handful of guys out there who are lucky enough to have found truly cool women to share their lives with. Hey, my hat's off to you, man, 'cause a brother knows it ain't easy. But, ladies, if you are scripting, demanding, complaining all the time, we aren't so lucky to be with you.*

*Finally, stop writing these mental scripts of what we would say if we "really cared." Don't expect any man to start reading lines you find in a romance novel. Women write these; women read them. Harlequin is a language guys don't speak and don't want to. Spare us the United Nations headset for translation. We'd rather learn Japanese—it's easier and will get us further ahead in the world.*

*In the end, ladies, we resent the shit out of your telling us what to say and do. If you—let me repeat—if you are sculpting your boyfriend, you have control issues. (See, we've picked up some of your psychobabble terminology. And you thought we weren't listening.)*

*Trust me when I tell you I never said any of this to my latest ex-girlfriend despite her many pleas to be "totally honest." Women say they want to communicate, but that's code for "I'm talking and you're listening." Men get the illusion of a chance to talk, too, but it damn well better be what women want to hear or we're "withholding emotionally." What happened to honesty?*

*Until next month, my friends, don't let the bitches get you down.*

I stared agape at the column long after I read the final words. What offensive, tired old stereotypes about women! What was the point? What trite, uninspired, unoriginal horseshit. Or was it? *Maximum for Him* was the number-one rated men's magazine in the country and *The Dog House* was a monthly column that, according to the letters to the editor section, really resonated with guys. This was all so confusing. There was a certain beauty and simplicity to my life of virtual hermitage. I wasn't sure I was ready for this. But one thing was certain. If I was going to venture out into this brave new world, I needed a guide. A guide dog, so to speak. I would hire Mike as a guy coach. A male consultant. I would run all ideas to impress Adam by The Dog for the sniff test. The Dog would be the harshest, toughest, meanest, most revolting critic I could find. If I could train with him, I'd be a champion.

# Chapter 8

Two weeks later, Mike the Dog had not returned a single one of my eight phone messages. His assistant, Gwen, was becoming annoyed with me, which I must confess was a tad thrilling. I'd never been a pest before. Gwen was a young woman with an English accent who seemed terribly bored with her job. "I will reissue your message, Miss Warren," she was burdened with uttering seven times.

Greta knocked on the door at 7:30 A.M., wearing faded blue sweatpants and a T-shirt with rhinestones warning, "Don't Mess with Texas!" I was squeezing the last orange for my breakfast drink. "I'm sorry, I'm running a few minutes behind," I offered. "I'll just put this in the fridge and we'll get going."

When I returned downstairs in my gray sweat suit (sans warnings), Greta held my yellow notepad beside the telephone. "Who, may I ask, is The Dog?" she asked with a suspicious brow.

"Oh," I hesitated, like a child who had been caught doing something wrong. "He writes a column for a men's magazine. I was thinking of calling him for some advice."

Greta used her tooth-trimmed fingernail to brush an overgrown patch of bangs away from her face. Her green eyes pierced accusingly. "Advice on what?" she asked but already knew.

"Guy stuff."

"Mona." She sighed with disappointment. "Please tell me you're not going for the male chauvinist seal of approval to appeal to that Adam guy. Because a man does a good job on your taxes doesn't mean he'll be a good life partner."

"Let's get running. We'll talk about it on the way," I offered, hoping we'd both gasp for breath so desperately that Greta wouldn't be able to grill me on my plan for The Dog to show me some new tricks. No such luck. Greta's slim body moved like a gazelle, and the run didn't tax her breathing in the least. I, on the other hand, hadn't been running since high school gym class, but promised Greta that part of my reinvention would be a commitment to my health. Running with Greta twice a week and a veggie dinner with her every Sunday night, she made me promise. She said a healthier lifestyle would help me think more clearly. I knew it would trim the extra ten pounds from my amorphous body.

"So, tell me, Mona," Greta began. "What on earth is so special about this Adam Zigfried that you've gone off the deep end like this? Give me three good reasons I should be rooting for this relationship to work out between the two of you."

"First of all, his name is Adam Ziegler, not Zigfried."

"Oh, now I'm convinced. What a great reason."

"It's not a reason. I just wanted to let you know so you can get used to saying his name correctly. After all, it'll be my name too soon." I smiled, mocking my own confidence.

"You plan to take your husband's name? Is there going to be anything left of the old Mona when you're done?"

"Greta, you've turned into a real drama queen." I rolled my eyes, huffing and puffing as the Pacific Ocean scrolled behind us. "I'm certainly not the first woman to take her husband's last name. It's not like I'm handing him my right leg." This particular limb came to mind only because of the pain shooting through it at that moment. We nodded to our fellow runners along the smooth ocean sidewalk. A cluster of tire-sized rocks formed a wall that separated us from the expansive white beach. I inhaled deeply, partly to get oxygen into my body, and partly to take in the paradise around us. Where else in the country were people jogging in T-shirts along palm tree–lined beach walks just a week before Christmas? My grandfather seemed to only make smart decisions, from buying a home on the ocean to being one of the pioneers of the canned tuna industry. San Diego, I sighed silently. God was definitely having a good day when he made this patch of the world.

"Women don't have to do things simply because others before them have," Greta treaded lightly.

"What happened to free choice?"

"What happened to free thinking?"

"You're so right, Greta. Taking Adam's name is going to evaporate my brain. My whole identity is going to be absorbed right into his. I am *that* stupid. Why are you so against this when you know it's going to make me happy?"

Greta didn't look in my direction as she spoke. Naval planes flew above her; nothing could distract her. "I don't believe in looking to other people to make yourself happy, that's all," she said, definitely with more than just Adam Ziegler in mind. "Mona, you are a wonderful person, but it breaks my heart that you don't seem to realize that. I noticed you never *did* give me those three reasons. And what in God's name are you thinking wanting to ask advice from that idiot, The Dog?"

"Have you read his column?" I asked.

"I've heard about it. He's frighteningly chauvinistic."

"That's exactly why," I said. "You always tell me to embrace what I fear. Believe me, I've read his column and this guy is scary. He's going to give me the insight into the way men think and not worry about political correctness. He's the real deal, the inside track into Guy World."

"Why would you want to be with a small-minded Neanderthal, though, Mona?"

"I don't. Adam isn't that way at all. Adam is sensitive and gentle and kind, but if I can understand men through the eyes of a total jerk, I'll be able to handle Adam, no problem."

"This makes absolutely no sense."

"It does to me, and frankly, I don't need your approval of this decision or any other. How's that for emotional health?"

"I'd say it's one step forward, two steps back."

We ran a bit less than a mile before my legs could take me no farther. "I don't have any patients this morning. Would you like to grab a cup of coffee at Starbucks?" Greta asked.

"Sure, but I've got to be honest with you, Greta. I have no patience either this morning. Can we drop Adam?"

"I'd love to drop Adam." She smiled. "Okay, I'll let it go. I know I can be a pain in the butt sometimes, but do understand it's only because I care about you." It rang with such genuine truth, I knew I could never stay angry at Greta for too long. Sometimes her timing was perfect.

I changed the subject as we walked the immaculate sidewalks of Coronado. "Hey, what ever happened with that guy in Austin?"

"What guy?" Greta asked.

"Hello. The guy you were living with. The guy it 'just

didn't work out with and I don't want to talk about it.'
Remember him?"

We walked in silence until we reached an empty Starbucks.
"Morning, Greta," said the clerk. "Mocha latte venti?" She
shook her head to approve. "And for you, ma'am?"

Greta stirred her whipped cream until it dissolved completely in her coffee. "I'm sorry, Mona. I know I promised
we'd drop the subject, but I must ask—how are you so
sure he's the one?"

"I'll make you a deal." I sighed. "I'll tell you what you
want to know about Adam if you tell me what was so
awful about your breakup that you had to move back
home."

Greta shifted her weight from one side of her seat to the
other. "The usual reasons," she said, unnaturally upbeat. I
wish I could have thick lips like Greta's, so full and uneven
on the bottom. Mine look like a Muppets—a sliced open
face with no rim to delineate the mouth. "We outgrew
each other, so it was time to move on."

"That's pretty boring," I said.

"True."

"That's really all there is to it?"

"That's all she wrote."

"I don't believe it," I said. "There's always more to it
than that."

"Not always. Okay, your turn."

"Hmm. Let's see," I began. "First, there's chemistry between me and Adam. You can't underestimate the power
of pure physical attraction. Second, he's from a *great* family. They're so close that Grammy said they all take vaca-
tions together. They even manage to have Sunday dinners
once a month. I think that's sweet. I want to bring children
into a family like that." Greta shifted again. "And, third, I
don't know. There's just something about him. He makes

my hair twirl. He makes me want to twirl my hair around my finger, flop onto my bed, and talk to him on the phone all night. I don't know, Greta. I just love him. I just do. I can't tell you exactly why, but I've got this gut feeling that he's the one. You know that feeling when you hear music that really resonates with you? You feel like someone drew a map straight to your soul, and the music travels the roads, seeps in through your pores, and follows every route to the very core of you. The part you rarely go to because it's so delicate that if you so much as inhale, you'll cry from the extraordinary, overwhelming sense of happiness. Do you know what I mean? That's how I feel when I think of Adam, and I have no logical explanation for it whatsoever. And I'm not one bit sorry about it either. I'm only sorry I waited so long to pursue it."

Greta took in what I was saying. I could see her mentally starting several rebuttals until she came up with this one. "You aren't pursuing it, though. Mona, you told me about Adam two weeks ago, and so far you haven't even picked up the telephone. Are you afraid the real Adam Ziegler won't be enough to live up to your fantasy?"

I tried to prevent my eyes from watering, but was soon looking at Greta through rising tears. "No. I'm afraid the real Mona Warren won't be enough." I took a deep breath and held back my tears. I try not to cry very often because when I do, it lasts for hours and exhausts the life out of me. When I really get going, I start gulping and sobbing and it's just an all-around mess. Every few years or so, I can't help myself, but as a general rule, I try to stop crying before it starts.

"Mona, I'm sorry," Greta said, running to the counter for napkins. "I didn't mean to upset you."

I rolled the brown napkin into a point and stuck it into the corner of my eye. I felt the tears jump onto the napkin,

escaping my miserable face. "I *don't* know what I'm doing,"
I said, sniffling. "I have no clue what I'm doing. That's
why I'm trying to hire The Dog, so he can help me figure
out what men want. I know I'm supposed to be focused on
what I want, and I will. I promise you, I will. But what I
want most is Adam and I have absolutely no idea how to
act around a guy. I've never even had a boyfriend, and I'm
terrified that I'll get to Adam's office and freak out from
the pressure and start talking like an imbecile, and blow it."

When we returned to the house, I glanced at my answering machine to see if The Dog had returned my call.
Greta picked up my pad of paper. "Waiting for The Dog?"
she asked.

"Kind of," I admitted. "I don't understand why he
doesn't call back."

"What would you say to spending Christmas day with
my family, the whole slew of us?" Greta offered.

"Okay."

"Okay, then. I'm going to do something for you now.
Let me restate that I think asking advice from a man who
calls himself a dog is absurd, but you're not going to truly
appreciate how useless he is until you see for yourself. I'll
get through to him and schedule your silly little appointment, but I guarantee he'll refuse your offer. I take that
back. After meeting him, you'll see that you don't need his
advice and won't offer anything other than a one-way trip
to the front door."

"But how? I've called him eight times already," I explained.

"Does tonight work for you?" Greta asked.

I nodded my head. "But how are you going to . . . ?"

"Should he come to the house or do you prefer to meet
at the coffee shop?"

"Um, here, but, he's not—"

She put her hand up to interrupt me and began dialing. "He's probably on vacation," I whispered.

Suddenly, Greta began speaking in an impeccable English accent. Impeccable enough, I hoped, to fool Mike's English secretary. "Yes, good morning. Please connect me with The Dog's office."

"Drop the accent, his assistant is . . ." I couldn't finish.

"Yes, good morning, Gwen. This is Felicity from Claudia Schiffer's office. Ms. Schiffer is a huge fan of The Dog's. She thinks his column is quite clever. She'll be stopping over in San Diego this evening and wonders if Mr. Dougherty would care to join her for dinner." She paused again. "Yes, of course I'll hold." Pause. Greta's facial expression signaled that Mike had picked up the line. "Yes, morning to you, too, Mr. Dougherty . . . yes, of course, Dog. Okay, lovely, lovely, Claudia will be delighted. Let me give you the address of the private home she will be staying at. I trust your discretion will be used with this information, correct?" Pause. "Wonderful. Let's say seven then." Greta gave him my address despite my repeated pleas to hang up the phone.

"What the hell did you do?!" I shouted when she hung up the phone.

"I arranged for you to meet with this Dog person. Isn't that what you wanted?"

"Greta, this is not a friendly dog! Read this column." I shoved my open copy of *Maximum for Him* at her. As she scanned the magazine, I continued, "He's going to come over here, see that I am the furthest thing from Claudia Schiffer, and God knows what." I started pacing around frantically as she read the article. "He's going to freak out when he gets here. Call and cancel. Give me the phone so I can cancel. He's going to totally flip out when he gets here and there's no Claudia Schiffer. Hey Dog, guess who's *not* coming to dinner? Instead you've got *me*?!"

Greta laughed as she looked up from the magazine. "Mona, this is what you said you wanted. If you want a male consultant, you have to meet him first. I set up the meeting, that's all. If this is what you want, you have to make it happen."

Is this what I wanted? Why hire a guy coach who's a dog when Adam is a prince? Was Mike like my New York? If I could make it there, I could make it anywhere? Or was I just using him as another delay tactic? Another excuse to prolong going for Adam?

# Chapter 9

When I told Greta I'd never had a boyfriend, I wasn't being entirely truthful. It was so long ago, though, it hardly counts as practical experience.

If I'd grown up in an American suburb, Todd would have been the boy next door. A product of the same farmhouse commune that I called home, he was the boy who slept on the other side of the children's dorm curtain.

My parents and their friends bought 110 acres in Montana just three weeks after Ronald Reagan was first elected president, and started building the house that spring. I was nine years old, and remember a lot of my friends' parents saying they were leaving the country, moving to Canada, starting a revolution, or something equally drastic. My parents, and three couples they went to college with, actually followed through. They said they would build a tremendous house in the middle of nowhere, raise animals, grow organic vegetables, sew their own clothing, make their own food, and live off the land. Live from their labor rather than relying on the outside world. Everything from food to furniture would be made by our new, extended family.

The first night in Missoula, Jessica and I found each other and became partners in cynicism about this whole weird commune idea our parents dreamt up. We each bet on how long it would last, and how it would end. My ten dollars said the animals would all run away right after eating all the vegetables. One year, tops. Jess thought the adults would all get on each other's nerves within six months, and we'd go our separate ways by Christmas.

Our hope for failure had the polar opposite effect on the house. (So much for Freddy's philosophy about thoughts manifesting reality.) Every night, there was more explosive laughter than the evening before. The adults constantly reminded each other what a brilliant choice they'd made. Asia recited her creation-of-paradise grace before every meal. Dinners were so plentiful they looked like knight's feasts. Only now can I appreciate the purity of eating dinners that we planted and grew ourselves. From plates that Asia threw, painted, and glazed. On a table my father built. With burning vanilla candles hand-dipped by my mother. In a house that we built. In a life they created. With the people we chose to make our family.

I don't remember exactly when it dawned on Jessica and me that Todd was gorgeous. There weren't grades to mark the time like we had in our previous life. It was the same year as Jessica's Red Party, though. I remember because she was embarrassed that he knew about her first period, so it must have been right around when we were both thirteen years old. We sat on the porch watching the men chop wood, pretending to read the assigned *Canterbury Tales,* but really peeking over the pages to watch Todd's tanned and newly developed chest as it contracted with every swing of the ax.

Todd had just taken his SATs and we all knew he'd be off to an Ivy League school in the fall. Everyone always said Todd was brilliant, but Jessica and I thought that was just a bunch of hippie talk. We thought he was pretty smart and seriously beautiful with his shoulder length wavy black hair and his Flathead Indian bone structure. But when Todd took his PSATs the year before and scored 1440, with a perfect score in math, we conceded that perhaps he really was brilliant.

The adults weren't thrilled about his desire to attend an Ivy League school, but they were also big proponents of letting us kids chart our own course. They felt Yale or Dartmouth, Todd's first choices, were too "establishment" and feared his good values would unravel there. Francesca assured them that if they raised the boy right, he could attend the University of Hell and still come out the same good person. Maybe even better. "That boy has spent his entire lifetime book-learning about privilege and power," Francesca explained at the dinner table as this issue was debated. "Let him experience it firsthand. He'll grow more compassionate in the environment. Let's not assume the environment will affect him. Todd is a strong presence that we must now share with the world. Imagine the love our boy will take out into the world." Her eyes welled with tears as Jessica rolled hers.

Todd and I never went on dates like normal teens. But we were definitely an item and everyone knew it. It happened the summer he turned seventeen. At his birthday party, in fact. Birthdays were huge celebrations in our family. Everyone got a big party with the theme of his or her choice. Babies and elders were especially celebrated with dozens of horns and rituals and poetry readings. They really knew how to celebrate life, I will say that. Anyway, Todd chose a beach party theme, which meant we built a tremendous bonfire and set blankets around it. Bags of cookies, marshmallows, and Hershey's chocolate sat promisingly in a crate. The sight of packaged food was an oddity in our home. We could hear Freddy lecturing the younger kids about the packaging of the sweets, asking them why they thought the manufacturers used an illustration of a teddy bear on its plastic bagging. "It's cute," my brother, Oscar, answered. "Okay, but let's take this a step further and talk about why the marshmallow company wants to put cute pictures of teddy bears on their bags." Freddy's inquiry was punctuated by Oscar's little head dropping to his lap.

My mother serenaded Todd that night, changing the gender in The Beatles "I Saw Her Standing There." When she sang that he was just seventeen, and asked if we knew what she meant, I blushed. I knew what she meant all right. I also knew that it meant that in one year from now, we'd be hosting his off-to-college party. Or so I thought. I don't know what Todd was thinking, but our eyes met from across the fire, stayed locked on each other a second too long, and we both knew the other was interested. The vibe, my parents called it.

Morgan drove an hour to buy two dozen lobsters, which Todd wanted for his birthday beach party. Todd had never tasted lobster, so it wasn't as though it was an old favorite. Rather, he was starting to dabble in the finer things so he wouldn't look like a sheltered Indian boy straight off a Montana commune. I think he had this wild notion that Ivy League kids were going to walk around campus talking about yachting and tennis, snacking on caviar and sipping champagne at polo games. I knew he felt terribly intimidated by the whole thing, but was going to go anyway. That's one of the things I really loved about Todd. He knew what he was afraid of, but didn't let it stand in the way from his doing it.

While we were sunbathing by the lake, he told me he wanted to attend an Ivy League university mostly because he wanted to measure himself against the standard that terrified him. Greta would have loved him. "Rich people scare me," he said, using his finger to draw a line in the dirt in front of us. "Everyone here tells me how smart I am, but I have to wonder what they're comparing me to, you know? My 'report cards' from them are always Groovy Plus, but what does that mean? I ask them if I would've been an A student at a regular school and they say that there aren't any letters to characterize my performance. I know what they're saying, but it doesn't really answer my question, you know?"

"Todd, you got a perfect score on your math PSAT," I assured him, reaching my hand to his forearm. He was lying on his stomach and rolled onto his side.

"Yeah, but I only got a 640 on English. You know what that means?"

"It means that you scored better than most kids in the country," I said. "Rich kids, kids who went to normal schools—most of them took the same test, Todd."

"Six-forty isn't that high," he said. "It's not Ivy League. And it's not like I'm the captain of the football team or have a whole lot of extracurricular activities. When they see that I only scored six-forty on English, they'll think I'm just some dumb Indian kid who has a head for numbers. I need the vocabulary," he said nervously.

Todd wasn't just talking about learning Latin roots and scoring higher on the English section of the SAT. When he said he needed the vocabulary, he said what all of us older kids thought—we don't speak the language of the real world. Our college classmates were going to talk about movies and television shows we'd never seen, and have favorite teams of sports we never saw. Of course, as my father's apprentice, Todd could make furniture. He was one of a small group of American teens who spoke Russian fluently. He played piano, bass guitar, saxophone, and harp. And he knew every plant and flower indigenous to the state of Montana, if not the entire country.

"Todd, relax," I said, thrilled to be his confidante. "You never even studied for the test. You'll buy one of those books, bone up on your vocabulary, and by the time the test comes around, you'll break 700 on English, I'll bet."

He sighed, then feeling guilty for monopolizing the conversation, switched gears. Todd penetrated me with his gaze. "You're beautiful," he said.

"See, I think you have a great vocabulary. I love your vocabulary." I giggled.

"I love the way I feel when I'm around you, Mona. It's so easy hanging out with you."

I adored my new role as his girlfriend. He was without a doubt, mind-blowingly amazing, and if he chose me, then I was wonderful by association. If he thought I was beautiful, I must be. After all, he was the genius. "I love your smile," I said somewhat clumsily, afraid to overwhelm him with the tidal wave of things I loved about him.

"I love everything about you, Mona."

"I love everything about you, too."

"I love you," he said for the first time.

"I love you, too."

Long after I'd graduated from college, I went to New Haven, Connecticut, for an engineering conference, and visited the Yale campus. I smiled with deep regret that Todd had never discovered that the students there ate Big Macs and wore hooded cotton Mexican tops just like his. Many of the kids wore frayed denim, hemp chokers and peasant shirts just like we wore. Commune chic.

We didn't celebrate Christmas at our home in Missoula because the adults felt the holiday had become too commercial. Instead, we made half-inch stars from tin foil and cellophane and hung hundreds of them with fishing wire from the ceiling. Freddy set the lighting so the stars would gently illuminate, creating a "winter nights" theme inside the house. My father and Freddy made a sheet thin moon from quarry rock, and backlit it with blue. We strung freeze-dried berries and wrapped mistletoe in ornate hand-made lace bows and knotty silk ribbon. The kids painted clay peace signs in rainbow colors and made God's-eyes from homespun, vegetable-dyed yarn. It looked like the holiday spread when *House & Garden* meets *Mother Jones*.

The only gifts we were allowed to buy were books. Everything else had to be made by our own talents. I saved up enough money to go to town and buy Todd the Barron's SAT study guide, then Asia helped me make a ceramic coffee mug for Todd's late nights of studying. I painted bright pink bitterroot blossoms on it before glazing it. He carved a chess set for me because we spent so many hours playing the game. In fact, we used chess as an excuse to stay up late and fool around after everyone else had gone to sleep. The first time we had sex, we tiptoed out of the house and into the barn, after the others had retired. Our excuse—as always—was an intense game of chess.

Todd and I talked about getting married after he graduated from Yale, which I think we both knew was more of a sweet fantasy than a realistic plan for our futures. I always figured he'd meet a blond, blue-blood from Yale, marry her, and have 2.3 kids. I was going to be a singer with an edgy alternative rock band, which now seems such an alien idea I can't even believe it was once mine. Though I realized Todd and I would probably go our separate ways, I always assumed we'd remain lifelong friends, which I suppose we did. I just never imagined that his life would be so short.

# Chapter 10

*Never bring flowers.*
*—Maximum for Him, October*
*Unless they're for Claudia Schiffer.*
*—December amendment*

The pounding on the door made my heart jump. My pulse raced; a layer of sweat appeared on my skin. It was the hour of reckoning. Seven. Dog time. Interestingly, he was right on schedule despite the fact that his dating rules include showing up ten minutes late with no excuses or apologies. I guess Claudia Schiffer is the exception to the rules.

I opened the door to the sight of a chiseled masculine face with soulful brown eyes and a five o'clock shadow. His dark blond hair had a slight wave and was flopped to the side in a scruffy, compellingly sexy way. His jaw shot out slightly from a centimeter under bite. He wore well-tailored casual pants, a cashmere high-neck plum sweater, and soft brown leather slip-on shoes. In his right hand, he casually held two dozen red roses with baby's breath and greens volumizing the impressive bouquet.

"Hey," he greeted me with polite dismissal, as though I must have been the supermodel's assistant. "Mike Dougherty to see Claudia."

"Come in," I offered. "Can I offer you something to drink? Lemonade? Beer?"

"I'll take a beer."

I poured his beer into the mug I had frosted before his arrival. He sat boyishly on my couch as I placed roses in a vase, feeling quite guilty for accepting flowers meant for a German supermodel who'd never step foot in my home. I returned to the family room, sat across from Mike, and thanked him for coming.

"Yeah, no problem," he snorted. "It's my pleasure. I'm real flattered she likes my column. Believe me, plenty of chicks don't." His focus swerved past me as Mike watched the stairs expectantly for Claudia Schiffer's descent. "She gonna be down pretty soon?"

"Look, Mike, I've got to confess something," I said. He said nothing. "I'm really sorry about this . . . it's just that you never returned any of my calls and this was the only way I could think of to get you here, and it really wasn't me anyway. My friend Greta called and said she was Claudia Schiffer's assistant and I was like, 'Stop, stop!' but she wouldn't listen because she really wanted me to, um, she thought it would be a good idea if we met because I really do have an exciting proposition for you, and, and . . . could you say something, please?"

Mike looked annoyed, but not entirely sure what I was saying. "So, you're Claudia Schiffer?" he clarified.

"Well, no . . . I'm not Claudia Schiffer. Of course, I'm not Claudia Schiffer, but if what you're asking is whether Claudia Schiffer is going to be here tonight, then, um, well, I have to apologize again, but, well, no. No, she couldn't make it."

"Couldn't make it?" he queried.

"Right."

"Couldn't make it? Or has no idea who you are, and never set up this bullshit meeting?"

My heart pounded like a frantic neighbor running to tell you the house is on fire. I desperately needed The Dog's help, and he was less than sixty seconds from the door.

"Um, no idea who I am," I stammered.

Mike stood up and grabbed his jacket. "Listen, I really wish you'd hear me out as long as you're here."

"Lady, I think you're psycho." He started toward the door.

I laughed nervously. "I assure you I'm not a psycho. I'm just very determined. Can't you respect that? I really wanted to meet with you because I value your opinion and want to make a business proposition. So I did what I had to do." As he got closer to the door, I knew I had about another thirty seconds to win him over, or become tonight's bar story. "Look, I've read a year's worth of back issues of your column and you're always complaining about how you wish women could think more like men. How cool it would be if women *really* knew what guys wanted? I'm offering an opportunity to do just that. You create the ultimate girlfriend. Think about what a service you'd be doing. You could write about the woman you're creating in your lab like Frankenstein's monster, um Frankenstein's bride?"

*Lose the whole Frankenstein thing. He already thinks you're a freak.*

"Like *Weird Science!* You know what I mean. Think about the material you'd get for your column." His body had stopped at the door, and his hand was on the knob. "Come on, Dog. I just want to make a guy unbelievably happy. Please. Six months. I'll pay you." At the mention of cash, he was ready to talk.

"How much?"

"A thousand a month," I offered.

"What do I gotta do for this thousand a month?"

"Advise me," I told him. "Just tell me what a guy wants from a girlfriend. Teach me how to become irresistible. We'll meet once a month and the rest we can do by phone. Ten hours a month, tops. Please, Dog. I'm desperate. I don't have much experience and I really need a, a guide."

"A guide dog?" He laughed. "You seem nice enough, but it's like workin' for the other side. I'm a guy's guy. I can't turn coat and be your fairy godmother."

"Two thousand?" I countered myself.

"I'm real sorry. I'm gonna have to pass." The knob turned.

"Twenty-five hundred," I wailed.

"Done." He smiled. Lifting his hand off the doorknob and shaking my hand, I enjoyed the most disempowered victory in the history of battle. "So, what's your name?"

"Mona." I smiled. "Mona Warren."

"Right. Why don't you cut me a check for December and we can get started right now?"

"Now?"

"Now a problem?"

"Um, no, no. Now is good. Now is great. I'll go get my checkbook. Grab a seat, Mike. Is where we were before okay with you?"

He didn't answer but returned to his place on the couch. "You think I could get another beer while you're up?"

"Yes, absolutely," I shouted from my office. "Should I order a pizza?"

"Sounds like a plan."

I returned to the couch where Mike had been partially absorbed by the burgundy chenille pillows. He leaned back, draping his arm around the back of the couch and resting his left ankle on his right knee. I sat primly in the corner, assuming about a fifth of the space. After I ordered pizza to Mike's specifications, he gave me his orientation. "Look, I'm the kinda guy who just tells it like it is. I don't do the whole happy talk at the front end, then finish on an up-note deal. I say what's on my mind. That gonna be a problem for you?" I shook my head to assure him that no happy talk would be needed. "If you're serious about this, I'm gonna have to lay the shit out there bluntly for you. You're not gonna cry if I hurt your feelings, are you?"

"No, no, absolutely no crying."

"Good, 'cause I gotta tell you, we *can* make you hot, but it's gonna take a lot of work. A lot. And I gotta just focus on my game and not worry about hurting your feelings, okay?"

"Okay. Do you really think I can be *hot*?"

He sighed. "It's doable. You're not half bad-looking, Mona, but I got my work cut out for me."

"I am ready to learn. Eager to learn."

Mike told me I was too passive, too accommodating. "You told me you were desperate and raised your price. You gotta get out of that mindset. I don't care if you're freaking out that I'm gonna leave, you've got to be cool about it, like hey, I'm offering something here. Take it or leave it."

"But you would have left it!"

"Sure 'bout that?" He smirked. A half hour later, our pizza arrived just as Mike was telling me I was devoid of any sex appeal. He continued chewing as he advised me on how to be more attractive. "You got a decent little body, Mona, but I really have to work to see it in that smock you're sporting." He swallowed and bit into another slice in the same breath. "You got a nice-looking face, but news flash for you, women are wearing makeup these days."

His eyes scanned me, assessing me from head to toe. "You gotta do something with the hair. It's just sorta sitting there doing nothing for me."

"Oh," I said sadly. "What's it supposed to do for you?"

"The deal is that you aren't gonna be sensitive about this. You want the truth or you want me to tell you a bunch of useless shit that'll make you feel good?"

"After you're done ripping me to shreds, you'll tell me what I'm supposed to do about it, right?"

I couldn't believe how much pizza this man could devour. How did he stay in such good shape shoving food in his mouth like letters through a mail drop? "First thing is you gotta start working out and get everything toned up. You could lose a few pounds, but no more than five, ten. I'm gonna hook you up with my sister on the clothing and hair thing 'cause I didn't sign up for the Queer Eye Fab Five team. I'm strictly a consultant on how to act, got it? Pay Vicki a hundred an hour and she'll take you shopping, hook you up with a good haircut and all that."

"Um, okay. Is she, um how should I put this?"

"Hot?" he finished.

"Well, I mean, is she—"

"She's a great-looking girl and if she's got the time, I'm sure she'll be willing to help me out."

"Okay."

"I think the best advice I can give you right now is to watch sexy women. Look at how they carry themselves. Watch how they move their bodies, how they dress. Look at their facial expressions. They're cute and they know how to use what they got. You should go to a strip club sometime and watch the girls work the crowd. They know how to play the game."

"Yeah, that's what I'm going to do." I rolled my eyes. "I'm going to a strip club with a wad of twenties."

"Go with a wad of twenties and you'll be very popular." Mike laughed. "My buddy told me his girlfriend took a stripping class and it was totally hot. Said she was like a whole different person. Had this 'I'm hot shit' attitude after a one-night class."

"But I don't want to be a stripper," I said. "I don't even think I'd strip for Adam. I'd be too embarrassed."

"You'd be *embarrassed*?"

"Yes, I'd feel completely self-conscious."

"You need the class, Mona," Mike insisted. "Trust me, you want to know what these girls know. You never have to strip for anyone, but get over the 'I'm embarrassed' thing." Abruptly, he looked at his watch. "My work is done here. My sister is in L.A. this week, but I'll have her call you first of the year to set up a time to shop and do the hair thing. Here's my cell phone and my home number if you need anything."

At the door, he looked softer than the last time we stood at the entry to my home. "You know, I kinda dug tonight. Maybe it's the holiday spirit or something, but I really feel like I'm doing something good here. Giving back to my community. Hey, have a good one. Remember, no cookies for Christmas, and sign up for that class."

As his car pulled out of my driveway, I leaned against the inside of the front door with a self-satisfied grin. "I did it," I said to no one. For a moment I questioned whether a guy like Mike could help me land a guy like Adam. One was my dream man; the other was every woman's worst nightmare. He definitely was my New York. I smiled remembering my first time in New York. I did make it there. I'd make it again and marry Adam just as I planned. For the first time in years, I felt a sense of peaceful assurance that everything would work out for me.

# Chapter 11

I have the absolute perfect birthday for someone who camouflages herself in the world. I share my big day with none other than Jesus Christ. Talk about being upstaged. Because of this gift from God (my birthday, not Jesus), I have never had to endure a cluster of restaurant waitstaff singing "Happy Birthday" to me. I have never had school or workmates taking collections for my birthday present. I always had an excuse not to throw a party. I took great consolation in this fact because it meant I would never have to suffer the humiliation of a poorly attended gathering.

Greta called early Christmas morning to wish me a happy birthday and make sure I still planned to attend dinner at her parents' house. Inspired by Mike's assurance that I had babe potential, I decided to run on the beach before showering and changing for Greta's. Rather than run along the cement walkway, though, I decided to climb over the wall of rocks and run barefoot along the shoreline.

My first Christmas with Grammy was spent dining in a hotel restaurant and window-shopping at closed stores, making us acutely aware that our family portrait was composed by tragedy. Something about getting away from home helped us escape the reality of looking at each other from opposite ends of an enormous dining room table. Grammy could've easily filled the seats with a dozen of her friends; it just seemed easier on both of us if we got out of San Diego. I suppose it was because the accident happened right around this time of year. We never really talked about it. It was always just assumed that Christmas would be spent anywhere but home.

There were years we stumbled onto very familial Christmas dinners. While I was on semester break from UCSD, Grammy and I stayed at a bed-and-breakfast about two hours outside of Dublin. It was possibly the coziest, warmest place on earth I'd ever visited. The Hennigan family ran the bed-and-breakfast, and Grammy and I were their only guests that week. They were a retired couple with five grown children who all lived within a three-mile radius with their own children. The Hennigans' walls were cluttered with framed photos and souvenir plates from places they'd traveled. A pewter mug with their family crest shared shelf space with a stuffed teddy bear wearing a knit sweater from a local preparatory school. A half finished game of Scrabble sat on a table where a silverware box was resting, waiting to be polished.

Grammy and I were like cats on a fishing dock, slightly tipsy and cuddled together under one of the many handmade quilts strewn across the Hennigan home. A fire blazed and people continued drinking, exchanging stories of the worst winters that ever hit Ireland.

Grammy and I also spent Christmas holidays in Jerusalem, Australia, Thailand, Athens, Rome, Barbados, and New York. Our New York trip was our last Christmas together. We were very much the tourists venturing through Central

Park In a horse-drawn carriage, taking in two Broadway shows and even going to the top of the red-and-green lit Empire State Building observation deck. I thought of how many couples planned to rendezvous there since *An Affair to Remember,* one of the only classic films I actually hated. I could never understand why Deborah Kerr didn't just show up in her wheelchair to meet Cary Grant. Grammy said I can't understand what a stigma it was to have a disability back then. She said it wasn't like these days when people in wheelchairs are in Kmart commercials. Still, if I were madly, passionately in love, I'd hope that my Cary Grant would adore me no matter what. I would crawl up every last stair of the then ADA non-compliant observation deck, panting and sweating, declaring, "I cannot walk, my darling, but I can still love. I can love you until I draw my last breath of life," or something equally dramatic. The kind of crazy talk you can only get away with in old movies.

Not only could I walk, I was able to run, and decided I'd better get to it if I was serious about losing that ten pounds Mike suggested. As my feet hit the wet sand, I noticed the imprint darken, then quickly fade. I thought about last Christmas and the one night I spent off the pages of the New York tour book—the first time I crawled out of my own life and into someone else's. Grammy said she wanted an evening to herself so I walked all the way from The Plaza down to Greenwich Village. I planned to hail a cab, but was distracted by the street vendors. I bought a blue fuzzy Kangol beret and scarf, which the Pakistani merchant said accentuated my eyes. A few blocks later, I picked up dangling earrings and a necklace made from old subway tokens. From the token lady, I also bought a belt made from MetroCards. On Thirty-Fourth street, a man named Gunther sold prints of the Statue of Liberty that he

designed with torn strips of subway map. Without notic-
ing the two-mile trek, before I knew it I was sitting in
Washington Square Park on an unseasonably warm night,
bumming a cigarette from a man who would've prompted
Grammy to clutch her purse.

As it turned out, the cigarette guy had a little street band
that performed in the park for tips while intermittently exchanging undersized envelopes with passersby. "What are
you dealing?" I asked.

"I deal nothing, sweetheart," he defended good-naturedly.
"What do you call yourself?"

"What do I call myself?" I laughed. It sounded as if I
had a choice. Then I realized that I did. "Um, Monique."

"Sit down, Monique, we sing a little song about Monique.
She take my smokes, she steal my heart." From the pocket
of his black wool coat, the young man pulled out a harmonica and his friend picked up his guitar from the ground and
tossed the rainbow-colored strap across his shoulder. I bal-
anced myself on the metal rail fence and listened as the
two improvised a song about "Monique, so beautiful, can't
hardly speak." I giggled. Mona would never hang out in
the park with drug dealers who write songs about her. But
Monique kind of liked it.

"I take requests, Monique," said my Jamaican Romeo.
"Like take out the garbage, honey. Kiss me here, kiss me
there. Change our baby's diapers. Love me all night long,
sweetheart."

Romeo was smoking something very potent, but I didn't
care. I could see he was a harmless musician who made
ends meet by dealing a little dope. Besides, we were in the
middle of a very public park. The worst thing that could
happen is I'd get arrested. "You look like a Beatles girl to
me, Monique. You like them Beatles?" he asked. Romeo
and his friends belted "A Hard Day's Night," serenading

me like a prop, a gimmick while people tossed coins in their guitar case.

"You a musician, Monique?" scaaky the guitarist asked.

"Musician? No. I'm an engineer."

"You tapping your toes and moving your lips like you want to play with the band, Monique. You want to play music with Romeo and me?" I shook my head in emphatic denial. "You head nodding no, but you feet tapping yes. What song you like? We play and you can hum along." He took chopsticks from his coat pocket. "You tap these on the fence and be the drummer."

When the guitar played the opening bars of John Lennon's "Across the Universe," my throat constricted. My mother sang this song to us kids most every night at bedtime. I knew every acid-inspired word, including the Sanskrit passage where most people just muddle through or fake it till the "Om." With the freedom of being Monique, I began singing until Scooby harmonized.

*"Nothing's gonna change my world . . ."*

The combination of Beatles music and Greenwich Village drew people to our little corner of the park, and inspired wishing well-like coin tossing. I stared at the ground to forget that people were watching, and tried to escape into the lyrics of this beautiful song and an even more beautiful memory.

Like my mother, I love to sing. It is my one true way of forgetting about the outside world and connecting with my core. I guess music does that for everyone, but singing is a special memory of my mother, who had one of the most intoxicating voices anyone had ever heard. She was a classically trained vocalist who everyone expected would sing for the Metropolitan Opera or something equally impressive. Instead, she sang lullabies to a house full of hippie kids. I sang in the shower. I sang in the car. But that night in the park was the first time anyone had ever heard my voice.

"Monique, you got some fine pipes on you, sweetheart." My Romeo laughed. "The people, they love you." He motioned to the crowd.

"Oh, they want weed," I dismissed.

As I relived last Christmas season, my only audience was the Pacific Ocean, quietly cheering me with its crashing waves. I raised my hands above my head. "Thank you. Thank you, Coronado. You've been great!"

# Chapter 12

Greta gave me two gifts for Christmas and my birthday—both self-help books. *Getting to Know You: A Woman's Guide to Self-Discovery* and *A Road Map to the Soul.* "Please take these in the spirit I give them," Greta half apologized as I was unwrapping the books. At least she had the good sense to give them to me privately, and not humiliate me in front of her fabulously well-adjusted family. Their book selections were certainly titles like *Being Perfect in an Imperfect World* and *We're Okay; They're Not.* Greta laughed at my characterization of her family. "Every family has its own issues," she said. "I'm not exactly the daughter my parents expected."

Greta's family didn't seem terribly disappointed with the way she turned out. There were at least a half dozen toasts celebrating her return to San Diego and her overdue breakup. Greta seemed uncomfortable the moment Terry's name came up. Her breath seemed trapped in her lungs and she shot her mother a look that pleaded to change the topic.

It had been more than a month since Greta returned from Texas and I still had no idea what had gone so wrong in her relationship that she had to leave. My guess was that Terry was unwilling to marry her, and after three years together, Greta probably realized it was never going to happen. If Adam and I shared so much history in one city, it would be hard to stay there with the constant reminders of places we'd gone and things we'd done together. Then, of course, there's the biggest reminder of all—him.

After dinner we sat in front of an understated Christmas tree decorated with small white bulbs and tasteful glass balls buried in the branches. Flames in the fireplace struggled to stay alive and chattering became quieter and less frequent. *A Very Perry Christmas* filled the air as Greta's mother handed us each a glass mug of spiced cider to "take the chill from our bones," she said, laughing.

"Would you ever consider playing soccer again?" Greta asked.

I laughed. "If you called what I did in high school playing, then no. I've never considered it."

"You weren't *that* bad." She teasingly shoved me.

I was a second alternate fullback, and the three times I actually made it onto the field during a soccer game, our opponents whipped right past me. Sometimes I lost my balance and fell just watching the other players running by. All the faking this way and cutting that way was dizzying. Our school made room on sports teams for every girl who wanted to play because extracurricular activities looked good on college applications. Greta was our starting goal keeper. In fact, she was recruited by several colleges and earned a full scholarship for soccer.

"Why do you ask?"

"I'm joining a women's league and thought you might want to get into it again. It might be good for you."

"Better mental health through soccer?" I joked.

"Well, the goals *are* loftier than marrying a stranger," was Greta's retort. "Seriously, it'll be fun. You'll meet nice women, get some exercise. Come on, you always say you have no life. Get a life. It's a social thing. No one's expecting you to be a star."

"I don't know," I hedged.

"When I signed up, a woman on the team told me that in addition to their regular games, they have scrimmages for women who aren't able to join the team for whatever reason. Why not give that a try?"

I scrunched up my nose. "I'll watch you play."

"Stop watching and start doing. Isn't that what this retirement is supposed to be all about?"

Soccer sounded about as appealing as an afternoon of mowing the lawn with my teeth, but I agreed to play in the following Saturday's scrimmage for a few reasons. It would burn a few hundred calories. I really did want to start making new friends. But the real reason was that I could use it as collateral with Greta. Or rather, I could prevent her from using my refusal against me. If I declined, she almost certainly would cite it as an example of my unwillingness to work on my own life. If I went to her soccer game, she couldn't say that I'm solely focused on Adam. I looked at Greta, eagerly awaiting my response, and was overcome with guilt. What a shitty friend I was, attending a soccer scrimmage as a preemptive strike. For whatever reason, it was important to Greta that we play soccer together again. I could extend myself in this way for one day.

"Okay, but they better know that I suck," I said.

"Fabulous!" She clapped. "This'll be *such* fun."

"And they'll know I suck, right?"

"Mona, I will most assuredly tell them that you suck, happy?"

"Not just yet."

I crawled into bed at midnight and had a great deal of trouble drifting off to sleep. I flipped from my back to my left side, then to my right. I spent a few minutes on my

stomach before deciding my problem might be tempera-
ture. As soon as I opened the window, I realized it needed
to be shut again. I conceded that perhaps I simply wasn't
tired yet. I scanned through a few pages of Greta's pop
psych books she selected for my lost soul. Road map to the
soul. Pul-ease!

> *Too many women today are looking outward
> for wholeness. What they have not yet realized is
> they are already whole and this God-given whole-
> ness can only be actualized from within. There
> are so many distractions from the self. Yet if we
> spent as much time looking at ourselves as we do
> turning to the mall, the bars, the office and the
> dating scene, we would discover that we do not
> need all of these outside sources to complete our
> lives. We are already complete. The truth is that it's
> easier to look outside ourselves for happiness. The
> hard work is looking at what we could do to make
> our lives better. The hardest work is really digging
> deep and figuring out what's missing within us that
> makes us seek validation from outside sources. The
> more women look outside themselves, the more
> they really ought to be looking within.*

Yawn! If Greta's agenda were any more in my face, it
would be my skin.

I logged on to the Internet to see what I could come up
with if I typed Adam's name in a search engine. In ten seconds, there were thousands of references to Adam P. Ziegler
listed before me. I giggled, almost guiltily, as though I'd accidentally caught a glimpse of his naked body. I couldn't
contain my grin at the sight of his name emboldened on
every blurb I saw.

"Let's see where you've been all my life," I said to no one.

"Gave a lecture on Congress' Corporate Auditing, Accountability, Responsibility and Transparency Act." I continued to read. "Death and Taxes: Tips for CPAs who file 706 forms on behalf of the deceased." I wondered if we'd have to file one of these for Grammy this year.

"Oh my God, how cute. Seen on the street. Says, 'I go for comfort before style.' The word he uses to describe his clothing choices: 'Sensible.' He is so unpretentious." I scrolled further.

"Wow, he wrote an article praising Bush's tax cuts for the middle class." I read a few paragraphs. "Hmm, some-one needs to clue my sweetie in on what middle class means." I smiled. At least he has an opinion and isn't afraid to pub-lish it. Grammy was a Republican, too, and she was per-fectly wonderful.

"Stanford, okay knew that from the degree on his office wall." Then a surprise. "Of his generous gift to the San Diego Chamber Music Society, Adam P. Ziegler says it is incumbent upon arts patrons to give all they can to this fine organiza-tion. Without music, our culture is a poor and soulless place where people simply exist but cease to live." Wow. A tad dra-matic, but what passion he has for music. Who knew?

A two-note chime came from my computer, like the ar-rival of a fairy. In the corner of my screen, a note alerted me that I had an instant message from MDog2@aol.com, and asked if I would accept it.

"Um, okay," I said before realizing I had to respond through my keyboard.

> *Hey. What are you doing on the computer on Christmas night?*
> *Mike?* I replied.

*Yeah, sorry. I put you on my Buddy List so I can bug my friends when I get tired of working online.*

*Oh. I was just doing a little work myself. How was your Christmas?*

*Average. Yours?*

*Okay. I got suckered into playing soccer next weekend which I'm not looking forward to, but other than that, nothing unusual.*

*A soccer player, ay?*

*I actually suck, but my girlfriend wants me to play.*

*Your girlfriend? Soccer? Did my invitation to this year's Dykefest get lost in the mail?*

*Don't I wish? Then I wouldn't need to rely on the likes of you! Imagine paying you to show me how to land a girlfriend! Seeing how you do such a great job at keeping the women hooked.*

*Ha! You've read January's column.*

*I've read every month's column.*

*Impressive.*

*Well, I wanted to know what I was buying.*

*A strong back and a good set of teeth.*

*And an ego that never quits.*

*That's called endurance, and believe me it ought to be on your checklist.*

*You're terrible!!!*

*You need a good helping of terrible. Hey, did you sign up for that class?*

*I'm not stripping!*

*Hold on.*

I waited as Mike undoubtedly went to the bathroom or grabbed a beer.

*Okay, I'm back. Mark January 8th on your calendar.*

*How come?*

*Stripping class. I enrolled you online.*

*I can't do that!!!!*

*What the hell are you paying me for if you're not going to take my advice? You told me you were Claudia Fucking Schiffer to get my attention, then nearly blockaded the door to get me to sign on as your Guy Coach. I cashed your check. Take my advice. It ain't cheap.*

I smiled at his rogue persuasion. "I cashed your check." I giggled.

*Okay. But let me seriously think through the stripping class.*

*It's one night, Mona! Three hours.*

*I suppose I could get through three hours. Do you really think this will help me?*

*Of course, I'll need a full report of everything that goes on in strip class. So I can do my job better, of course.*

*I've got to get some sleep. It's nearly two.*

*Night. Merry Christmas.*

*Good night, Dog.*

# Chapter 13

The morning grass was slick with dew and sunshine was fighting its way through a mild fog. I adore San Diego, where my biggest weather complaint was that it was too bright and a bit nippy in January.

Seven women, including Greta, stood in a circle passing a neon yellow soccer ball to each other. A guy in a rugby shirt was fixing the net to the goal box, shouting at two dogs that chased each other around the field. As I approached the group, I couldn't hear exactly what the women were saying, but it was the cadence and tone of sports taunting and bravado. That friendly ass-slapping banter among comrades. Several of the women wore sports bras and one had the most perfectly sectioned abs I'd ever seen. It was perfection beyond human capabilities. Like the physical specimen posters from high school biology classroom posters.

I entered apologizing. For being late. For sucking. For not having cleats. "Hey don't worry about it. We're just kickin' the ball around today," said the abs set, Brooke. "Get in here," she coaxed. I tried to pass the ball to Greta but it flew toward Lucy. The upside of passing the ball in a circle is that no one was sure where I was aiming, and by default, it always wound up in the general vicinity of someone.

During the game, Brooke ran down the field on a break away so I shadowed her, desperately hoping she would never pass the ball to me. Of course, she did. It came straight to me and I surprised myself when I stopped its course with my foot and gained control. With a clear field in front of me, I began to dribble the ball as fast as I could. I ran full throttle toward the goal and felt the sheer exhilaration that comes with the potential for victory. I saw myself at the net, shooting the ball past the goal keeper. I saw her dive toward my cannon shot and land on the grass just after the ball grazed the tips of her gloves. I saw my team carrying me off the field on players' shoulders. I saw a microphone and a television camera in my face, asking "Mona Warren, you've just won the World Cup. What are you going to do now?" I saw myself with perfect abs, mugging to the television cameras. "I'm going to Disneyland!"

What I didn't see was Jenna barreling toward me to steal the ball about two feet from where I'd taken possession of it. Our shoulders bumped, which left me on the ground watching Jenna run toward the goal. Although I was playing offense, I couldn't stay in my zone. This was personal. I ran as fast as I could toward her and tried to recapture the fantasy she'd so cruelly snatched from me. My determination and skill were not well matched though, and I ended up sliding into Jenna's back, then onto the grass and scraping the entire top layer of skin off of my right knee. It was one of those injuries that no one can really see, but hurts like hell. The skin looked as though it was just a bit tender with hair-thin scratches of blood extending down the shin. After the fall, there was no longer any skin to protect my leg from the sting of the elements. Clean water and fresh air felt like acid tearing the paint off of a car. The nearly invisible blade etchings sliced straight through my leg with pain.

After she shot her goal, Jenna came back to help me off the ground by extending her hand and giving me a firm pull. "You got hustle, I'll give you that, but in a real game you'd've gotten called for that," she told me.

The Kickin' Chicks forgave my many illegal moves, writing me off as Greta's talentless friend who could fill in for an occasional low turnout scrimmage. I wasn't especially surprised when the only invitation I received from the team was to come watch them play during the season. That and to join them for a round of beers after the scrimmage.

"To Mona," Greta lifted her beer mug.

"To Mona," my soccer mates joined in.

"You don't even know what I'm toasting her for, you bunch of lushes. Let me finish the toast, then we'll drink."

"Here, here," shouted Brooke. "To the patience of lushes."

"Now, you probably won't believe this, but my dear friend Mona did *not* want to play soccer this morning."

They all burst into laughter. "Well, the girl sure was filled with desire on the field," Jenna said, chuckling.

"Okay, so I'm not an athlete," I defended with mock annoyance.

"Don't get me wrong, girl. You got the soul of an athlete," she added.

Brooke's laughter escaped through her nose. "Just not the feet."

"Anyway." Greta stretched the word to regain the floor. "Mona tried something a little different. She went a little beyond her comfort zone, and I, for one, am very proud of her." She lifted her mug to let the others know that now they could toast.

"And let's not forget about our newest Kickin' Chick at the goal today." Mary Ellen raised her mug. "Some nice save there, Greta. Looooooking goooood, baby!"

Greta feigned embarrassment, holding her hand toward her chest as if to say "who me?" She batted her lashes, then snapped. "You all are full of it. I gave up one too many goals." One sneaked past her.

"Hey, Mona," Jenna switched gears. "I meant to ask you. Y'ever box?"

Jenna nodded, unfazed by my shock at the question. "Yeah, you know?"

"Hello. Did you see me out there on the field today? I'm hardly an ass-kicker."

"Girl, you *are* an ass-kicker," Jenna replied.

Brooke couldn't help adding, "Not a ball kicker, though."

"Nah, seriously, girl, you only shoved me like twenty times out there," Jenna said.

"Yeah, you shoved me, too," Mary Ellen added. "And we were on the same team."

"I'm so sorry!"

"Nah," she dismissed with the wave of a hand. "Not like anyone got hurt but you. I wonder if you might not get a kick out of going to the gym and beating the shit out of a punching bag."

"I doubt it."

"Eh, don't write it off so quickly. Give it a try. It's a hell of a workout. You go to any gym these days and check out the boxing classes and they're like ninety percent women."

"Well, I'll think about it," I lied. "Thanks for letting me play with you today. I had fun."

That evening, I headed toward the beach to unwind and catch one of the first sunsets of the new year. I predicted it would be a brush of grape cotton candy, but would have been equally satisfied with a flaming sinker where everyone on the beach would stop and applaud when the last sliver of gold disappeared behind the Pacific. I decided not to shower, somewhat savoring the dirt marks on my body and loose blades of grass clinging to my ponytail.

"Good evening to you, Miss Mona," said a deep male voice in front of the house. I turned from locking the gate to see a full head of white hair and a forest green alligator cardigan. It was Grammy's friend, Captain John. "Lovely evening we're having."

"Yes, lovely. Did you and Mrs. Brower enjoy the holiday, sir?"

He knit his brows. "You haven't heard."

I shook my head.

"Anne died in September, dear. I'm sorry."

"Oh my God! No, *I'm* sorry. Please accept my condolences, sir. If I had heard I certainly would have stopped by to pay my respects. I'm so sorry for your loss."

"Thank you, dear. She had a good life and we had many fine years together. We do have to thank the good Lord for our time with loved ones." He looked older than I'd remembered. "It was good to see you, Mona. Happy New Year to you."

"Yes, Happy—Yes, it was good seeing you, too, sir."

When I returned home, my message light was blinking. "You have two messages," said my electronic friend.

"Hi, it's me. Thanks for being such a great sport today. I know you didn't want to play soccer, but you did it for me and I wanted to tell you that I really do appreciate it. You're true blue, Mona, and I'm so happy we've reconnected. On another note entirely, I've been meaning to ask whatever happened with The Animal? Did he freak out when he found out you're not Claudia Schiffer? For the record, I think you're just as pretty as—" Beep.

My answering machine automatically cuts people off before they can finish a lie. I had to pay a bit extra for the feature, but I've found it to be worth every penny.

"Hey, Mona. It's Mike. I need to go with you to this class tomorrow night and, errrr, audit. You know, so you feel you got a friend by your side, ha. To support you in your three hours of need. No, seriously, good luck. Take lots of notes for me. Really. Lots of notes, 'cause I'm going to wanna hear every detail, got it? I know—" Beep.

I picked up the phone and dialed. The line rang once. Twice. Three times. "Hello," he answered.

"You know what?"

"What?"

"Your message. You got cut off right after you said, 'I know.' What do you know?"

"Oh, hey." I could see him just now registering my voice. "Look, this isn't a great time. I'll call you soon, okay?"

"Oh, yeah sure. No problem. We can talk whenever. No big deal. Go back to what you were doing," I hung up. Or *who* you were doing. The poor woman, I thought, imagining his flavor of the week sprawled beside him. Does she have any idea what she's in for with The Dog?

# Chapter 14

The ballet studio was nestled in an alley in Pacific Beach off a main street lined with trendy bars, vintage clothing shops, and funky restaurants. Ten minutes late, I ran up the staircase into a sauna-smelling white lobby where a thin woman with her hair in a black bun sat at a reception desk. Three swanlike women in leotards and toe shoes clustered around the desk, reaching their wiry arms toward their extended feet. The pounding of my sneakers announced the arrival of an imposter before I'd ascended the stairs. In my ponytail and sweatpants, the straps of my high heel shoes dangling from my right hand, I was obviously not there for a ballet class, but was still reluctant to state my reason for being on their turf.

"I'm here for, um, the class," I said as embarrassment washed over me like a wave.

"Exotic dancing?" The bun perked, exchanging amused glances with the other ballerinas.

"Vicki's taking that class," one said to another. "I've got to ask her what she thinks."

"Right that way." The bun pointed down the hallway.

I turned the corner of the hallway and peeked in a small

glass window. Women were sitting on the floor in a circle, lips moving, hair being braided, laughing. A sisterhood of wannabe strippers. This was crazy. I looked to see where the nearest exit was, but to leave the building, I'd have to pass by Swan Lake again. I could imagine them giggling uproariously as I dashed by with my swollen eyes and five-inch platform shoes.

Buying the shoes on Saturday was humiliating enough. When the posh-looking elderly saleswoman at Neiman Marcus asked if she could assist me, I told her I was having a difficult time finding the brand of shoe I was instructed to bring to class. "I've never heard of this line, but I need to find CFM shoes," I explained. Her face quickly became as white as the silk scarf tied around her loose neck. She placed a hand on my shoulder and turned me so both of our backs faced the showroom.

"Someone is playing a little joke on you, dear," said the saleswoman.

"No, they're not," I said. "I'm taking a class and I was told I need to bring CFM shoes."

"I don't know what kind of class you're taking, dear, but I assure you, Neiman Marcus does not carry *that* type of shoe. I suggest you try Colette's Closet downtown." Not only did Colette's carry Come Fuck Me shoes, but skimpy lingerie and accessories that all shouted the same general invitation.

The door to the ballet studio opened and a breeze of laughter rushed out. As always, I missed the joke. "Oh, hi!" The teacher waved, a honey blond cheer captain type. "We're getting started now. Have a seat. You must be Mona."

"Why?" slipped out. It was bad enough that Mike enrolled me in a stripping class, but had he called in advance to describe me to the instructor? He was probably trying to impress her with his Mr. Sensitivity routine. I could hear him now. "My dear, sweet, frumpy, and awkward friend will be attending. Please be gentle with her." I became enraged at the thought.

"Excuse me, what didya say?" said Tabitha. I could see why she was successful at stripping. Not only was she adorable looking, she seemed so thoroughly happy to chat with me. I almost handed her a twenty to keep looking at me.

"Oh, um, I just wondered why you said I must be Mona. Did, um, someone tell you I was coming?"

Her face lit up with a touchdown smile. "The attendance sheet did, sweetie pie!" Tabitha held up her clipboard. Yours was the only name I didn't check off yet. Have a seat in the circle. We're going 'round telling our names and what we hope to learn tonight."

I sat on the hardwood floor, surrounded by fellow classmates. At the front of the room was a wall of mirror; at the back was a ballet barre. Pushed in the corner was what I later learned was a port-a-pole. Much to my relief, looking at my classmates was not like flipping through *Playboy* magazine. A sixtysomething woman introduced herself as Myra and got a laugh from the circle of women when she said that taking the class was the last stop before filling her husband's prescription for Viagra. Her oversized T-shirt bore an illustration of a cat sitting atop a pile of books. "So many books, so little time," it lamented. We were all conspirators. Secret keepers for one another. Certainly no one in Myra's book club knew she was at a stripping class. When her husband's boss asked if he had any special plans for the weekend, he surely didn't answer that he was going to witness his wife's first striptease, hoping it would help cure his impotence.

Kelly wore black Betty Paige bangs and multiple tattoos

on her arms. Pale foundation accentuated the heavy black liner on her top eyelids. Chewing a fresh piece of Juicy Fruit, Kelly said she was getting married in three weeks and wanted to surprise her new husband on their wedding night. "Ahhhh," the women sweetly sighed as if she'd just sold her hair to pay for his watch chain.

Hidden beneath a mane of tangled brown hair was Olivia, a stocky woman who said it was her sixth time taking the class. "I'm an addict," she said. I refrained from leading the group in "Hi, Olivia." For the last three years, Olivia worked at the metal supply company where they manufacture poles for strip clubs. Two years ago, she filled in for a delivery guy and became fascinated with the club scene. "It was a forbidden underworld of sexy women and ogling men, where all the rules of the outside world don't apply. I was hooked from go."

Fern was in her forties and looked like Cher might have turned out if she hadn't enjoyed the comforts of fame. Her long frizzy hair screamed, "I bartended in Reno one too many years," and her eyebrows were so over-plucked, they looked almost terrified to try to grow back. She had the kind of face that was always smoking, even when there was no cigarette dangling from her dry lips. Fern said her husband promised he'd stop going to strip joints so often if she learned to dance for him. He even bought an extra large coffee table with a detachable pole in the center.

"Wasn't that a million dollar idea?" offered Olivia, who quickly let it be known that she was the ultimate authority in all things exotic. Over the course of the evening, poor Tabitha couldn't get two sentences out without Olivia piping in to share *her* favorite strip music, *her* online source for clear-heeled platform shoes, and *her* demonstration of the hip roll.

"I love to dance. I love making love, and I love feeling sexy," said a middle-aged Latina whom I imagined managed a family restaurant by day. "When I heard about the class, I told my lover we got to do this for each other," Maria said, gesturing to the woman beside her.

Together? But they don't let men—oooooooh, she's a lesbian. I see now. As must be Ginny, the embarrassed-looking woman beside her.

Vicki was the only one in the class who actually wanted to be a stripper, which I wondered if her ballet friends knew. "I've been dancing all my life, but I could never join a ballet company." She gestured to her cantaloupe boobs. We all laughed, a bit envious of such problems. "I dance with a modern jazz company but the pay is for shit so I need to supplement," she explained. Vicki was exactly what one would expect a stripper to look like, right down to the perfectly arched Hollywood brows and platinum blond hair. She had the Paris Hilton look, walking the thin line between sexy and cheap.

"I've got three kids under six and I need to wake things up in the bedroom or my sex life is going to be finished," said an exhausted-looking women.

"And what about you, Mona?" Tabitha asked.

"Oh, um, okay," I stammered, hoping my body would move more skillfully than my mouth. "I guess I just want to get in touch with that, you know, that other side of myself."

"Your untapped sexuality," Tabitha said.

"Um, yeah, I guess." How humiliating that she could immediately see how "untapped" my sexuality was. It was plain to see I was as appealing as a keg of old, tepid beer.

"Within each of us is a sexual goddess who is waiting for us to connect with her," Tabitha delivered through her thousand-watt smile. "Ten years ago everyone was talking about the inner child, which is totally great, too, but modern women have disconnected from the power of their sexuality because we want to be judged for our substance not our style. Don't get me wrong. I am all for substance, but embracing substance doesn't have to mean sacrificing our style, our sexuality, that special something that makes us light up a room when we walk into it."

"Confidence," Olivia added. It had been a whole forty seconds since her last pearl of wisdom.

"Pizzazz," Tabitha continued. "I only dance fifteen hours a week, but the rest of the time, I'm always using what I learn at the clubs. When I'm out in the world, I'm using the same skills I use when I'm on stage. It doesn't matter if I'm at the supermarket, the dentist's office, or church."

*Church?!*

"Church?" Yvette beat me to the punch. "What kind of church you go to?"

"Catholic, sweetie pie," Tabitha said as though using exotic dancing skills while accepting Holy Communion was the most normal thing in the world.

Yvette pressed, "What are you doing at church that you learned in a strip club? Not to be disrespectful or anything, I'm just curious what they let straight women get away with these days while my lesbian ass is kept in the closet."

"It's not so much what I do, it's how I feel, how I carry myself," Tabitha explained.

"What are you doing, strutting down the aisle or making sexy eyes at the priest or something?"

"Of course not, silly!"

"You kneeling at the alter all suggestive and stuff?"

"You are too cute!" Tabitha sparked. She pointed to the diamond-encrusted cross dangling from her neck. "Here's the way I see it. This cross was a gift to me from another dancer, who, like me, is highly, highly spiritual. She said something I will never forget to this day."

*Especially since it was said yesterday.*

"Kitten said that the cross represents the spiritual and the sensual and where the two sticks intersect is where the powers meet."

*Leave it to Kitten.*

"That middle part is a square, which if you think about it is kind of powerful because there are only two forces that meet to create a four-sided shape, so it's kind of like the spirituality and the sensuality double when they're together."

*Gorgeous bodies are wasted on imbeciles.*

"Some people are missionaries and they go to poor places giving out food, and that is such a beautiful thing to do. Dancers are kind of like sexual missionaries."

*No pun intended, I'm quite sure.*

"I'm giving positive sexual energy to the world and I make people really, really happy. This class is about so much more than stripping. It's about life and giving and sharing your gifts." Part of me thought Tabitha was an adorable but ridiculous child blessed with a killer body, who was desperately trying to force a spiritual message from hustling money from horny guys. Another part reluctantly admitted that she may be onto something. The whole intersection of the spirituality and the sensuality creating a double-whammy of super-duper Jesus power was a bit much, but the idea that a person could be wholesome and pure and good, and simultaneously very in touch with her sexuality was something I hadn't considered.

"Life is a striptease," added Olivia, who really needed to shut up very soon.

"I thought it was a cabaret," shot Kelly, the least tolerant of Olivia.

Tabitha acted as if she hadn't heard a word. I was reminded of the scene in *Legally Blonde* where Elle taught her hairdresser the "bend and snap." Tabitha's signature move was the "ignore and proceed," which she undoubtedly had to use when lecherous men wanted more than a lap dance from her. Bubbling with enthusiasm, Tabitha handed us each an agenda for the class. "We're going to start off with the entrance and walk, then move on to hip rolls, booty shaking, crawling, sliding, and pole work. Everybody ready to turn up the heat and hustle some bucks?!"

*What would Jesus do?*

"Let's do it!" shouted Olivia.

Tabitha walked to her CD player, but before putting on a hard-driving rap tune, Tabitha lined us up in front of the mirror like a chorus line. "What you need to know about men at strip clubs is that they will suck your soul dry if you let them. Most of them don't mean to, it's just the nature of the business. They're there to take pleasure and you're there to give it, but if you're not very, very guarded they'll take something precious from you." She paused to let that sink in, forgetting that with the exception of Vicki, none of us had any intention of dancing professionally. "Another thing is that for every lap dance you sell, five guys are going to turn you down, and that feels like shit. It doesn't matter how pretty or sexy you are, most of them are just too cheap to spring for a dance. It's not you, it's them. It's that simple. You *cannot* take it personally, or it will drain you. I have a little ritual I do before I dance," she perked. "I sing Christina Aguilera's 'Beautiful' to myself in the changing room before I go on. I watch myself in the mirror and belt it out. 'Words can't bring me down!'"

she began to sing. "Then I think about what I'm going to buy for myself with the money I make from them and I turn the guys into that thing before I go on stage, so I'm never really looking at men, I'm looking at furniture, diamond earrings, whatever! It may sound a bit cold, but these guys are there to take, take, take, and if you don't protect yourself, you'll find yourself, well, taken. Okay then!" Tabitha beckoned us with a sweeping motion of both arms. "Who's feeling sexy?"

I didn't. I felt foolish and embarrassed to be staring at my own reflection in a line of wannabe sexpots. "A lot of you are probably feeling pretty crazy for being here right now, like, why did I sign up for this class. Am I right or am I right?" A round of nervous laughter was comforting. "No matter how you're feeling—whether you are bloated from your period, or you just had a big fight with your boyfriend, oh, or girlfriend, or you've got a big pimple on your butt—no matter what you feel inside, you have got to come out with an attitude that you are the hottest thing on the planet and these guys are lucky to be looking at you. If you can pull that off, I don't care how old you are or what you look like, you are going to be smokin' when you dance."

"That is so true," said Olivia. "It's all about the attitude." Vicki shot me a look as if to say, "There's one in every crowd, isn't there?" I refrained from looking behind me to see if she was really gesturing to one of the pretty girls.

By the second hour the class had become a sisterhood of booty-shaking hoochie mamas. During the first exercise, the "step, roll, drag" walk, Violet brought us together when she collapsed in tears during the very first exercise. Each of us had made flirtatious eye contact with our reflections in the mirror when we saw Violet fall to the ground and burst into tears "I can't do this," she cried. Immediately, the women scampered to huddle around her. Stripping was a learned skill, but crisis management was second nature for women. Betty Paige, Reno Cher, and Mrs. Viagra draped their arms around Violet and told her how brave she was, and how she *could* strut her sexy little ass toward herself in the mirror. I could hear Mike's voice in my mind—"*Leave it to a bunch of chicks to take something sexy and make it into some big emotional drama.*"

When Violet sobbed on the ballet studio floor, I couldn't understand why she was distraught at the sight of her strutting self. But twenty minutes later, I too was terrified by the vulnerability of my own image desperately trying to be something I wasn't—sexy. There's something exquisitely fragile in the attempt. In the desire. Any one of these women could have broken me with a word. When Violet got off the floor and wiped her nose with her shirt sleeve, it was as though we'd all been initiated into a secret sorority. We weren't really sure why, but we now had a vested interest in the other's success.

With every dance move I did, it was as if a layer of old wallpaper was being peeled off. The hip roll was like tearing sheets of Grammy's elegant floral pattern from the dining room. The crawling move felt like a metal spatula removing another layer, a gold finished pattern under the flowers. Twirling provocatively around a pole was like tearing wood paneling off of the commune walls with my bare hands. Underneath was a pink velvet wall covering as gaudy as a brothel's. I would never actually decorate my house with such tacky paper, but a small part of me reveled in the hard sexuality of it. Loathe as I am to admit it, there was a piece of me that loved the cheap and tawdry side of sex—a part of me that longed to create one room in my tremendous home that looked as though a mud-flap silhouette lived there.

Even Olivia ingratiated herself to the group when she helped a few of us with our hip rolls. She placed her hands on my hips, moved them as though they were suspending a hoola hoop, and assured me that it took her hours to get the hang of it. Vicki immediately mastered every move, but took herself way too seriously, seducing her own image in the mirror with pursed lips and squinting eyes. When she ran her hands through her hair, then ran them down her Danskin-clad breasts and crotch, I shuddered at the lack of subtlety. "Too much?" she asked me with the tinge of insecurity that won me over.

"Well . . ." I hesitated. "You're a beautiful woman. You don't need to try so hard at it. I think you could definitely pull it off sexier if you took it down two or three notches."

For our final exam, each student had to perform one number for the class. Tabitha dimmed the lights, moved the port-a-pole to the center of the room, poured everyone a glass of wine, and gave us each a fistful of Monopoly money. I was the last dancer, which meant I had the chance to sip two glasses of wine and witness that, even after taking the class, only Vicki deserved real money for exotic dancing. Despite a hip roll that was as sexy as churning butter, the "Vicious and Voluptuous Violet" was the class favorite. The group burst into wild applause when Violet stumbled on her five-inch CFM heels and momentarily lost her balance. In her best trucker voice, Olivia shouted, "I likes me a good clumsy woman." We laughed.

Vicki hooted in a husky drawl, "Womens is all sexy when they wobbly."

When Tabitha motioned that it was my turn, my giddiness sobered into terror. I pointed to my watch to let her know we were already five minutes over time. "Time to dance, sweetie pie," she whispered. "Next we have a real work of art for you. We won't have to wonder what you're smiling about when you see the magnificent and mysterious Mona Lisa." Tabitha zipped out before pressing the Play button on her CD. I recognized Mary J. Blige's voice urging, "so just dance for me," and silently coached myself. "You are the hottest thing on planet earth, and these diamond rings are lucky to be looking at you," I repeated in my mind. I began with a modest hip roll then twirled around the pole a few times before sliding my arched back down it as though my hands were chained together over my head. The stripping sorority began cheering and calling me over to tip me with pink dollars in the elastic of my sweatpants. Soon, the wine buzz returned and I let loose. Mona Lisa stopped at all the right breaks and mugged the famous enigmatic grin while placing my hands mischievously over my shirted breasts. I tossed my head to make my high ponytail whip around like a helicopter propeller. Sliding my hands from my thighs to my knees, I bent at the waist and pretended my butt cheeks were washing a windshield, as Tabitha had instructed earlier. As I heard the song winding down, I decided to be the only one in the class who used the slavelike crawling move we were taught. I did a few more small teasing moves before gently slipping into my submissive pose. Well, it was supposed to be a gentle slip but I ended up losing control and slamming my knees against the wooden floors. "Shit!" I screamed, realizing I had landed on the same spot where I'd removed my skin during the soccer game. "My knee, my knee is bleeding!" I cried. The Monopoly money fell to the floor, and this time it was me in the center of the maternal huddle. "Are you okay, sweetie pie?" Tabitha rushed over.

The tired mother reached into her purse for Blue's Clues Band-Aids.

Betty Paige rubbed her hand across my back and told me to count to ten.

Vicki told me I looked pretty sexy until I screamed in agony.

# Chapter 15

On our wedding night, Adam carried me over the threshold of the honeymoon suite of the Hotel Del Coronado. He set me onto the king-sized pink velvet bedspread where a silver bucket of ice chilled a bottle of champagne. We laughed for no particular reason, just giddy to be alone together. "Would you forgive me if I tore these buttons from your gown?" Adam asked.

"Oh, don't," I begged, though I was thrilled he was so eager to undress me. "I want to save the gown for our daughter to wear at her wedding."

"You torment me, Mona. There've got to be a hundred little buttons down the back of that thing."

"This *thing* is a work of art, Adam! And there are exactly 142 pearl buttons for your beefy fingers to unfasten if you want me," I teased.

"*You* are a work of art." Adam sat me on the edge of the bed and brushed the loose hair from my *Breakfast at Tiffany's* bun away from my neck. My breathing became labored as my body slipped into a bath of warmth and intensity. "One button," he said as I felt the bodice of my gown loosen ever so slightly. "Two," he said, popping the second button loose. Three, four, and five felt as though my body was being freed. First the touch of the air on my skin, then Adam's fingers delicately, surgically separating the button loops from the pearls. Each time his finger grasped another button and pressed it through the loop, I felt myself swell and split with desirous, desperate invitation. It was divine torture.

Then the phone rang. "Who would call us on our wedding night?" I whined.

"Let it ring," he whispered as he began slipping the sleeve from my shoulder.

Then it rang a second time. "Ignore it, Mona."

I slid back into my wedding night, the perfect balance of anticipation and satisfaction.

After a few seconds, the answering machine beeped like a siren. "Hey, Mona Lisa," Mike's voice blared through the room. "Did you have a good time last night, hot stuff?"

Why the hell is Mike Dougherty calling me on my wedding night?! How dare he call demanding the intimate details of my first night with Adam—while it's still going on no less. And why in God's good name would he leave a message like that on the answering machine when he knows Adam is with me?! Wait a second. There's no answering machine at the . . .

"Shit!" My eyes shot open. "I can't even have a romantic night with Adam in my dreams." I picked up the phone, furious with Mike for interrupting my dream. "Do you mind?!" I shouted into the phone. "I was trying to sleep!"

"Whoa," he said like such a dumb guy, he actually sounded like someone doing an impression of a dumb guy. "I'm sorry, did I accidentally dial my ex-wife?"

"I didn't know you have an ex-wife," I said with less of an edge, but still annoyed. "You never write about her."

"Yeah, well I've got an ex-wife who would sue the shit

out of me for whispering her name in a confessional," Mike said.

"Well I can see why. You are completely rude and self-centered!"

"How the hell was I supposed to know you were still sleeping? It *is* almost nine o'clock. Some of us who have jobs have been up for hours," he snapped back. "I wanted your take on last night."

"Oh yeah, right. You are so interested in how I did in the class, right? Soooo concerned with how I handled it because you, you're just so caring. You just want to hear about all of the hot naked women I saw last night." I mocked his request with a dumb guy voice. "Take notes. Tell me everything."

"Is this what you're like in the morning? Here's a free one for you, don't let your boy see your charming morning personality. You need some serious coffee or Valium, or something."

I sat up in bed and threw my blankets off of my body. "I do *not* need some coffee or Valium or anything. You were completely rude to me the other night."

"What are you talking about?" Mike asked.

"I called you and you completely dismissed me like I was some sort of intrusion on your life. Like 'So sorry, this is not a good time for me right now. I'll call you when it's convenient for *me*. Me, the center of the universe." I was pacing the house madly, thankful to be barefoot, lest he hear the angry staccato of shoe heels in the background.

"You are whacked!" Mike shot. "I don't know what the hell you're talking about. I was busy. I told you it wasn't a good time to talk and that I'd call you back. Now I'm calling you back. Where's the problem?"

His question was like a slap in the face. Not the slap of an abuser. But the kind of slap a buddy gives you when you're freaking out. The kind of slap where you snap back to your good senses and say, "Thanks, man. I needed that." I couldn't say that to Mike, though. I'd painted myself into a corner and now seemed like the hysterical women he writes about in his column. I had to find an excuse he'd understand.

"Hey, I'm sorry, Dog. I was just having a sex dream and you called right when I was about to, well you know. You can't blame a girl for being a bit cranky after that."

"Oh," he digested. "Okay."

"Okay, like okay, you're over it? Or okay like, 'Okay, whatever. You're whacked but I don't want to get into it'?"

"Is there a difference?" Mike asked.

"The difference is that one is like, 'Oh, okay, I can understand where you're coming from and we're fine now' and the second is like, 'I don't know what you're talking about, but I don't really give a shit either, so I'll say okay so we can change the topic and move on to things that I actually care about like whether the women in strip class wore G-strings or went totally nude.'"

"Uh, the first one," he answered.

"The first what?"

"The first thing you said. The one about I get what you're saying and it's all good."

"Are you sure?"

"Okay, the second one," Mike panicked.

"Do you have any idea what I'm even talking about?!"

Mike began to laugh. "Look, I hear you, but I gotta be honest, I have no idea what you're talking about." At that point, I laughed, too. "Mona, I'm a pretty simple guy. All this 'what did you mean by this, what did you mean by that' is really wasted on me. If I say okay, it just means okay. Maybe this would be a good time for me to clue you

in on guy truth number two: We're really not all that complicated. If we say we're hungry, it's 'cause we're hungry. If
we say we're tired, we're tired. We don't do the whole sub-
text thing the way women do."

"What's the first truth?" I asked.

"The what?"

"Mike, do you have a thirty-second memory? The first
guy truth. You said the second was that you people are
dog-shit simple. What's the first?"

"Oh, yeah. That we're thinking about sex most of the
time."

"Well, then you should appreciate that I didn't like having my sex dream interrupted." I sank into my chaise lounge
and kicked my leg onto the wooden arm rest.

"Nah. So what was this sex dream about anyway?"

"Never mind. So who was over last night when I called?"

"Never mind. Hey, Vicki told me you got into it last
night. Said you were kinda hot, Mona Lisa."

My spirit free-fell at the thought of Mike and Vicki talking about me in stripping class. Certainly they had a few
laughs at my expense. I wondered if Vicki offered an imitation of how ridiculous I looked. I wondered if he told
her how much I was paying him. I wondered how the hell
Mike even knew Vicki!

"How the hell do you even know Vicki?" I demanded.

"Fuck, am I in trouble again?"

To an observer, it would appear as though I was doing
nothing. I sat motionless, saying nothing. The nothingness,
though, was the center of an isometric pull of equal com-
peting forces. Part of me was furious, humiliated, and be-
trayed by the fact that Mike sent a mole to report on my
performance at stripping class. I wanted to tear through
the phone line, grab the skin on his face, and bang his head
on a wall—repeatedly. Another part didn't want to seem

as though every little thing set me off. I had already spent my drama on the "what does okay mean?" ordeal. I didn't want him to think that every interaction with me was going to be wrought with conflict.

"No, I just want to know how you know Vicki from dance class. You hadn't mentioned you knew someone in the class already. Was she there to, to, you know, check up on me? Who is she anyway, your girlfriend?"

"Nah. Vicki's my little sister. I told her about this gig with you 'cause of the whole shopping and hair thing. When I told her about the stripping class she said it sounded cool and she's always thought dancing would be an easy way to make money. So I told her where it is, and turns out she's been taking ballet class there forever and never knew they did a monthly strip night. Anyway, I told her you were gonna be there but that you were shy about going so it'd probably be best if she lay low and didn't say anything about knowing me. You're pissed at me again, aren't you?"

"No," I said and meant it. "That was nice of you. I almost ditched the class before I even got to the door, so I'm glad I didn't know your sister was there. It *would've* made me nervous. What did she say anyway? Did she say I looked like an idiot? She was really good, by the way. *Really* good. I wasn't that good. Did she tell you that?"

"Nah, she said you were cute."

"Cute?" I tossed the small scraggly fish back into the ocean.

"Good," Mike tried again.

"Did she really?!" I reeled in. "I've never done anything even remotely like that before so naturally I wasn't as good as Vicki or anything. Did she really use the word good?"

"Yeah, she said you seemed a little uncomfortable at first, but once you let go and got into it, you looked sexy, I mean good."

"No, sexy is good, too," I said. "Did she actually say sexy or are you just interpreting?"

"Hey, I got an idea. Why don't you drive your psycho little ass across the bridge and let me decide for myself. I really can't remember if she said good or sexy, or good and sexy. Who knows? Man's gotta see for himself."

"Very cute." I smirked.

"Cute?! Cute?!" He imitated my voice. "Do you mean cute or do you mean clever? Cute or sexy? I'm not so sure how I feel about cute."

A rapping on the front door interrupted. "Shit! It's Greta," I told Mike. "I've got to go. We're supposed to go running and I'm not even dressed."

"Mona Lisa, you are a Grade-A cock tease, you know that? Listen, call me later for Vicki's phone number. She says she's got time to take you shopping this weekend."

Running down the stairs and toward the door, I welcomed Greta sheepishly. "I'm sorry I'm late. I overslept. I can be ready in five minutes."

"Not a problem. Take your time, Mona."

"Guess who I was on the phone with just now?" I shouted downstairs.

"Your future husband?" she mocked.

"Nope! Mike the Dog. I hired him. He's my guy coach." I giggled. "And guess what I did last night?"

"Tell me," she shouted.

"I took a dance class." I popped my head down the stairwell to catch her expression.

"Fantastic, Mona!"

"Exotic dancing," I said, in a Barry White sexy low voice.

"Jesus Christ," she sighed.

"Totally approves. Really, wait until I tell you what this

stripper Kitten has to say about how exotic dancing is really the path to spiritual enlightenment."

"Kitten?" Greta raised her brows.

"Kitten," I said as I descended the steps. I felt like sliding down the banister on a single cheek.

"So, Dog's your guy coach and Kitten's your stripping coach?"

"Kitten wasn't the teacher. She was the teacher's friend."

"I think you're missing the point. You're letting a bunch of house pets run your life. Dare I ask what's next?"

"Um, maybe more soccer with the Kickin' Chicks." I smiled.

"Oh you're such a little smarty pants." She chased me, trying to swat me with a dishrag.

# Chapter 16

After seven weeks, Greta and I were running three and a half miles every other day. By the last week in January, I no longer felt as though someone was stabbing my right rib while stuffing cotton into my head. With my loss of seven pounds, I also noticed that my ass was joining the rest of my body for the run instead of following in a separate cart known as Hanes briefs. Greta insisted we have Sunday dinner at a health institute in Lemon Grove where people with cancer go to heal themselves with wheatgrass. On Sundays, they open their doors to the public for dinner. Greta seemed to think the three-dollar meal was a real bargain, but when a place is serving raw vegetables, "seed cheese," wheatgrass juice, and some mucky water concoction called Rejuvelac, how much can they really ask people to pay?

To the great disappointment of my cynical side, I actually liked wheat grass juice and started ordering flats of grass from the health food store. I bought a viselike contraption to squeeze my own juice and also purchased a vegetable juicer so I could become a devotee of liquid salad.

After our run, I invited Greta in for juice. "So, guess

where I'm going this weekend?" I prompted Greta as I fed a carrot into the slot of my juicer. The metal teeth squealed with delight as it pulverized the carrot and spit an ounce of vegetable blood from the chute.

"Okay, I'm game. Where are you going this weekend?"

"Mike's sister is taking me shopping."

"So now you need a shopping consultant, too? Can you make any decisions on your own?"

"Says the mental health consultant," I quipped, hoping to shift gears.

"Oh Greta, you've never even met Mike or Vicki. He's okay when you get past all his bravado, and she's nice."

"I don't need to meet Mike to know him. He's a classic misogynist," she said.

"Is that how you treat your patients? You classify them as a type and don't bother getting to know them as individuals?" I asked.

"That's a very different relationship and you know it," Greta said as I watched her scan her brain for a reason. "When people are in therapy, it's because they want to gain insight about themselves and understand themselves better. Any man who preys on vulnerable women, pretending to have valuable advice on the male mind, is a con artist."

"Mike hardly preyed on me, and I don't consider myself a victim of a con artist, Miss Claudia Schiffer's assistant," I smugly retorted. The noise of the juicer seemed louder in the absence of conversation. The air was heavy with awkwardness. I groped for any words to break the silence between us.

Greta said softly, "It's just that I would've gone shopping with you for free. Don't you care for my taste in clothing?"

"Of course I do!" I lied. The truth is that Greta main-

tains a classic professional style, even when she isn't working. It worked for her, but I was looking for something in
between her style and Vicki's wardrobe of fireworks.

"It just seems your makeover is all about your appearance, and you're not spending any time working on your
inner life."

I surprised myself and Greta by slamming my palms
onto the brown granite countertop of my kitchen. "I *am*
looking at myself! Didn't I play soccer with you a few
weeks ago? Didn't I read those goofy pop psych books you
bought me, and cull through the mountain of crap to find
the few things that were helpful? Didn't I eat garden scraps
because you said a healthy body was important to mental
health? What more do I have to do to show you that I am
putting as much energy into the inner me as I am the outer
stuff?! Just because I want to look better and put a little
pizzazz in my wardrobe doesn't make me shallow. You're
a beautiful woman. You can get all the male attention you
want simply by stepping out the door. I can't. You've
known me for sixteen years. You know I prefer blending
in. But now for the first time in my life I do want some attention, and I want it from Adam Ziegler, the man I love.
And I'll tell you what else, I'm going to get it. I'm going to
do whatever it takes and get what I want. Greta, I love you
dearly, but I offer no apologies for what I'm doing. I'm
going shopping this weekend and if Vicki tells me that an
outfit makes me look pretty or sexy, I'm going to buy it.
For God's sake, Greta, I'm not hurting anybody. I'm not
doing anything illegal or immoral so please, once and for
all, get off your high horse and stop acting like I'm committing treason against myself for buying a few skirts and
a couple of cute tops."

Greta looked at the cup of juice, which was overflowing
onto the counter after I madly stuffed carrots into the

juicer without paying attention to output. I grabbed a cloth and began wiping. Greta placed her hand over mine gently.

"Okay," she said. "Just promise me you won't lose yourself trying to become what you think someone else wants?

"Deal."

What I loved about shopping with Vicki was that she didn't feel any sense of obligation to stay and look at clothing in boutiques if she knew right away that she wouldn't be interested in anything there. After I'm in the shop I feel as if I have to examine a few items and feign interest when saleswomen go on about the designer's artistic genius. Not Vicki. She isn't at all averse to walking into a store and making a U-turn like a model strutting the catwalk.

At every store, all eyes followed Vicki's monochromatic second layer of skin—tight pink jeans, a pink beaded cropped sweater, and pink platform shoes with bows. Vicki slinked over to items I would have never considered, touched the fabric, then held it up against her chest with a beaming smile that asked what I thought. At a hundred dollars an hour, she would get my unedited feedback. "Too low cut," I dismissed.

"Low cut? *This?* You're crazy. Try it on. You don't have to buy it." This was Vicki's response to all of my concerns with her selections. I said too tight; she said try it on. I thought too slutty; she said slip it on for a quickie in the dressing room. I protested that colors and patterns were too bold; Vicki said I should have a fling with a brazen sweater.

"I hope you won't take this the wrong way, Vicki, but I don't want you to make me over into you. I need you to help me figure out my own style."

"Oh," she said, disappointed. I hadn't purchased anything in our first hour and she was in need of a cash register buzz. "Okay, I'm with you on working out your own style and all, but what did you mean by not wanting to look like me?"

It was a horrible time for me to feel a sense of conquest in deflating the pretty girl's ego. It's just that women like Vicki never valued my opinion. They never even asked for it. I had to confess that I felt a smidge of vindication that I hurt her feelings. Vicki had been nothing but kind to me, but in a moment she became every bitch at the Academy who called me a nerd, a freak, a hippie drug addict, and a lesbian. Then I looked at her waiting for my response, and Vicki was just Vicki again.

"I'm sorry," I said as we sat on the wooden benches outside Forever 21, a store crowded with teens and middle-aged women. "Your look expresses who you are, but I want something that says me."

"God, Mona, you are so full of shit," she returned neutrally. "Why don't you tell me what you really think of the way I dress? You won't hurt my feelings."

Hadn't I already? And why was she telling me I wouldn't hurt her feelings? Was it that I was just a client, not a real friend? Was it that I was frumpy and my opinion was therefore meaningless? Or was she simply begging me to tell her what she already knew—that the way she dressed revealed too much about Vicki's desperate need for attention. I inhaled, mustering the nerve. "Vicki, you're a very sexy woman. There's no doubt about it. It's just the way you dress screams 'trying too hard.' Your whole stomach is showing in that sweater. And that pink rhinestone Playboy bunny hanging from your bellybutton." I shuddered. "It's like you have no idea that people would look at you even if you didn't invite them to. Please don't take this the wrong way. All I'm saying is that you look good enough just with what you were born with. See these girls?" I pointed to a pack of teen girls with ironed hair and nondescript faces. "They need to try. You don't. I think you'd be sexier if you went with a more conservative look. Like the really hot investment banker with the black wide leg pants suit and square toe shoes with tassles."

"I want to look like a woman," she protested.

"Trust me, no one is going to mistake you for a guy no matter what you're wearing. Did I offend you?"

"Mona, I am basically unoffendable," she postured. "Have you ever thought about getting your hair straightened?"

I shook my head, wondering if we'd finished the conversation about Vicki's clothes.

"Can I ask you a question, Vicki?" She nodded. "What's with all the pink?"

She laughed. "I had my colors done once and the woman said I should only wear pink."

"Really?"

"Yeah, why?"

"Vicki, you'd look good in any color. Aren't they supposed to give you a whole season or something, not just one color?"

She shrugged. "Yeah, I guess I got the cut-rate deal. Do you really think I'd look good in any color?"

Could she really not know this? Or does she just need to hear it again? In any case, there was only one answer that I would give. "Yes, Vicki, you'd look good in puce."

She smiled and bit her lip, then began shooting beauty tips rapid fire. "You've got a nice rich chocolate color to your hair. We should get you in for that Japanese hair straightening deal. Hey, after we get your new clothes, let's

go to the MAC store and ask them to give you a total makeover, then we can see what kind of makeup you should
buy. Have you ever thought about shaping your eyebrows?"

Within minutes we were flipping through outfits at Ann
Taylor. I bought a form-fitting black cotton sweater with a
white embroidered looping design and matching pants, three
spring button-down linen tops, a tasteful denim skirt, and
a spunky little pair of wedge heels. By the end of the day, I
had five shopping bags filled with outfits that were my brand
of sexy—not Vicki's. And she had a few new pantsuits that
showed less skin and more Vicki. She dropped the pink
and went from stripper chic to elegant sexy with an ease I
envied.

"Wanna catch a movie?" Vicki offered as we walked to
the mall parking lot to deposit our purchases in our respective car trunks.

"Off the clock?"

Vicki smiled. "Definitely off the clock. I had a good time
today. I wouldn't charge you unless I had to, but I'm strapped
for cash right now, which is why I'm doing the whole stripping thing. I don't want you to feel like we're not friends
or anything. I feel kind of bad charging you."

"Vicki, I was just kidding about being on the clock. You
provided a service today. I'm happy to pay you for it. Really.
Are you really going to get a job dancing?" I giggled nervously at the thought that one of my classmates was going
to take her rhinestone studded diploma and put it to use.

"Got an audition tomorrow. Manager said to come on
in, he'll take a look at me and if he likes what he sees, I
need to be ready to give him a three-song routine right
there and then."

"Wow. Maybe our class should take a field trip and
watch you some night," I elbowed her.

"Assuming I get it," she said, genuinely unassuming.

"You're kidding, right?" I raised my eyebrows and opened my eyes wide to suggest her doubt was completely unfounded. "You are exactly what they're looking for. You're gorgeous, plus you picked up every dance move like it was second nature."

"Thanks." She smiled, realizing I was probably right that she'd ace the audition. "But don't bring the class. Can you imagine Olivia there, 'Errr, uh, excuse me, but I brought my own CD the girls could dance to. If anyone's out sick today, I would just loooove to fill in.'"

We laughed conspiratorially. "I'm so sure a group of women would be welcome at a strip club. Can you imagine?" I tried my best old drunk guy voice, which for some reason came out sounding like Shrek. "Ah, come on now, ladies. First The Citadel, then Augusta, now strip clubs? 'Ow 'bout lettin' us boys keep one safe 'arbor, ay?" We giggled like Wilma Flintstone and Betty Rubble—chirpy and playfully contemptuous of the cavemen with whom we share the planet.

"Speaking of chauvinist pigs, how's it going with my brother?"

"So far, all he's done is sign me up for the stripping class, which I have to say was not an altogether terrible idea. He was right about me getting in touch with a different part of myself. Can I tell you something?" She nodded. "I have been having the hottest dreams since I took that class, not just when I'm sleeping either. For like two days after that class, all I could think about was sex."

"I take it that's not the normal state of affairs for you." Vicki smiled.

"That's an understatement."

"Going through a dry spell?"

"Yeah, like a sixteen-year dry spell."

"Sixteen years?!" She gasped. "Why? Do you have the world's best vibrator or something?"

"I just never really got close to anyone after my first boyfriend. I just could never . . ." I trailed off.

"Broke your heart?"

"No, he died. He was killed, actually. Him and the rest of my family. There was an accident. No one survived." It felt weird to say this aloud.

"Whoa!" Vicki absorbed this. "That's horrible. I mean, you hear about things like that, but I've never met anyone who . . ." her voice trailed off. "I'm so sorry, Mona. How awful for you." She paused, knitting her brow. "So you had sex with, I'm sorry what was his name?"

I hadn't said it since the last time I spoke to him. "Todd," struggled to escape.

"So you had sex with Todd, he was killed, and you haven't been with a guy since?" I nodded. "I hope I don't seem too crass here, but you're not thinking you're like the fuck of death or anything, are you?"

I burst into laughter. "The fuck of death?! Oh my God, Vicki, I can't believe you said that!"

"I'm sorry."

"God, no. Don't be sorry. Everyone always walks on eggshells when they find out about, you know. No one's ever accused me of being the fuck of death! Priceless."

Vicki had clearly switched gears. "Mona, I hope you don't take this the wrong way, but don't get too attached to Mike, okay?"

"Attached? We have a business relationship, that's all."

"Okay, whatever. It's just I've seen a lot of girls get shit on pretty badly by Mike. Not that some of them don't deserve it, but you seem like a decent person. I don't want to see him hurt you."

"Hurt me? Mike's an employee. He couldn't hurt me if he tried. Vicki, I've hired him to help me appeal to another guy, remember?"

"Okay, my mistake."

When I returned home that evening, there were two messages from Greta. The first asking how my day of shopping went; the second reminding me of the Kickin' Chicks game the next weekend.

# Chapter 17

---

*Gone Are the Good-Time Girls*
*—Mike "the Dog" Dougherty*

*It's a sad day for dogs everywhere. The last of the good-time girls have gone the way of bridal registries and joint checking accounts. Due to some cruel twist of fate or imperfection of nature, even the hard-core good-time, casual sex party girls have been domesticated. Now, even they want a commitment from guys.*

*Cyberporn chicks now want a committed relationship with their voyeurs. What's the world coming to?*

*I logged on to my e-mail account the other day and saw this subject line that read, "Want to see hot sluts get it on?" Not-so-coincidentally, the answer to that question was a resounding yes. I know how porn works. They give you a little glimpse, then want you to join some club for beaucoup bucks. No surprises there.*

*What I didn't expect was that I'd be unable to log off the freakin' site after a few minutes. Like*

*a thousand relationships in the past, I found my-
self frantically clicking "End Task" to no avail.
Hot Slut would not shut down. She would not
go away. Suddenly, I'm getting images of credit
cards she accepts. "End Task," I pound. "Quit,"
I press. "Exit. Exit. Exit." She would have none
of this. She was here to stay. She wants a commitment. She wants my money. She wants to introduce me to her slutty friends. Finally, I decide
the only choice I had was to hit Control, Alt,
Delete. And with the rest of my system, Hot Slut
went away. An hour later, I log on again, and
guess who's back? You know it. It's her and an
army of e-sluts accosting me with offers. They
tell me they just want to have fun, but I know
what they really want—a long-term relationship
with my Visa card.*

*I ended up having to put Hot Slut on my spam
blocker, which is the electronic version of a re-
straining order.*

*Has the world gone completely nuts? Where
are the good-time girls that were stashed in magazines under my dad's side of the bed? The ones
who wouldn't utter a single word, but stood
there posed naked for me to look at, then quietly
left when I had something else to do?*

*Perhaps what's so tough about this was that I
always trusted that porn girls were most like us
guys. They don't talk much and when they do,
it's all about us and our dicks. They never need
us to do household chores. They don't have cats.
Basically, they're us with righteous female bods.
When fantasy meets reality is where dreams end
and nightmares begin. You cannot take a scrump-*

*tims fantasy woman and give her curlers and
a rolling pin because the reality completely can-
cels out the fantasy. Here's the equation. Pamela
Anderson plus commitment equals Madge, the
Palmolive lady. Sad but true.*

I had to re-read Mike's column after my lunch with
Vicki. Was this man dropped on his head as a baby or
something? Then I tried Greta's pop psych picks. I would
never admit this to her, but the books she bought me for
Christmas had some interesting exercises. It's not that I
want to deny Greta the opportunity to be helpful; I just
know how impossible she'd be if she knew I bought any of
her psychobabble. She'd have a reading list for me and
three referrals for therapists. I went online and found a
book with a title that jumped out and grabbed me: *Feel the
Fear and Do It Anyway!* It was the first time I'd ever con-
templated that fear and action could coexist peacefully. I
always thought I had to get over my fear before doing anything, but according to this Dr. Jeffers, I should embrace
my fear rather than swatting it away like a swarm of flies.

It was time for me to call Adam for my tax appointment—the perfect time to feel my fear and do it anyway. I
felt a nausea so strong I thought I might actually vomit. I
paced the house and rehearsed exactly what I would say.

"Hello, Adam. It's Mona Warren," I practiced.

"Mona," he'd sink into his chair with a smile, "how
have you been? I was sorry to hear about Caroline. How
are you getting along without her?"

"Thank you, Adam. Naturally, it's been difficult. The fact
that Grammy had eighty-one years and lived such a wonderful life is a great comfort to me. Tell me, will you need
to file a 706 form for me this year?"

"You sure know my business, Mona. I'm impressed, but

not surprised. You always seemed to understand the financial matters I explained to your grandmother. You are a very smart woman."

"Not that smart, Adam."

"Why is that?"

"Because I've let seven years go by without telling you how I feel about you. That's pretty dumb in my book."

"Oh, Mona. I have been in love with you since the day we first met, but your grandmother forbade me to pursue things with you until she passed away."

I hadn't worked through why Grammy would make such a ridiculous request, but for the sake of the fantasy, I went with it. There was something wildly romantic about the reconciliation of forbidden love. Years of separation bred a passion between us fed by hunger. Adam and I then hang up our phones, jump into our cars, and drive toward each other, unable to be apart one moment longer. As he's driving to Coronado and I'm heading toward downtown, we stop right in the middle of the bridge. We run toward each other in slow motion, arms open and waiting. He gallantly jumps over the concrete divider and embraces me, lifting and twirling my bow-arched body as my newly straightened hair whips gracefully in the breeze. Car horns blow and people cheer. Adam gently holds my face and looks deeply into my eyes. "Marry me, Mona Warren. Make me the happiest man alive and marry me."

"Yes." I laugh, my hair still blowing in the wind, but never getting caught in my lipstick. "Yes, Adam Ziegler. I will marry you!"

A lacy cursive line begins writing. "The End."

"Adam Ziegler's office," a nasal female honking interrupted the rolling credits.

"Oh, yes, um, thank you," I struggled. "May I speak with Adam please?"

"May I tell him what this is regarding?" she grilled.

"Oh, yes. Please tell him it's Mona Warren. I need to make an appointment to discuss my taxes."

"You don't need an appointment, dear. I'll fax or e-mail our questionnaire and we'll handle everything electronically."

Certainly this nasal woman had no idea that my life, my future happiness, was hinging on this tax appointment. She couldn't possibly know the panic, angst, and rage her words were causing. I took a deep breath and remembered Greta pretending she was Claudia Schiffer's assistant. She must have had at least a mild case of the jitters, but she did it anyway. To get through this call, I would pretend I was cast in the film *Life of Mona,* playing the role of crafty and resourceful Greta. I'd mix in a bit of Vicki's confidence and create my own character who could handle this situation far better than plain old Mona.

"You can e-mail the questionnaire, but I really do insist on an appointment with Mr. Ziegler. My grandmother passed away and he'll need to fill out a 706 form this year."

"He can do that without your having to come in, dear. Our new office manager organized a system that helps us maximize efficiency and save our clients' valuable time," she honked her canned response.

*Breathe deeply. Do not cry.*

"Please put me through to Mr. Ziegler. Tell him it's Mona Warren." Remaining silent after this was the toughest part. I wanted to apologize for my tone of privilege and entitlement. I wanted to confide in her, woman-to-woman, that I loved Adam and *wanted* to be as inefficient as possible with last year's tax returns. Instead, I said nothing and listened to the thick dead air of offending the receptionist.

"Good morning, Mona. What can I do for you?" It was

Him. He knew it was me on the phone demanding to speak with him, and he still thought it was a good morning. The sound of his voice uttering my name made me regret that I wasn't taping the call for repeated replay later. His sound was warm and deep with the slightest undercurrent of sleepy crackle, like a thunderstorm. And he wanted to know what he could do for me. Marry me. Love me forever. Enter my Christmas scene proclaiming that, with me, it's a wonderful life. See the world with me. Father children with me. Grow old with me. Be devastated when I die at 106 and follow me three days later, so our great grandchildren can tell future generations about the greatest love story ever. But first, forgive me for being such a bitch to your receptionist.

"Good morning, Adam. I'm sorry if I was a bit pushy with your secretary, but she didn't seem to understand that we always do our taxes with you in person."

"No problem," he said. "But I believe you'll enjoy our new system, where—"

"I realize it's quicker with your new system, but I really feel more comfortable doing things the old-fashioned way."

*You know, hire a male consultant, reinvent myself, meet for taxes, get married, and live happily ever after.*

With no hesitation he replied, "Of course, Mona. That's not a problem. It's always a pleasure to see you. Let me grab my calendar. Let's wait until after February fifteenth when your interest statements are in."

"That long?" I sounded disappointed. Trying to rehabilitate, I said, "I mean, I really wanted to wrap up my taxes early this year."

"You want to do them right, though, Mona. I don't want to have to come visit you in prison." I remembered the scene in *Midnight Express* where the incarcerated American drug smuggler's girlfriend comes to visit him in the Turkish prison and shows her breasts through the glass divider of the visitor's booth.

This prompted another ill-timed giggle. "Okay, how's the sixteenth for you then?" I asked.

"How does ten sharp sound?" Adam asked.

Like a symphony. Like eternity. Like heaven.

"Sounds frine," I said.

*Frine? Did I just say frine? This is why I have always chosen to evaporate from social settings. I say things like "ten sounds frine."*

"Okeydokey. We'll see you at ten sharp on the sixteenth. Do you need a confirmation call?"

I refrained from laughing. "No," I said calmly, careful not to butcher the two-letter refusal. I dared to continue speaking. "Thank you. It's on my calendar. I won't forget. I'll look forward to it."

*See how responsible I am? I'd never forget your birthday, your dry cleaning, or our children's piano lessons.*

I hung up the phone and began jumping around my kitchen like a game show contestant who won the big spin. With fists tightly clasped, I jumped up and down, kicking my own butt. "Eeeeeeeyyyy!!!!" I squealed. "I'm going to see him. Just twenty-one long and painful days standing between me and Adam Ziegler. I could die. I could just die from the thrill."

I stepped into the sun-flooded backyard and called Mike, who said he was on his way to the gym. I was so happy about everything that his boxing match sounded fascinating. Mike sounded like a prince. Birds were actually singing my favorite song and a butterfly landed on my shoulder. Okay, maybe not, but I was utterly euphoric, which must explain why my next statement seemed true. "I've always wanted to try boxing," I bubbled.

"What's got you so excited?" Mike asked flatly.

"Well, if that's as interested as you can pretend to be, then I'm not telling," I teased.

"Okay. Why don't we talk when I get back from the gym? We can slate our next meeting and go over some notes I jotted."

I playfully whined, "No! Pretend you're dying to know what I'm so happy about. Ask me. I'll tell you this time, I promise."

His pause shoved me away. Then he sighed, tolerating me for the money. "All right," he rallied only slightly. Then with the over-the-top phony enthusiasm of a radio commercial, he continued. "Gee, Mona! What's your big news? I'm on the edge of my seat."

I deflated. My news seemed trivial. "Never mind."

"Fuck, Mona. Tell me or don't tell me. I'm not in the mood for another chick fucking with my head this morning."

"What's going on?" I asked.

"Who knows?" he said. "I never know what you people are talking about."

"Maybe you should hire me as a female consultant."

No response.

"No, seriously, Mike. What's going on?"

"My girlfriend's bitching that I don't 'communicate' with her. Says I'm an emotional tightwad, I don't know. I don't know what you people want from me. I talk. I listen. I communicate."

"I didn't know you still had a girlfriend. In your column, you said your girlfriend moved out."

"Yeah, well I write those three months in advance. Lucky me found someone new to mess with my head."

"Someone who's telling you the same thing the U-Haul girl did?"

"Fuck off, Mona."

I hung up. "No, you fuck off, Mike," I said to the dead air. I dialed Greta's office. Answering machine. "Hey Greta, it's me. I did it. I called Adam Ziegler and made my tax appointment. I'm beyond excited. And nervous. Anyway, call me when you can. I'm dying to talk to you. This is all starting to feel very real now and I'm in total knots about it. Oops, my other line is ringing. We'll talk later, okay sweetie pie?"

Click.

*Sweetie pie?*

"Hey," Mike said. I said nothing. "Sorry about that. Can we let it go?"

I couldn't help smiling. "Yeah, we can let it go, but I want you to know that I refuse to be treated like that. I am not a doormat, Mike Dougherty. I'm a person with feelings and it really hurt me when you—"

"I thought we were gonna let it go," he said.

"Mike. In case you haven't noticed, I am a woman. This *is* letting it go. Anyway, I am a person with feelings and you cannot just curse at me when I say something you don't want to hear. Do you think I want to hear that I'm not sexy? Do you think I want to hear that my clothes look frumpy? No, but I listen because for some unknown reason, I think you have some valuable insight for me. You can listen to what I have to say every now and then, got it?"

*Yikes, back off psycho girl. You need this man. If he quits, you'll be a ship without a captain. Apologize before he—*

"Okay."

*Okay?! Okay, okay? Or okay, I'm dismissing you and this subject because I'm sick of both?*

"Okay," I said, then pinned down my bottom lip with my teeth.

"Did you say you wanna try boxing?" Mike asked.

"Yeah, how come?"

" 'Cause I just got here and the schedule says there's a class in fifteen minutes. It's mostly chicks that take classes, so you won't feel outta place or anything. Why don't you take the class and by the time it lets out I'll be done here, we can down some chow and go over the game plan with your boy."

Down some chow. The game plan with my boy. When he spoke to me, I was like one of the boys. I got to see a side of Mike that other women didn't. Or did they?

Mike gave me directions and I was on my way to his gym for boxing class, which was simultaneously terrifying and thrilling. When I arrived, Tio, the instructor, gave me bright red gloves and led me to a room with six other women warriors. I saw the reflection of myself and giggled. I felt as though someone should take a photo of me and hang it in a pizza joint.

The first time my glove hit the punching bag it was as if a part of me engaged, shifted gears. I gripped the metal rod inside the glove and threw my fist forward with an intensity that frightened me. I flooded with anger. When I connected with the bag, a shock wave traveled through my hand, then up my arm, then through my entire body. The feedback from my own hit rushed through my entire being. An explosion of fury took over and I became enraged at the punching bag. I stepped back and gave it another shot, this time following my right hook with an immediate left. "Take that, you useless sack of shit," I whispered through gritted teeth. I tucked my chin into my chest and began moving back and forth as if I was trying to duck a punch from the bag. The thud sound of my punch was so pure it was intoxicating and addicting. As soon as I heard the smack of my punch, I instantly needed another. Inexplicably

filled with insane hatred for this punching bag, I went into
a trancelike state and have no idea how much time passed
until I heard Tio's comment.

"You're a natural fighter," said Tio. "I've never seen
you here before, you new?"

"I'm a guest," I said, never stopping my attack on the
bag. I knew it was a half hour class and this punching bag
was due a serious ass kicking. "My friend Mike comes to
this gym." Whack.

"You've got grit," he said.

With that I excused myself and ran to the restroom. I
frantically searched for a place where I could be alone, but
the locker room and showers were filled with naked women.
I thought about jumping into the pool fully clothed so I
could scream at the top of my lungs under water, but knew
Mike would get in trouble for inviting a lunatic as his guest.
Finally I saw that the sauna was empty and ran into it,
buried my face into my hands, and sobbed. "Five minutes,"
I promised myself tearfully. "Five minutes of crying and
that's it."

# Chapter 18

---

"Just calm down and tell us what happened, Mona. Then we'll get Teddy's side of the story."

"Teddy's side of the story? Teddy doesn't have a side of the story!" I shouted. "That little shithead just chopped off half of my ponytail. My hair is gone! What side of the story does he have?"

I was twelve years old and had just started caring about my appearance. Jacqueline and Freddy's nine-year-old devil child had decided to experiment with scissors against my sleeping head and left me with a paint brush-length of bristles just above my ear. We had no access to makeup, nail polish or stylish clothes. I had no subscription to *Seventeen*. None of us even had braces. The most we could hope for was good hair and more than anything I wanted long, flowing hair for Francesca to braid like Bo Derek in *"10."* I wasn't allowed to actually see the movie, but when we were in town, I saw the same movie poster that everyone in America was familiar with—the image of Bo Derek running down the beach with dozens of beaded cornrows framing her chiseled features. When the movie came out, I had a bowl haircut, but vowed to let it grow long enough to braid. Three years later, it was just long enough to cornrow until Teddy decided to give me a partial Mohawk.

"We'll see what Teddy has to say, Mona. First tell us what happened from your perspective," my father said in a voice that was so calm it was infuriating. His daughter had been viciously attacked. Why wasn't he upset by this? His diplomacy was supposed to breed tolerance, but had the opposite effect. I hated him for standing by passively and even entertaining the idea that there could be two sides to this Sampsonian butchering.

"My side? Okay, I'm sleeping and then I hear my hair being cut. I open my eyes and Teddy's holding a pair of scissors in one hand and a big chunk of hair in the other. End of story."

"Is this when you hit Teddy?" Jacqueline asked as she sat in a chair made of twisted tree branches.

"I didn't hit him, I pushed him away," I protested. "He was cutting my hair off!"

"She hit me," Teddy corrected.

"I didn't hit you, you little freak, but who could blame me if I did?"

"It sounds as if you may have hit him, Mona," my father said, his eyes wide with disappointment. "Did you hit Teddy?"

"He cut my hair off! I didn't hit him. I shoved him, but if—"

"She hit me," the scruffy little runt said again. I looked at his little face, a rim of snot crusting around his nostrils, translucent blue eyes and raisiny little lips that kept forming the same sentence. "She hit me."

"I didn't hit him, but I'd have had every right to. Why doesn't anyone care that this little shithead chopped off my hair for no reason?!"

Jacqueline asked me to please watch my language in

front of her son. My father told me that Teddy had a reason for cutting my hair off, it just wasn't a good one. As the older one, I was responsible for acting responsibly, he said. "Hitting is never, ever okay," he began in a gratingly mellow voice. "We brought you kids here to keep you away from the violence of the outside world. We're trying to create a place of harmony, peace, and love here—not a war zone."

"This is not who we are, Mona!" said Jacqueline. "We don't curse at each other and hit children."

"But we cut each other's hair off?! Why am I the only one getting in trouble?"

Even as I spoke the words, I knew there was no such thing as trouble in our own private Woodstock. Teddy and I were told to take a walk in the woods together and work out our differences. Ironically, the adults were doling out the cruelest punishment we could have imagined. We were instructed to talk about our feelings about "the conflict," what brought on Teddy's desire to cut my hair and how things might have been handled differently. Less than an eighth of a mile into our walk for world peace, Teddy and I broke our silence. He told me he was going to cut the rest of my hair off when I went to sleep that night. Then we threw rocks at each other for another half hour before we agreed to pretend we'd worked it out, so we could get home in time for lunch.

I stepped out of the gym sauna and rinsed my face with cold water, ready to return to boxing class. My heart raced with lust when I turned the corner and saw the dull gray bag waiting for me. "Ready for an ass kicking?" I asked, smirking silently.

At lunch, Mike asked me what I was so worked up about on the telephone that morning. I told him I had set my tax appointment with my future Mr. Married and Filing Jointly. "Let's get our plan together," Mike said as he began shoving an overstuffed turkey club sandwich into his mouth. "You look great by the way," was muffled by food. "The new clothes are working for you. Looks like you took off a few pounds, too."

"Yes! Seven, so far. Do you notice anything else different about me?"

"Straight hair."

"Yes," I perked. "I can't believe you noticed."

"Vicki told me you were getting it done. Looks good." He wiped his mouth with a napkin and took the longest sip of soda I'd ever witnessed.

"I really like her," I smiled.

"Yeah, she dug you, too. Even though you sent her home looking like a freakin' Washington lobbyist."

"I thought the suits looked great on her. Hey, did she get that . . . did you know she was going for a job interview, at um, that—"

"At a club?" Mike relieved me. I nodded. "Yeah, I know about it, but I'm not thrilled about my kid sister' stripping."

"How come?" I asked.

" 'Cause I been to strip joints. I know what guys are like when they're there. I'm one of 'em, remember?"

"Mike?" I leaned toward him, lowering my voice to ask him permission to continue. Instead, he kept chewing.

He feigned annoyance. "What?"

"I can't help wondering if there's more to you," I said.

"More than what?"

"More than this 'I'm a dickhead who can't understand women' routine. I can't help thinking there might be someone, I don't know, real underneath it all."

"Nah," he dismissed. "This is basically it. Every woman

I've ever known—except my mom—asks the same thing, but this is the real me, Mona. There's no Mr. Sensitive underneath. Y'know, if I could teach you one thing that would really separate you from the rest of the pack, it'd be to back off on the whole 'breaking through' routine. Guys hate that shit. We've all heard it a thousand times." Mocking a female voice, he continued, " 'Let me in emotionally, take off the mask, you don't have to be afraid to show me the real you.' It's really kind of annoying, to tell you the truth. Most chicks seem to think there's this whole emotional inner life that guys have that we're afraid to share, but the fact is it's pretty much what you see is what you get with us. Differentiate yourself a bit, Mona, and be the cool one who doesn't do that shit. Believe me, you people are genetically capable of it, 'cause I've met a few who don't do the whole gold-mining routine. Vicki doesn't. My mom doesn't. Most of you do it, though, and truthfully, it's a big turnoff. Be that ass-kicking chick I saw at the gym today. Be the cool one that doesn't hyper-analyze shit, and read deep hidden meaning into nothing."

"You watched me at the gym?"

"Oh, yeah. You were looking pretty tough in that class." He smiled and put his hand on top of mine like Greta always does, "Tell me, Mona, was that the *real* you?"

"Very funny." I pulled my hand back.

"Let me in." He tilted his head and spoke softly, teasing. "A good man can help you work through your rage and get through to the real you, Mona. The soft, gentle Mona who's simply afraid to love."

*Oh my God, he's right. It does sound barfy.*

I shot back, "The soft and gentle Mona has spent half a lifetime afraid to do anything. I need to be the tough and strong Mona. The new and improved Mona, who I assure you will never again ask about the real you."

"Atta girl!"

" 'Cause I don't really give a shit." I laughed. "You're my employee, here to serve me and my needs."

"Even better." He double high-fived me over the table. He laughed, clutched his hand to his heart, and wiped away an imaginary tear. "Sometimes I really feel like I'm making a difference in this world."

"Oh stop!" I swatted him.

When the waitress brought our check, I realized we hadn't discussed my strategy for the first meeting with Adam. "Hey Dog, this lunch has given me some good info, but I really need to get a game plan for my tax meeting. Can you stay an extra fifteen minutes?"

"Let's go somewhere else," he offered. "Ever play air hockey?"

"Never lost a game." I crossed my arms and raised an eyebrow to challenge him.

"Prepare to."

# Chapter 19

Freddy and Jacqueline bought an air hockey table for us kids after we all signed a treaty agreeing that there would be no fighting over use, no score keeping, and no gloating. These rules, of course, went straight out the door after the first week. The sound of the puck was like firecrackers when us teens played. The banging, the shooting—it was invigorating.

Todd explained how to use geometry to excel at air hockey, sketching directions on how to shoot the puck at the center of the side of the table, so it ricocheted straight into the goal. He explained that hitting the exact right spot was difficult, but if I could get the puck there, the angle would never fail me.

Mike slid the puck to me from across the table, bowing chivalrously to give me the first shot. As I gripped the knob, I felt the cool familiar breeze gently wafting from the table. A couple of kids stood beside us and put their change on the edge of the table to reserve the next game. The cacophony of the arcade was distracting but energizing. I pretended all of the bells, sirens, and buzzers were sounding just for me—my personal cheering section.

When I told Mike I'd never lost a game, I wasn't lying.

It's just that I hadn't played in sixteen years. Grammy wasn't exactly an arcade gal and Greta loved "real sports" far too much to indulge me in plug-in games. It had been a long while, but when my hand gripped the knob, the adrenaline rush was as familiar as the feel of cold water. My first shot blurred past Mike as I heard the gratifying sound of the puck blasting through the goal. The swish. The back and forth spatter of the puck struggling to escape its inevitable fate. The flat dead thud of defeat as the puck hits the bottom of the goal return slot.

"Lucky shot," Mike said before wailing the puck back toward me. The cadence sounded like applause. My arm flung the knob for a shot then returned to defend my goal. Mike instantly caught on to my angle shot and learned to defend against it. I switched sides and started aiming for the left side of the table. Whack. Goal. "I am excellent!" I shouted, holding my hands over my head and wailing while doing a short victory dance.

Swoosh. Clunk. Mike shot the puck straight into my goal while my hands were overhead. "Hey!" I shouted. "You can't do that! You have to ask if I'm ready before you shoot."

"No, I don't," he dismissed. "Come on, shoot."

"You totally cheated. You saw I wasn't ready for you to shoot. That was completely unfair."

"Hey, you were busy with your little touchdown dance, so I exploited the opportunity. That's the way the game is played. Come on, shoot. This thing is on a timer."

I gritted my teeth. Swish. Plop. Score. I held my knob right in front of the goal, leaned back into my hip roll, waving my left hand overhead. "I am excellent!" I revised my dance.

"Hey, nice hips. You learn that in stripping class?"

"I most certainly did," I continued, then sang, "I am excellent, no matter what they say."

"Hey, you can carry a tune, Mona Lisa." Mike smiled.

"Come on and shoot the puck, Dog. This thing is on a timer and I want a nice wide margin of victory so you can't piss and moan about how you almost beat me. I want to make it perfectly clear—when it comes to air hockey and Mona Warren—you *couldn't* have been a contender!"

That Sunday, Vicki came to my house in the morning to pick me up to watch the Kickin' Chicks game, starring Greta as goalkeeper. Mike said he would "try" to make it, but that nine was awfully early for him on a weekend. Vicki stopped at the entryway and scanned the foyer, slack-jawed. Taking mental inventory, she let slip, "Is this place yours?"

"No, I'm the governess," I said with what I thought was obvious sarcasm. When she accepted it, I had to correct her. "I'm kidding, of course it's my house. It was my grandmother's, but it's mine now."

"Your grandmother's." She scanned again. "Okay, that makes sense."

"What do you mean?" I asked.

"Oh, no offense. Don't get me wrong, this is one sweet crib to be sure. It's got that, you know, old person feel to it. I'm sure you'll do it up with your own style soon." She caught my reaction and apologized for what she assumed was offending me. "I'm sorry, I shouldn't have said that. The place is beautiful, really. Very elegant."

"It's okay," I assured her. "I've been thinking about redecorating. This is going to sound weird, but I kind of feel disloyal changing things. Like I'd be erasing my grandmother's memory from her own house. That probably sounds bizarre."

She walked in and sat on the same area of couch her

brother took just before Christmas. "No, Mona. But she
died and left it to you. That means you can do whatever
you want with it. Don't you think that I want you to make
the place your own?" She scanned the new room. "Jesus,
Mona. Do you know what I'd give for a place like this?"

People always ask that question and have no idea of
their own answer. If Vicki knew what the house really cost
me, I doubt she'd trade places.

"What would you give?" I asked.

"A lot!" she laughed at the absurdity.

"Like what? What would you give up for a place like
this? Your parents? Two brothers? Your first love? Your
youth?"

"Yeah, I'd definitely give up my first love," she said.
"He could fuck off if I could have a place like this. Did I
say something wrong?"

"No." I lightened up. "So how's the dancing going?"

"Okay," she dragged out. "Not really what I expected."

"What did you expect?"

"I guess I thought the guys would be more, more atten-
tive," she said. I loved Vicki's candor. Not only was she
willing to admit that she craved adoration, she wasn't
afraid to confess that she wasn't getting it. "Sometimes
they watch sports games and look right past my practi-
cally naked body when I'm dancing. I'm like, you think I
color my hair, tweeze my eyebrows, wax my bush, go to
the tanning booth, and put on six coats of lip gloss so you
can ignore me?!"

"I will not be ignored, Dan," I said in my best imitation
of Glenn Close in *Fatal Attraction*.

"What?" Vicki asked.

"Never mind, go on."

"Most of the guys who come in are pretty nice." She
perked up, "Then there are the losers who want to save

you and take you 'away from this life.'" She giggled, apparently remembering a recent knight. "Every now and then there's a drunk guy who gets grabby. That only lasts a second before they get their asses kicked out, but it's still annoying."

"It sounds awful," I commiserated.

"Sometimes," she said with a lilt. "But other times I feel really powerful, like my body is casting a spell over these guys. Like my boobs are cash magnets." She laughed. "This is going to sound crazy, but sometimes I feel like a super-hero."

In a damsel in distress voice, I called, "Help, Naked Girl! The bank is being held up by armed robbers. Eeeeek!"

"Okay, maybe not a superhero," she said.

I ran to the couch to hug Vicki. "No, sweetie pie, I'm just kidding. I'm glad you're finding it empowering, too. Really. I was just teasing. It's my way." As the words came out, I realized that they were true, but the notion was newborn. I'd never been the intimacy-through-insult type. I'd only been to New York once.

"Hey, how did we get onto this? We should get moving or we'll miss the game."

We arrived at the field just after the first quarter started and unfolded our chairs next to Mike, who was already there. "Hey, I thought you guys were blowing me off," he said, lifting his coffee cup from the pocket of his folding arm chair. Greta saw us and nodded her head to say hello.

"I'm sure you would have done fine on your own," I said as I patted the back of his well-worn rugby jersey. As I ran my fingers across the blue cotton I realized that, to my great dismay, I enjoyed the feeling of Mike's body moving under my hand. It was more than his Downy fabric softener that excited each line of my fingerprints.

*Good God, he has nice shoulders,* I lusted. *Adam has*

nice shoulders, too, and a solid set of values and a lovely family to marry into.

Mike's snorting retort snapped me back to reality. "What are you kidding? Twenty-two sweaty lesbians pushing and shoving each other. I'm in heaven here."

"Hey, that's my wife out there, dude," said a guy with a pumpkin stomach and an outgrown bleached mullet. "She's no lesbian."

"Lighten up, man," he shot back. Then, glancing at the man's wife on the field, Mike continued, "I'd be cranky, too, if I was married to her." Vicki and I feared that this soccer match was about to get very European in a few seconds.

"Whaddya say, dude?"

Mike sat back in his chair, lifted his sunglasses, and continued. "I said if that was my wife—"

"Dude! You write the Dog column in *Maximum For Him*! I'd know your face anywhere!" Mike nodded. "Your shit's hilarious. I read you every month."

"Hey, thanks, buddy." He reached for his hand. They did this ridiculous hand-slapping, grabbing, shoulder-bumping nonsense that they must have thought made them look cool. "I didn't mean anything by the lesbian thing."

"Hey, don't sweat it, bro. Don't I wish it, right?"

Vicki and I rolled our eyes at each other. "Has he always been like this?" I asked her.

"A dickhead? Yes," Vicki said a little too loud for the other spectators' comfort.

The Goalin' Grrrls fans rose to their feet and started yelling. A yellow jersey passed the ball to another who shot a ball that grazed Greta's gloves and dropped into the goal. For the rest of the game, Mike and Mullet Man bonded through beer and lawn chair coaching. Vicki and I were on our feet, screaming like a teen sighting of Ricky Martin.

We had soccer fever and we had it bad. Vicki hungrily watched the tactics of the game, while I was simply interested in the Kickin' Chicks winning. By the end of the half, the score was two to one in favor of the Chicks. Vicki and I were like mad women, chanting "Kickin' Chicks!" like it was a battle cry. We recruited about a half dozen fans to join us, and unsuccessfully tried to start a wave of twenty people. The others thought we were simply insane as we screamed and hugged each other with every goal for the home team.

# Chapter 20

*Ditch The Bitch*
*—The Dog House, February*

February is the shortest month of the year, but the first two weeks feel like eternal damnation for us guys. The countdown to Valentine's Day begins, and women around the world are yapping to each other about what "special and beautiful" plans they have with their boyfriends. It gets mighty competitive, let me tell you. One girl says her boyfriend rented out an entire restaurant for just the two of them, then another chimes in that her guy is taking her to dinner in Paris. Soon, a third pipes in that her boyfriend is buying her a ring.

Normally, I'd say so what. Who cares what chicks are talking about among themselves? Most of the time it's harmless chatter about period cramps and toenail polish, but when they start in with the battle of the boyfriends it affects us. It affects us because when they start playing in the romantic Super Bowl, guess who the only *losers are? Men! There's no way we can win because some woman is always going to exaggerate about how "special and beautiful" her Valentine's Day was, and the rest of them are going to come storming back to you complaining about your meager box of cookies or fistful of daisies. These standbys won't do anymore. Guys are expected to be creative. We've got to constantly jump a bar set higher and higher by women.*

*I say enough. It's time to draw the line. This year, let's turn the tables and make Valentine's Day one that women will never forget. Now, this'll only work if we all do it, so none of you better wimp out on me, got it? This year bag the flowers, eat the Oreos yourself, and ditch the bitch. You read right—ditch the bitch. If every guy dumps his girlfriend right before or the evening of Valentine's Day, we've set the bar right where we want it—low to the ground (hell, on the ground!). It's kind of like going on strike. Our union, Guys Local 428, is staging a walkout, brothers! This may sound cruel and inhumane, but management has abused its power long enough.*

*I can hear you right now. Dog, if I dump my girlfriend how am I going to get laid? Dog, I kind of like my girlfriend, I'm not ready to dump her just yet. Or, the truly pitiful, Dog, I'm married. I'll address your concerns in reverse order. If you're married, you obviously can't get rid of her so easily. And hey, a guy does need his laundry done, so just skip the Valentine's Day gift. No dinner and no card either. We've got to stick together and make this a dry Valentine's Day for wives and girlfriends alike. Second, even if you dig your girlfriend, dump her anyway. You'll get her back if you want. Just call a few days later and tell her you're sorry, you were afraid of your own feelings, whatever line of shit you can come up with. And finally, you will get laid again. Don't let the fear of never getting laid again turn you into a whipped man. You will get laid. As long as there are women in bars and booze flowing, you will get laid again. Have faith.*

*Why ditch the bitch? Because if every woman in America gets shunned this Valentine's Day, guess whose carnations and Reese's Pieces are gonna look pretty freakin' amazing next year? They're not gonna lower the bar for us. We've gotta do it. For ourselves. For our future sons and theirs to follow. Ditch the bitch for a better tomorrow.*

The first time I read Mike's latest column was in late January when it arrived in my mailbox, but I had to revisit it after Mike called just before 8 P.M. on Valentine's Day— minutes after his new girlfriend dumped him. When I first read the article, it seemed like just another one of Mike's chauvinistic musings, but now it really irritated me. Not just because it was unkind, poorly written, and completely devoid of any humor or insight, but because it was so unreflective of the Mike I knew. He swears that what you see is what you get with him, but what I was seeing and getting were two entirely different breeds of dog.

Mike and I were on the phone lamenting our respective failures with the opposite sex. My problem was lack of opportunities. Mike's was that he screwed up all of his. Tonight, he proved that was true.

Kelly, the new woman Mike was dating, was in the midst of cooking a sweet romantic dinner for the two of them at her apartment. I imagined her taking Cornish game hens out of the oven and gingerly brushing soy sauce on the crisp skin. I saw her reaching into her cupboards for wineglasses, her long blond hair languishing down her arched back. I saw her excitement growing as her perfect body strutted to set the dinner table. Instinctively stepping, rolling, then dragging in her CFM shoes. I imagined Kelly pushing up her boobs, making her Wonderbra work double-time when the phone rang and her friend read Mike's moronic column to her.

I told Mike I didn't blame Kelly for dumping him, especially since she was guaranteed the same fate over a meal she slaved to prepare. Mike didn't see it this way. He explained that his column was entertainment, not advice. "Mike!" I yelled. "You *advised* these men to go on strike. You said you were some sort of guy's union going on strike. You were like Norma Rae standing with a sign over your head with a picture of a heart and a slash mark through it. What's worse, your assumption about why women talk about their Valentine's Day gifts is so wrong. It's not so we can show off about how we've got you whipped. It's because we love you, and when you do sweet things for us it shows you love us, too. What's wrong with wanting to tell people about how wonderful your boyfriend or husband is? What's wrong with wanting to shout from the rooftops that you found a real prince out there? Honestly, Mike, sometimes I don't know why I hired you. You just spout out all these clichés about men and women, and I suspect any advice you have for me about Adam is going to be as useless as your column is to your readers."

"I know." He sighed. He sounded like a man who was exhausted by living the life he prescribed, but I'm sure that was just wishful thinking on my part. I'm sure he was simply hungry and bummed that he wouldn't be getting sex that night. "I know I'm a fuckup, but I also know the difference between real advice and a humor column. When I give you a game plan for your boy, it'll be effective, believe me."

He seemed a bit down so I refrained from giving him my advice for future "humor" columns—try to inject something funny. "So Mike," I said instead, "what happened with your ex-wife?" I leaned back into my bed and pulled the blanket up to my neck.

"Whoa, that's outta left field," Mike returned.

"Not really. I've been wondering ever since you told me you were once married. What happened between you?" Backing off only slightly I said, "I mean, did she ask too much of you on Valentine's Day?"

He sighed. "I don't want to get into this, Mona. What's done is over."

"Don't ever say that in front of Greta." I laughed.

"Who?"

"My friend," I reminded. "The goal keeper, remember?"

"Oh, the dyke?" he recalled.

"Greta's not a dyke," I shot.

"Yeah, you're right. The femme," he corrected himself.

"The what?"

"The femme, the femme," Mike said impatiently, asking with his tone what rock I'd been living under that I'd never heard the term. "The femme. A pretty lesbian. You know, the girlie one."

"What are you talking about? Just because Greta plays soccer doesn't make her a lesbian."

Mike laughed. "Whatever gets you through the night, Mona Lisa. Surely your friend is familiar with the term denial." He snickered again as if he pitied my inability to see what was so obvious to the rest of the world.

"You're just avoiding the question. Whatever happened with your wife?"

He told me he was married for six years to a woman named Rachel he met in college. She had fiery red hair and green eyes with a look that was pure Irish. "She was really amazing at first. We clicked on everything. We'd go out and get so wrapped up in whatever we were talking about that after we got home, we'd sit in the driveway for an hour afterward. I almost killed us once by forgetting to turn off the engine." Mike's voice softened as he spoke about Rachel, then got heavy, and he stopped. I urged him to continue, and after a few protests, he talked for another two hours about all of the things he loved about Rachel. They met on campus where he worked at the student newspaper, and wrote a story, "Where the Naked Chicks Are." One such place was Rachel's art class. Rachel was revolted by his assignment (an idea which he failed to mention was his own), but couldn't resist the chemistry between them. I imagined there was something about his rough arrogance combined with his enchantment with her that Rachel found irresistible. With her aspirations to become a professional glassmaker, she was an exotic delicacy for him. For her, Mike was, well, a hot dog.

"So what went wrong?" I asked. "D'you cheat on her?"

"No, Mona. I didn't," he said in a way that suggested it was she who strayed.

"Did *she*?"

He sighed a heavy confirmation. "Yep," was all he said, but it sounded like the air rushing from the truck tire that had been slashed. "Said I was an 'emotional vacuum.' Didn't 'share' enough with her. You know, a guy's got problems and doesn't want to dump 'em on his wife. S'at a crime?

So she signs us up for couples counseling, which is a disaster. The guy is sitting there asking me how I feel about what Rachel's telling me about our problems. So I say, 'Not good.' I guess that's not what he had in mind because Rachel rolls her eyes and he's looking at me like, 'wrong answer, Tonto.' So he goes on. 'What I mean is how does it make you *feel*?' So I tell him real slow, 'Not. Good.' So he says, real impatient, 'Does it make you feel hurt, rejected, sad?' I don't know, maybe I should have said it did. Maybe that was the right thing to say, but honest to God all I felt was not good. After three times, I told Rachel I didn't want to go anymore because I thought we could work things out on our own. She seemed okay about it, but said she was going to keep going by herself, which was okay by me. Then, about ten months later, she comes home and tells me that she's met someone else and she's thinking about leaving me."

"Thinking about it?" I asked.

"Yeah, she says she's still in love with me, but I won't let her in and she wants to connect with someone. She's lonely, she says. Then, right after she tells me this, she says, 'Please say something to make me stay. Tell me it will be different. Tell me you'll try to make it different. Tell me you want me to stay.'"

"Did you do it?" I said, rolling onto my stomach to hear the rest of his story.

"I don't like being told what to say," he dismissed. "It's fake and I feel like an idiot saying a bunch of shit Rachel's therapist thinks I should say."

"Did you say anything?"

"What's there to say to a wife who's cheating on me?"

I felt Rachel's desperation in trying to get more from Mike. She told him a dozen times that they were drifting apart and she wanted to reconnect. She waited for years for things to get better between them, but they never did. And he never tried to make them better. Finally, Rachel resigned herself to the painfully inevitable truth that Mike wasn't going to lift a finger to make their relationship work. What she didn't know was that he had no idea how. When Rachel pleaded with Mike, it was like the stranger who approaches you asking for directions in a foreign language. She urgently tugs your arm, rattling off what sounds like Spanish or maybe Portuguese or Italian. You know she needs your help, but for the life of you, you have no idea what she's saying.

"Why not? Weren't you still in love with her?"

"Yeah, she was my wife, of course I loved her. But she was getting boned by some other guy and had her mind made up, so there was nothing I could do about it."

What Mike didn't know was that if Rachel begged him to say those things, there must have been more that she left unsaid. How could he not understand how humiliating it was for Rachel to lay emotionally naked before him, and have him counter with indifference? I imagined Mike shrugging his wide shoulders at her questions about what went wrong. Mike's recount is that his wife cheated on him and left for another guy, but the reality is that Mike cheated Rachel of intimacy and left her for the cold comfort of macho detachment.

"God, you're an idiot!" I shouted. "This is like a romantic tragedy with your big fat head causing all the trouble, Dog. She hadn't made up her mind. There was plenty you could've done about it. You could've just said you'd try, then done it."

"Nah. That would've bought me six months, then she'd've taken off with that other guy anyway," Mike dismissed. "Mona Lisa." He sighed. "Why do I always end up telling you more than I want?"

"Because you can."

"That it?" Mike returned.

"You know it is. Know what else? I think we never tell people more than we really want."

"Getting a little deep on me here, Mona Lisa."

"Mike?"

"Yeah."

"From what you've told me, it sounds like you left her long before she had an affair."

"That's what she said."

"Are you ready to hear it this time?"

"I don't know. Listen, before we switch roles entirely and you become my girl coach, I'm going to get my sorry, dumped-on-Valentine's Day ass some chow and hit the sack."

And with a joy I shouldn't have felt, I smiled that he was going to bed alone that night. Before I went to sleep, I led the Adam Ziegler pep rally, enthusiastically listing all of the reasons it was him—not Mike—who would make the perfect lifetime companion for me. Attraction is fleeting. Love is solid.

# Chapter 21

Ileft my stomach on the ground floor of Adam's office
building as the rest of me was lifted by elevator to the
eighth floor of a mirrored downtown high-rise. The receptionist sat unassumingly at the front desk, humming as she
stuffed envelopes, then lifted her head with its mass of
white cotton-candy hair.

"Good morning," she honked. "May I help you?"

"Mona Warren to see Adam Ziegler please." I borrowed Mike's introduction for his Claudia Schiffer visit.

"Ah yes, Miss Warren." She smiled. "I'll let Mr. Ziegler
know you're here." I assured myself I was just being para-
noid and that she was not smirking at me with pity, thinking that Adam was out of my league. I wrote it off to a
one-two punch of fatigue and anxiety. Plus, I was looking
pretty good these days, I thought. Even Mike said I had almost reached my "babe potential" thanks to shedding a
little excess baggage, waking up my wardrobe, and applying a little color to my face. I was boxing twice a week,
which scared the fat off of my arms entirely and left me
with a nice little cut under my bicep. I was now able to
make it through an entire class without inexplicable bouts
of crying, but still crept off to the sauna afterward to drop

tears on the hot coals. I was nervous that laser teeth whitening would hurt, so Vicki promised if I went through with it, she'd get me a special surprise. To complement my new pearly whites, Vicki bought me a lip pump, a little gadget that looked frighteningly similar to a speculum. After the first two disastrous attempts, I finally got it to work without bruising my face. I placed my lips into the mouthpiece and watched my lips get sucked forward like a duckbill. It was such a powerful force, the pump even sucked some saliva from my mouth, which should have let me know it was time to release the suction. But I figured if the instructions recommended two seconds for "pouty, kissable lips," ten would make me a regular Angelina Jolie. Instead I looked like the finalist in one of those blueberry pie eating contests where people aren't allowed to use their hands, much less silverware.

I loved Greta without question, but what I liked about Vicki is that she accepted my vanity without analysis. She didn't automatically assume that because I wanted to improve my appearance, I was a shell of a woman, pathetically unaware of any inner life. I also appreciated that Vicki pulled no punches. When I told her I didn't like my lips, she didn't do the old *Oh no, they're lovely* routine. Vicki agreed immediately, without even doing the pro forma examination before commenting. She wasn't even looking in my direction when I told her I hated my lips. She didn't need to turn around when she said, "They *are* thin." Then she bribed me with a lip pump.

As I followed the receptionist back to Adam's office, I adjusted the fluid filled "ex-plant" trying once again to escape from my bra. After the chicks-only Audrey Hepburn film festival in my living room, Vicki slipped me a Victoria's Secret bag and advised, "Pop these babies under your boobs and they'll give you an extra cup size," as she winked. They definitely delivered the extra cup size, but seemed to have a mind of their own and had places to go and people to see—none of which were in my bra.

The door to Adam's office opened and I swore a choir of angels sang. What was I ever thinking lusting after Mike's silly shoulders. This man was very handsome and sturdy. If I told Adam I needed to talk to him, he'd be there, not busily, absently protecting his male ego. He glanced up from his desk and smiled brightly, genuinely happy to see me. Adam stood, then came around from behind his desk and extended his hand to shake mine. "Good to see you, Mona. Please have a seat."

*See! Talk about available.*

Adam was shorter than I remembered, but I'm not exactly statuesque, so this wasn't a huge deal. His red-and-blue-checkered tie arrived a full three seconds before the rest of him. Still, the sight of him was so incredibly welcoming, like an oasis.

"How have you been, Mona?" he said as he returned to his desk. "Anything new and exciting going on in your life?" *Make me an offer.*

"I left my job in December," I said, silently coaching myself to breathe slowly and steadily. *In. I am the sexiest woman in the world and he is lucky to be sitting across the desk from me. Out. In. I am calm, I am cool. Out.*

"That's big news. What are your plans for the future?"

I had to remind myself that this question was not actually a marriage proposal, and that I should not leap across his enormous mahogany desk and kiss him. "I'm not sure what I'm going to do," I said. *Sounds flaky, come up with something.* "I mean, of course, I'll be terribly busy volunteering for worthy causes." *Sounds like a rich old lady.* "And partying." *Partying? What are you, sixteen?* "I mean working for the party."

"The Grand Old one, I hope." He winked.

"Of course," I bubbled back, hoping he would never find out that I'm a registered member of the Green Party. "So, what have you been up to, Adam? Did you have a nice Valentine's Day?" *Could I be more obvious?!*

"Life's been pretty fair. Spent the good part of the morning trying to win Ozzfest tickets off the darned radio to no avail. It's crazy how fast these things sell out," he said, glancing at his watch as if the mere mention of time reminded him that he needed to speed things along with me.

"I've got tickets to Ozzfest," I blurted in a moment of panic. "Do you want to go?" I asked, wondering what the hell Ozzfest was, and how I would produce the sold-out tickets. "Just as friends. It wouldn't have to be a date or anything."

In a second that would determine a lifetime, Adam smiled and told me he'd love to go. Well, he agreed to it, at least. The love would come later.

"I, uuh, you, uuh, sort of dropped something," Adam said, darting his finger at my ex-plant that jumped liked a frog out of my bra and onto his desk. As I sat facing Adam, fully aware that one breast was noticeably fuller than the other, I groped for an explanation less humiliating than the truth. The gelatin-filled sack stared up, mocking me, laughing at its successful attempt to expose me for the B-cup fraud I am.

After far too long a pause, I explained that it was a cold compress prescribed by my doctor. "It's to reduce swelling," I said. "I have a breast infection."

*A breast infection?! A breast infection?! How completely unsexy is that?!*

"It's actually a sports injury. I play soccer and the ball knocked me pretty hard in the boob," I stammered. *Stop talking immediately!* "Which is how this one got infected,"

I gestured toward my left breast. "But it's almost better now. The cold compresses have helped a lot." *Please shut me up!*

Mercifully, Adam buried his head in my tax file and changed the topic. "If I'm going to go to a concert right in the middle of tax season, I'd better get moving on your filing, Mona," he said. "Do you have all of your interest statements?"

Adam leafed through my papers, promising he'd do everything within the law to reduce my tax liability. "I'll tell you, I think it's criminal that people like you are hit with such a high tax bill. Your grandfather helped build this city. I think people who bring jobs to the community and build the local economy should really get a break, you know? If you have a lot, it means you've probably already given a lot." He shook his head with dismay at the amount of taxes I'd need to pay. "That's what I believe."

"Oh, okay." I filled the dead space, wondering why I felt like I was being courted by the Republican National Committee.

"No really, you worked hard for your money," Adam said, his face still buried in papers.

"Well, I inherited it," I reminded him. "And the life insurance."

"Your grandfather worked hard for it then, with the tuna fish business," Adam said.

"You're from back east, aren't you?!" I was thrilled to shift gears.

"We moved here when I was twelve. Why do you ask?"

"You said tuna *fish*," I said. "People from back east call it tuna fish. It just sounds so funny, 'cause of course it's fish. Out here we just say tuna. The fish is assumed. It's a silent fish."

*Oh God, please strike me mute right now.*

"Tuna, then," Adam returned flatly. "Anyway, I'll look for some ways to help protect your money, Mona. We've got to watch each other's backs. That's what I believe."

"Hallelujah!" I laughed.

He stared back, blank.

"It's just that you said that's what you believe, so I was like 'Hallelujah! I believe.' It was just a joke," I shuffled. "I don't know what I'm saying. The antibiotics make me a little loopy sometimes. Okay, well you've got everything, so I guess I'll see you this weekend for the Oz festival."

"Mike!" I shouted into my cell phone as soon as I saw the square of daylight allowing me to exit Adam's garage. "It's me, Mona Lisa. Guess who I have a date with?" I heard nothing. "Are you there? Mike, I'm leaving Adam's building where he just asked me out on a date. A date! Do you hear me?"

"I hear about every other word you're saying," Mike said coolly. "Something about a date."

"Yeeeesss!" I screeched. "A bona fide, tell-the-grand-kids-about-it first date. The first date of the rest of my life. A pick-me-up, take-me-to-dinner D-A-T-E. Just one question for you, what's Ozzfest?"

"You're going to Ozzfest?!" Mike now matched my level of enthusiasm. "That concert's been sold out for weeks."

"Back up," I said, my anxiety level rising. "Then tell me when it is, and how I get tickets."

"Oh shit!" He laughed. "*You* gotta get the tickets?! What's up with that?"

"I told him I had tickets already, okay? I offered to give them to him, but he insisted that we go together and that we have dinner beforehand. Somewhere quiet, he said, because he wanted to spend time getting to know me," I lied.

"He said he wanted to get to know you? He talks like a girl."

"Shut up!" I snapped. "I'm excited about this. Just tell me where this band is playing and how I can get tickets."

"It's not one band, Mona. It's something like twenty heavy metal groups. Ozzy Osbourne, Metallica, Korn, Marilyn Manson, you know."

"No, I don't know. That's why I'm asking."

Mike laughed. "Ozzfest is this weekend and the only way to get tickets at this point is from a scalper or off eBay."

"*What* bay?"

"You're kidding? You've never heard of eBay?" Mike gave an incredulous chuckle. "The online auction?" Silence. "EBay, eBay," he said, as if repeating it would refresh my memory. "You've never heard of eBay? You don't know about Ozzfest. Mona Lisa, I gotta ask, where ya' been?"

"Listen, if I was worldly I wouldn't need you, now, would I?" I shot playfully. "You're cashing my checks, now answer the question."

"Mona Lisa," Mike danced me with his words, "I gotta tell ya, I'm *liking* this new attitude."

Mike was freshly showered with his hair still wet when he met me at the house to show me how to register as an eBay buyer. He smelled like soap. Reaching his arms around my back to help guide my roller ball, he helped me set up my secret cyber-life as MonaLisa31. Mike also opened a PayPal account for me so I could simply tap the code "Monasbux" and money would painlessly transfer from my Visa to cyber-vendors. Something about the immaterial nature of the transaction and three degrees of separation between me and the actual cash gave eBay the distinct feeling of something clandestine and sexually charged. Like

an affair of cash. PayPal did it with Visa, who got it auto
matically every month from the bank.

"Five hundred dollars?!" I shouted. "They want five
hundred dollars for these tickets?! I thought heavy metal
was a bunch of poor pimple-faced teenage boys. Who's
buying five hundred dollar tickets to this, this, this festival
thing?"

Like a surgeon performing an operation through my
keyboard, Mike remained steady with his hands and calm
with his voice. "Let's find out." He rolled the ball around
and started clicking to see who had bid on the tickets.
Suddenly, I was looking at all of the other purchases the
little pimple faces had made, and more important, their
bidding style. "You got three snippers in on this auction,"
he said. I raised an eyebrow as if to say *If I didn't know
what eBay was, I certainly don't know the jargon.* "Oh yeah,
sorry." He read me right. "Snippers come in at the very
last minute and outbid everyone else. You gotta be right
here at the keyboard ready to pound those fuckers."

I giggled then silently kicked myself for momentarily
wondering what the weight of Mike's body would feel like
on top of mine.

*Adam, Adam, Adam. Mike is sexy and exciting, no
question. He would have been a fun guy to date in college,
but in the long run he is totally wrong for you. Hell, he's
wrong for every woman who gets within two feet of him
emotionally. Mike: Wonderful night. Adam: Wonderful life.*

I cleared my throat for no particular reason. "Okay, um,
how do I, um pound the fuckers?" Mike smiled as if he
knew I'd just imagined the feel of his penetration. "I've got
something in my throat. I'm going to grab a glass of ice
water. Do you want a beer while I'm up?"

"No thanks." He smiled smugly. "I could use some cold
water, too, though."

I returned to see Mike clicking away at my keyboard. "You got three main competitors here. Nothingface is a clipper, but he's never made a purchase above two hundred bucks so I think he's out. These two guys, Metalman and XTC420 buy lots of heavy metal shit *and* they've bought tickets online before." I placed the ice water by Mike's side where he left it without touching the glass. "Here's what you gotta do. The auction ends at 11:23 tonight. Log on tonight, type in your bid of a thousand bucks at 11:20 and confirm it right when the clock on the computer says 11:22 P.M. Not the clock on the wall, got it?"

"I'm supposed to pay a thousand dollars to see a heavy metal concert?" I sank my head into Mike's shoulder. "Who's ever heard of a Republican accountant who's into heavy metal anyway? Aren't they supposed to dig Lawrence Welk and Frank Sinatra?"

"Hey." Mike patted my head like a kid sister. "I'm a Republican. Ozzfest rocks and so does Frank."

"A thousand dollars," I mock sobbed.

"Poor baby." He patted me again before reaching for his glass of water.

# Chapter 22

As instructed, I was on the eBay auction for Ozzfest tickets at the stroke of 11:00 that night. Truth be told, I logged on at 10:15 and got into a bidding war for a pair of Aerosoles wedge boots that were absolutely adorable, despite the fact that they were a size too big and a color I didn't really need. I already owned black boots, but after forty minutes of sifting through nearly 200 pairs of cowboy boots, baby booties, and a vinyl of "These Boots Are Made for Walkin'," I felt lucky to find a pair so close to what I was actually looking for. My intention was to bid twenty-five dollars and forget about it, but as soon as I confirmed my bid, a message from eBay popped up. "You have been outbid by another bidder," it informed me. "Oh yeah, who?" I asked the screen. I remembered Mike looking at an area called "bidding history," so I went there to find that some shoe-thieving little tart known only as Shoe-Princess had declared war over *my* boots. I clicked back to the bidding section and upped the ante to thirty-five dollars, and within seconds received a message from eBay, again informing me that I'd been outbid again. "What?!" I cried, outraged, before going back to the bidding history. "ShoePrincess," I grumbled. When I was outbid a third time,

I found myself shouting, "Die ShoePrincess, die!" Not since the Wicked Witch of the West stalked poor Dorothy for her ruby slippers had a pair of shoes been so highly coveted. Clearly, I had Oz on the brain. Like a sprinkling of fairy dust, I heard the two-note arrival of an instant message.

> *Good girl, Mona Lisa.*
> *Mike?*
> *Who else calls you Mona Lisa?*
> *What are you doing?*
> *Just earning my keep, making sure my girl is where she needs to be. You haven't bid yet, right?*
> *No, but I'm doing battle with some bitch named ShoePrincess who seems to have nothing better to do than park herself on eBay and outbid me the second I try to buy these cute go-go boots. Every time I bid, she's right there taking me down. She does it in seconds. Like it's personal. She's just so right there in my face.*
> *Ha!*
> *What ha?*
> *You know she's not really sitting there at her computer, right?*
> *What do you mean?*
> *Oh man, I almost don't want to tell you.*
> *Tell me!!!!!*
> *You see the area where it asks how high you're willing to bid? Hers must've been higher than what you're putting in, so eBay automatically lets you know if you want to stay in the game, it's time to step up.*
> *Oh.*
> *Still want the boots?*
> *I'm not sure.*

*Are they black?*
*Yes.*
*Leather?*
*Yes.*
*Be sure. Be very sure.*
*How come?*
*Very sexy. Take the bitch down at the end of
auction. When does it end?*
*Two days.*
*Mona Lisa!!! Get outta there and go buy your
Ozzfest tickets. Stop pissing around and go back
when the fucker's ready to close in ten minutes.
Have I taught you nothing? Go bid on Ozzfest
and come back. I got an idea for you.*

I placed my high bid at a thousand dollars, as Mike suggested, and hit confirm just as the clock on my screen read
11:22 P.M. I stopped to absorb the fact that such a slight
motion—the clicking of my roller ball—had just set in motion my new life with Adam.

*I won!!!!! I won the tickets, Mike!!!!!*
*Congratulations. How much did you pay?*
*What do you mean? I bid a thousand like you
said.*
*You had to pay the full grand? That sucks.*
*What do you mean? I didn't even check. I as-
sumed I paid the thousand I offered.*
*Hold on.* After a minute he returned with the
news that I had won the tickets at $755. I jumped
out of my chair for the victory dance, elated that
I'd not only won my passport to a wonderful
life, but saved $245! *Happy now?*
*Thrilled!!!!*

*Make sure you click on payment instructions so you can get that squared away before the weekend. Fourteen hours of heavy metal. Man, I envy you.*

*What?!*

*What, what?*

*You wrote fourteen hours of heavy metal. Are you serious?*

*Very. I told you it's twenty-some bands.*

*Good God, that's a lot of heavy metal to absorb.*

*Yep. Hey, I got an idea I wanna tell you 'bout. I was thinking about what a smooth move this was, you tellin' your boy you're into metal, and all. Not too many chicks are into that. So, I'm thinking, how do we build on that cool heavy metal chick thing we got going?*

*I'm terrified.*

*You gotta make this guy think you got an interesting past. Like you got a wild side. So I'm thinking you hire an actor who's doing the part of the rock star, and he "accidentally" runs into you guys before Ozzfest and starts going off about how you two had all these wild times and how you dumped him and he's all broken up about it still. I'm telling you, this is gold. If I'm out with a chick and some linebacker for the Chargers or Grade 8 bass player starts in on my woman, I'm thinking, man, I got myself a hot little commodity here. She dumped him, but she's into me. That makes me one lucky guy to be out with her. Get it?*

I hated Mike's strategy of having Adam trump the rock star, but I had to admit, it did make sense. Mike suggested

I go to a community theatre group and pay some guy a couple hundred bucks to talk me up at the restaurant Adam and I were at before Ozzfest.

The next morning, I drove downtown to write a check for two tickets to hell, and find an actor to play my brooding, dumped ex. When I met Tim, I assumed he would refer me to another actor with his company, but instead he said he'd love to "tackle this challenging role." I couldn't help wondering whether the challenge would be transforming his boyish looks into a metal bad boy, or pretending to be brokenhearted over me. Tim posed such a stark contrast to the giant tattoo from whom I'd just purchased my Ozzfest tickets that I had my doubts about his ability to pull it off. He looked like a hick, but I told myself it was just the overalls he wore and the fact that I pulled him away from painting a set with a sign reading "Welcome to Bedford Falls."

Tim kept asking ridiculous questions about our fictitious relationship, like how long we were together and why I dumped him.

"Look, you don't need to get into all that at the restaurant," I assured him. "I just need you to walk up to the table and make it clear that we once dated and that you're not over me yet because I'm unforgettable."

"Mona, I understand that I'm not going to discuss our history together, but if I'm going to be convincing, *I* need to know all of this background," Tim explained. The more he spoke, the less confident I was in his ability to pass himself off as the next Motograter drummer. "Mona, I want to take this role seriously. Impressing this guy is important to you, and I want to make sure I play the part with authenticity. You *are* paying me more for one night's work than I'll receive for the entire run of our show—and I'm the lead."

Tim must have sensed I was having second thoughts about him because he offered to take on the "research" himself. "Why don't I create a history for us and develop my character on my own? When I run into you, just let me take the lead and don't contradict anything I say. Remember, don't deny anything I say; stick with a 'yes and' strategy."

" 'Yes and'?"

"I say we met at a museum. Now don't you go and say, 'no we didn't, it was a concert.' You say, '*yes and* it was love at first sight.' Got it?"

"Okay," I said hesitantly. "Can you do something with your hair, though?"

"Oh don't worry about it, Mona. I am going to scream heavy metal. Trust me, I'll leave my overalls at home Friday night. Give me the address and leave the rest to me."

# Chapter 23

"Ozzfest? You once referred to heavy metal music as the soundtrack for trash collection," Greta said, her sneakers pounding the pavement in perfect cadence with mine. "Hey there, Jack." She waved to an older runner and his dog. "Do you have any idea what type of filthy people will be there?"

"I don't think heavy metal people are dirty," I mused. "I think it's the grunge folks who don't shower."

"My point is that *you* are not one of these metal people. You don't even like this type of music."

"Maybe I'll like it," I said, hoping.

Adam didn't exactly choose a candlelight-and-wine type of restaurant for our first date, but considering we were on our way to Ozzfest, our attire wouldn't have been appropriate. He wore jeans and a plain white T-shirt with etchings of a few skeletons pulling each other with puppet strings. Still, Adam looked like an accountant with his unpierced face and arm hairs that looked like he may have actually combed them. Vicki lent me her torn low riders and a T-shirt with a skull wearing a red bow.

As our menus were placed at the table, in stumbled a

drugged-out leathered-up freak, muttering in an absurd accent that slid from English to South African to Australian. His red hair was gelled into about ten spikes, so his head looked like a medieval instrument of torture. His shirt must have been purposely torn in several places because it was otherwise brand-new, crisp and white. His black leather vest matched the armful of spiked wristbands that crept up to his elbow. God knows why, but the lunatic had a press-on tattoo of Hello Kitty on his bicep.

"Ay there, is't moy Mona?" the bur-head shouted across the diner. *Oh God, tell me it's not*—"I thought that was moy love, ay love," he slurred. Tim stumbled to the table with slightly more grandiosity than Dudley Moore's Arthur. When he arrived at our table, he held out his arms to hug me, trying hard to reveal the track marks he'd made along his arms. "Mona, Mona, Mona," he said, sounding far too out of it to recognize anyone from his present, much less his past. He flung his hand toward Adam and spat, "Who the fuck is this, moy motherfucking replacement?" *Oh God, please stop!*

Adam knit his brows, then looked at me with a questioning concern. "Adam Ziegler," he extended his hand. "I assume you're an acquaintance of Mona's."

Tim's voice raised an octave, making him sound like something from a Monty Python movie. "An acquaintance?! An acquaintance, yeh say?! S'at what she told yeh, mate?" His hands were jittering and he kept winking at me with both eyes, like Jeannie granting a wish.

I jumped in to interrupt and redirect. I had to tell Adam that Tim was a schoolmate, a former coworker, or someone I casually knew. "Adam, this is—"

"Poison," Tim sprayed us.

*Poison?! Did that jackass just introduce himself as Poison?!*

"Um, hello Poison, it's nice to meet you." Adam stood uncomfortably. "Would you like to sit? You're unsteady on your feet."

"Fuck the fuck off, mate!" Tim pushed Adam's helpful arm away.

*Just for the record, if you're telling someone to fuck the fuck off, he's not your mate. Leave, leave, leave!*

"Sorry mate," Tim plopped his leather-wrapped ass down at our table. "It's just so bleeding hard to see moy lovely little Mona out with another bloke. I could slit moy bloody wrists right 'ere," he threatened with a smooth butter knife. "Y'ever been in love with the most beautiful girl who shows yeh how fanfuckingtastic life can be, then leaves yeh with nothing 'cept yer memories of the best days of yer life?" He leaned back in his seat as if he was getting settled in for a long night. Inadvertently, Tim wiped his nose with his wrist. I took great delight in seeing him flinch at the first contact with his spiked band.

"Would you care for a tissue, Poison?" Adam offered, reaching into his pants pocket.

*Why does he keep calling him Poison, like it's a perfectly normal name?!*

"What I'd like is the bloody love of moy life back," he snapped. "What do yeh say, Mona? Those three years were the best bloody years of moy life. Can we give it another shot? I promise I'll tell the boys of Gower's Pharmacy to stop making plays fer yuh, not that I can hardly blame them, you sexy thing, you," he winked hard. "Gower's Pharmacy, mate. Y'ever heard of us? Our first CD went straight shit!"

*Three years?! A band named after a pharmacy? Players who hit on me? Where's that knife?*

"This really isn't the time . . . Poison," I muttered the

name. "It was nice running into you, but we've really got to get going."

"Ozzfest?" he asked. I quickly nodded. "Watch out for this lassie in the mosh pit, mate," he winked at Adam. "She's a whore!"

"Okay," I said sternly. "We really need to get going. Good to see you . . . Poison. Gotta fly now."

Tim winked again. "Gotcha, love. If yeh ever want to mend my broken heart, yeh got the number. Just dial the love sha—"

"All right! Good-bye. We really need to leave now."

The waitress approached our table. "Ready to order?"

Tim skulked out of the restaurant and shouted, "I love you, Mona!" as the door swung behind him.

"What a disturbed fellow," Adam said.

"He's a musician," I dismissed.

"He's a troubled man," Adam said, genuinely concerned. "Maybe we should've helped him out. Did you see the track marks up his arms? I think that guy's a drug addict. We all suffer when people like that go without rehabilitation. That's what I believe. You think that guy earns a nickel?" He shook his head. "He's at the public trough or dealing drugs to kids—or both!"

I held my head in my hands, wishing I'd never staged this without clearly outlining what I expected from Tim. Adam did not look at all impressed by the fact that I'd dated this heavy metal band guy. I seemed dangerous in the worst sense of the word. "Did you ever share a needle with this guy?" Adam asked.

"No! Of course not. We were together very briefly."

"Poison said it was six years."

*Stop calling him that!*

"Three years," I corrected.

"Three years is a long time, Mona."

"We weren't together three years. It was more like three months. The guy's on drugs. He's deluded. He's troubled. You said so yourself. Let's talk about something else. How's your family doing? Do they still do those—"

"Have you been tested for AIDS?"

# Chapter 24

Vicki was quite a performer, genuinely loving the excitement of being watched, loved, cheered. There were others who looked exhausted by the constant hustle, but Vicki seemed to revel in the energy of it. Perhaps it's because the coach only put her in for the second half of the game, but when she ran onto the field, she whipped off her jersey like post-World Cup Brandi Chastain and ran the periphery of the field high-fiving the thirty or so Kickin' Chicks fans. She seemed a good fit for the team. I watched the other players to see if there were any side glances or eye rolling at their slutty new midfielder, but they seemed to get a charge out of her flare.

After the game, Vicki, Greta, and I went to dinner together, our second outing as a trio. We promised we wouldn't get quite as drunk this time, and vowed absolutely no Audrey Hepburn films. A few months ago, we found ourselves sprawled out on the floor of my family room watching back-to-back Hepburn films finishing with *Roman Holiday*. At midnight, I was sobbing that Gregory Peck had just let Audrey Hepburn go without a fight. Vicki, who became extremely cynical when she drank too much, slurred that the princess and the reporter were from two different worlds and there was no point hoping for the happy ending "No point?!" I said, taking on a bit of that classic film leading-lady affect. "What about him? The point is love, Vicki. How can he just walk away from true love?!"

"What was he supposed to do, stand there and beg her to give up her life as a princess? Come on. Get real, Mona."

Greta was taking mental notes, I could tell. A fact confirmed by her later diagnosis that Vicki had attachment issues and I had displacement problems. Doctor, heal thyself, I thought.

If I weren't drunk that night I would have never blurted that it was obvious that Vicki and Mike came from the same gene pool. "You Doughertys are a heartless, cold lot," I said.

"That much is true, but it's got nothing to do with the gene pool." Vicki laughed. "Have you ever noticed that Mike and I look nothing alike?" Mike was adopted, she told me. I regretted making the comment about their heartless genes, but like most things, this just seemed to roll off Vicki's tongue as if it was no big deal. "Don't look so freaked about it, Mona. Mike was just adopted. My parents didn't buy him off the black market.

When the waitress approached our table of two grass-stained soccer chicks and me, she asked if we'd like to start off with something to drink. Simultaneously, we all refused. "Maybe if we stop at one bottle," Vicki suggested, looking to each of us for approval.

"Last time got a wee bit too saucy," Greta reminded Vicki.

"Let's stop at one bottle," I reaffirmed Vicki's plea for moderation instead of abstinence.

"Okay," we said in unison. "*One* bottle of your house Chianti, please," Vicki spoke alone. Then turning to me, she asked about last weekend's date with Adam.

"Ah yes, little miss metal." Greta laughed. "Do tell us about Ozzfest."

"Let's put it this way, we'll have to tell our grand-children about our second date. Adam looked like he was having a great time, screaming along lyrics I could barely understand. 'Said you're a liar!!!! Kicked my face with love. Rat from hell . . . damned blood stained throat' I sang. What the hell are these guys so angry about?"

"Middle-class suburban white boys who grew up to be rich white boys." Vicki laughed. "All pissed off about nothing."

"*I'm* pissed off about the fact that I may be permanently deaf in my left ear! The worst part was that freaky actor I hired to pretend he was my ex-boyfriend," I reported. "Your brother's idea. Anyway, he's screaming and cursing, and he took the role sooooo seriously, he put track marks up his arm with strawberry seeds to look like little scabs."

"Ewwww!" they said together.

"How could you tell they were strawberry seeds?" Vicki asked.

"They were some type of seed because they started falling off and I saw these little glue marks where the faux scabs were. Adam felt sorry for him. Thought we should buy him a meal. Until, of course, Tim took his part of brood-ing, disturbed ex a bit too seriously. After he left the diner, he threw a rock through the window and shouted, 'The money's in the newspaper!' We didn't even have a newspa-per."

"What?!" Vicki was dumbfounded. "What does that even mean? What money? What newspaper?"

"Who knows?! The guy was a total freak. I've got major damage control to do now with Adam. Would you believe this lunatic wants me to pay for a replacement window for the diner?"

"Honey, this is where a good prescription comes in handy." Greta seemed relieved and amused. "So, I take it you've learned an expensive lesson and won't be pursuing this cockamamie scheme any longer?"

"Absolutely," I assured her. "Next time I hire an actor, I'm going to make sure I really go over what's going to happen. We're sticking to a straight script next time."

The waitress returned to uncork our bottle. She handed the cork to Vicki, who looked at Greta and I as if to say, *Here I am with two rich girls and they give* me *the cork to sniff.* Vicki then fulfilled her role as head of the table and approved the sip that was poured. "Very nice," she said, mocking herself. When the waitress left, Vicki leaned in toward the center of the table and whispered, "They are so barking up the wrong tree here. If it gives me a buzz, it works for me."

Our meals were placed on the table as I was explaining how I would impress Adam on our next date by demonstrating what a solid citizen I was. "I call this one Project Good Samaritan," I started. "When Tim called to ask me to pay for the glass window he broke, I went slightly ballistic on him. 'How exactly did you think that my having an ex-boyfriend who vandalizes diners would impress Adam?!' I shouted. 'How did you think telling him I was a mosh pit whore was going to be a good thing for my image?! You were deranged, Tim. People going to Ozzfest thought *you* were a freak. Do you know how hard it is to stand out as a mentally ill person at a heavy metal concert?!' Shockingly, Tim was surprised that I was displeased with his performance and offered to do another gig absolutely free. Of course, I declined, but decided to use another actor from his theatre company for a more low-key assignment."

My pals nibbled as I told them about my next stunt. "So

this weekend, Adam and I are going to the zoo and while we're there, an actress is going to collapse to the ground. Then I'll jump in, give her CPR, and save the day. Adam will see me as competent, responsible, and totally adorable. What do you think?"

Vicki nodded, raising her eyebrows with approval for my image-neutralizing plan. Greta did not think it was such a good idea. "Why can't you date the man and see where it leads? Why the need to stage everything and everyone?" Turning to Vicki, she continued, "Don't you find this whole scheme a bit controlling?"

"Anyway, so that's the plan," I said, dismissing Greta's question. "It looks like you're really enjoying yourself out there on the field, Vick."

She leaned in toward us and whispered that she needed some advice. It seemed the manager at Field of Dream Girls was not thrilled with Vicki's new position on the soccer team, and asked her to quit. "He says the bruises on my legs aren't sexy," she began. "I've been covering them up with foundation, but look at this beauty." She stood, lifted her shorts, and revealed a mark the size and color of an eggplant right on her left butt cheek. "I'm not really sure what I should do. This is how I make my living, but I love playing soccer. I twisted my ankle last week and high heels were totally unmanageable, but who wants to see a stripper in Birkenstocks?"

"It seems you have a dilemma," Greta said in full-on therapist mode.

"What should I do?" Vicki turned to her.

"What do you want to do?"

"I don't know. Find better makeup, I guess." Vicki shrugged. "I feel like I should dance as long as I can 'cause I probably only have another four, five years at it. Then again, I don't want to wait another four or five years before playing soccer again. I don't know. If I could make as much money in a field where I don't need a flawless ass, this'd be a no-brainer."

"What else can you see yourself doing?" Greta asked.

Vicki leaned her scrunched mouth into her fist and pondered the thought. "That day I went shopping with Mona, I felt really useful. I felt like I was really earning my money helping her pick out outfits that bring out her best features. You know what I'd really like to do, though?" The intensity of Vicki's voice heightened with her last thought. "I would love to revamp that sweet crib of yours. I can't even tell you how many ideas I have for that place. It has sooooo much potential, Mona."

"I love that house," Greta said, defending Grammy's decor.

"I like it, too, but you've got to admit it's a bit dated. Maybe you'd let me do a room? Like one of the downstairs guest rooms, maybe? I was thinking the little guest room where the three steps lead up to it we could do in a *Wizard of Oz* theme. We could get rainbow carpet for the steps up, a yellow brick road rug, a poppy covered duvet, and do murals all over the place—Munchkinland, Emerald City in the distance, Dorothy and Toto skipping, a piece of the Kansas house in the corner with the witch's feet peeking out from under it, what do you think?"

"Mona's house is lovely as is. Plus I think we all have had enough of Oz for a while," Greta offered.

"I like it," I lied. It wasn't an outright lie. What I liked was seeing Vicki come alive at the thought of redecorating my house. I knew it was past time I did something to make that house my home. "I'm not sure I'm into the whole *Wizard of Oz* theme, but I think it's kind of kitsch to do the guest rooms in movie themes. How 'bout if I hire you to do both downstairs guest rooms?"

Vicki nodded emphatically. "What do you think of a *Psycho* bathroom?" she stabbed.

"A *Psycho* bathroom?" Greta shrieked. "You two have gone completely mad. And I'm qualified to make that diagnosis."

"What do you say I put together some ideas this week and we can talk before the game next weekend?" Vicki asked.

"Our soccer game or the 'Mona saves the day' game?" Greta asked.

The number on my cell phone showed it was Mike calling. "Hey." I smiled as I answered. "I'm having dinner with Greta and your sister. Can I call you later?"

"No big," he said. "I got an idea for your next scam."

"It's not a scam," I protested. "It's public relations."

"Whatever. I got an idea for you. Call me later." He hung up without saying good-bye.

That night, I actually changed into the cute pajamas I bought myself for Valentine's Day. After I dialed Mike's number, I hung up and collapsed into my pillows. My heart was pounding like the drum section of a virgin sacrificing ceremony—hard and steady. *Stop it now!* I commanded myself. *Mike is completely and totally wrong for you. He is a Dog who will shit all over you. You will get emotionally attached and he will remain unavailable, and you will die from the pain. Adam is a sensible choice. He's sweet, kind, and solid. Wonderful night versus wonderful life—the choice is simple.*

Or it should have been. Preferring Mike to Adam was not part of my plan and it was pissing me off big time. I was furious with myself for sabotaging my future happiness, but more angry with Mike for reasons I could never pinpoint.

"Hey, Mona Lisa," he said when I gathered my resources and called again.

"What did you want?" I said flat and cool.

"Wanted to give you an idea for your boy. That's why I get the big bucks, right?"

"Fine. What is it?"

"Is something wrong?" Mike asked. "You sound mad."

*Don't pretend you care, you heartless piece of shit. You're all the same from Gregory Peck to you—totally and completely disengaged from your feelings.*

"Nothing at all," I said. "Should there be something wrong?"

"No, I guess not. Anyway, I was thinking that the next time you see this guy, you should act like you dig sports. So I want to load you up with a little sports jargon."

*See how they switch gears so quickly? No sensitivity whatsoever. Completely out of touch with how I'm feeling. You think he'd be any different in a relationship? Puleeease!*

"Sounds good. Lay it on me, buddy."

# Chapter 25

*Spring is here and love is in the air . . . or maybe it's the smell of fertilizer being sprinkled on my neighbor's lawn.*
*—The Dog House, March*

There are only a few ways to tell it's springtime in San Diego—the animals at the zoo are in a perpetual state of sexual arousal. Our trees are always in bloom, but only in the spring does our African gorilla hump his mate right in front of a group of Head Start kids. In March, it's not the snow that's melting around here. It's the heart of the female orangutan that looks dreamily at her nappy companion, and thinks maybe—just maybe—he really does care.

"Don't you just love springtime in San Diego?" I asked Adam as we rode the Skyfari toward the polar bear tank. "I mean, San Diego is beautiful any time of year, but there's something magical about this city in the spring."

*Like the fact that you're here next to me. God, you know you're in trouble when your inner dialogue sounds forced.*

Adam shrugged. "Yeah, I hate to be argumentative, but I don't share your love of San Diego."

*What? Who doesn't love San Diego?*

He continued. "Don't you ever get sick of sunny and beautiful?"

*Never!*

"Um, sometimes. But it rains here occasionally. Back in November we had that big storm, remember? And just last week, it was cloudy most of the afternoon."

He continued. "San Diego has such a small-town feel to it. It's a city with an inferiority complex, and frankly, it should have one. That's what I believe." He snorted.

Then Adam said what I knew was coming next. "Sometimes I feel like if I don't get out of this town, I'm going to bust. I want to move to a real city, someplace like Tulsa."

*Tulsa? Tulsa, Oklahoma? Where did that come from? I was waiting for Chicago, New York, Los Angeles, or Paris. Isn't the weather pretty moderate in Tulsa, too?*

"Why Tulsa?" I asked as our carrier descended.

As we walked to the polar bear tank—where Julie, the actress I hired, was scheduled to pass out at the stroke of noon—Adam told me about a convention he went to in Tulsa. Three days of learning about detecting fraud at savings and loans, nine meals that included red meat, and a day at the rodeo, he recalled as if he were dreaming of his reentry to heaven.

I spotted Julie watching a polar bear press his giant purple pads against the glass tank and backflip for her. She acknowledged me discreetly, then brushed her hair behind her ear, her signal asking me if I was ready. I was to cough once for yes, and twice for no. It was such naughty fun, I almost wished we had reason for more clandestine communication. Maybe I'd coach Adam and my children's Little League team and use secret signals with players.

When I coughed, Adam asked if I was okay. With that I knew I'd set my sites on the right guy. "I'm fine." I smiled. "But that woman isn't!" I pointed to Julie who had fallen a little too slowly and landed in a pose that was a smidge sexier than it needed to be. Her hip jutted out like Mae West and she actually placed her hand on her forehead.

I ran toward her and announced to the other zoo guests that I knew CPR and would assist in saving this stranger's life. *Because that's the kind of wholesome and good-hearted gal I am.*

"Stand back," I exclaimed. "I can resuscitate her!" I knelt before her limp body as a crowd gathered around to watch. "Give her some air." I searched her neck for a pulse. As I leaned my mouth toward her, I felt a strong hand on my shoulder.

"Are you a doctor?" demanded the darkest black man I'd ever seen before. His head was sheared and his teeth and eyes were so bright they were blinding. The voice was so commanding, I was terrified.

"Um, no, I'm not a doctor."

*But I play one on dates?*

"I am," he said, shoving me aside. He felt for Julie's pulse at which point she opened her eyes. The crowd clapped.

"What happened?" Julie asked.

Dr. Mean Guy turned to me and shouted, "She had a pulse and her breathing was fine. This woman did *not* require CPR."

"Um, okay, sorry." I sunk into my shoulders like a child being reprimanded by her teacher. The crowd had not yet dissipated, so he continued lecturing them, using me as the example of why laypeople should not attempt such heroics. "Anyone with a double-digit IQ can pass a first aid class, but before running in to perform unnecessary CPR—that could have caused this woman serious harm—ask if there's a doctor available, people! That *is* why we go to medical school." He turned to me and repeated, "You could have

seriously injured this woman, I'm sure your heart was in
the right place, but next time, try using your head."

By this point, the crowd was glaring at me as if the reason Julie was lying on the ground in the first place was because I jumped on her back and strangled her. Two kids
sneered at me. One mother shook her head with disgust.
Adam was on his cell phone calling for an ambulance.

The person who was most upset with me, however, was
Julie, who called me the next day, hysterical that she spent
four hours in the hospital emergency room being evaluated
because both Dr. Mean Guy and Adam thought it was best
to take the precaution. "I don't have health insurance and
my driver's license has been suspended, Mona!" she cried.
"They say I can't have it back until I've gone six months
'episode free.' How am I supposed to get to rehearsals,
Mona? How am I supposed to pick up my son from
school?!"

Doctors are so arrogant. My parents were right when
they used to rant about doctors believing they were ordained by God. Four of the kids got very sick one extremely
rainy winter and we were forced to call a doctor from
Missoula in to examine them. Two weeks of soup, herbal
steams, and prayer weren't doing the trick so they brought
in the big guns. The doctor did little other than criticize us
for living in such close quarters, and nearly freaked out
when he discovered only half of us kids were immunized. I
didn't hear most of the conversation because it took place
behind closed doors, but I distinctly recall my mother
telling the doctor that they were only seeking his medical
advice, not a commentary on their lifestyle. As she closed
the front door, she sighed. "Such arrogance. We want to
fight a virus, they want to fight us. The almighty medical
establishment knows what's best for everyone."

As Adam and I drove back to Coronado, I tuned my

radio to a college basketball game. "Who do you think will be this year's final four?" I asked.

"A hoops fan?" Adam smiled. As I looked at Adam, I saw someone who would never leave his family. There was something very attractive about how firmly grounded he seemed. I didn't agree with everything he was grounded in, but I liked that he was anchored. Mike was like a vapor. Anytime I tried to wrap my arms around something real with him, I realized it just wasn't there. Or if it was, the mist was so fine and so fleeting that I couldn't feel it for more than a second.

"Nothing like that March Madness." I giggled nervously as I recited my line of utter bullshit.

"Oh yeah?" Adam seemed pleased. Mike was right about this one. Wonder of wonders, he was right. Adam seemed to love the fact that I knew a little something about basketball. "Who are your teams?" he asked.

I took a deep breath, knowing this time it was me who was the actor reciting lines. "Everyone loves the powerhouses like Duke and Arizona, but I'm an underdog kind of gal. I think Syracuse has just about the best freshman in the country right now."

*So far, so good.*

"Carmelo Anthony," Adam relieved me of remembering the name.

"You gotta love the six-eight swing guy who plays both the three and the four. He's unstoppable in the post and can shoot the threes," I said, hoping I'd recited my lines just as Mike had written.

Adam looked thrilled. "You're right about Syracuse, but you know Jim Boeheim can never pull out the big win."

*Jim Boeheim?! Jim Boeheim?!*

I shrugged, hoping Adam would dismiss the whole Jim Boeheim conversation. "Come on, Mona, name the last big game Boeheim pulled out."

*Can we talk about Anthony's high school record?*

"See, you can't name one, can you?" Adam asked.

"Um, well, he's just one player," I said

"What?"

"Um, you can't expect one guy to be responsible for the success of the whole team," I said softly.

"I can if that guy is the coach."

# Chapter 26

---

A dam told me that the two dates we had were the best he'd ever had. I wondered if this was just a line—how this could possibly be true—but there seemed to be no ulterior motive for him to say such a thing. He didn't need to borrow money. He was not pursuing a sexual relationship with me. If Adam Ziegler had an agenda, I could not figure out what it was. He seemed genuinely happy to spend time with me.

I, on the other hand, woke up feeling gutted after both dates. Adam was such a good choice for a mate, and from a distance I felt such chemistry with him, but the more I spent time with him, the more he bored me. Any sparks that flew were a result of my frantically rubbing sticks together to create them. Yet, Adam seemed perfectly content and asked to see me again the next weekend. On mission autopilot, I agreed but dreaded it. Part of me thought my reluctance was the pressure of having to come up with a new public relations stunt. Another part knew it was just the simple realization that Adam was not blowing my hair back the way I'd expected.

My mantra these days seemed to be that passion was fleeting, but the more I said it the less I believed it. A reverse meditation of sorts, bringing me further from the place of inner peace and contentment I so desperately sought. I thought about Grammy and my grandfather's re- lationship and how perfect they were together despite what appeared to be a very formal, polite acquaintance. I re- membered my father grabbing my mother by the waist every time she passed by, pulling her in for a kiss on the neck. She swatted him playfully and chided him, but her body language clearly communicated her sheer pleasure with their sustained mutual attraction. But even as their passion lasted, they did not. I came up with a new, more positively phrased mantra for myself. Instead of focusing on passion being fleeting, I would repeat that stability was enduring. Enduring, I liked that word. I wasn't giving Adam a fair chance. I needed to focus on all of the wonderful qualities that attracted me to Adam in the first place.

I hung on to the hope that perhaps the first dates with Adam fell flat because of the venues. Death was preferable to Ozzfest, and like most San Diegans, I'd been to the zoo only four million times before, and was burnt out on Horn and Hoof Mesa.

Last week, Greta complained that her married women clients gripe about the lack of excitement in their relation- ships. The thrilling roller coaster of courtship has been re- placed by the mundane teacup ride of domesticity. "They always think if they married someone else, their lives would have turned out differently," she complained recently dur- ing one of our beach runs. "I see women married to good men, shitty men, philandering men, boring men, alcoholic men and they all think there's someone different out there who would have been better for them." She sighed. "They seem to think if they married their ex-boyfriend or the phantom prince, their entire lives would have turned out like a fairy tale instead of a cookbook," she said. "What they don't get is that if they hadn't chosen their current partner, they would have wound up with the same guy wearing different pants," she said, laughing.

Greta could see I wasn't following. "What I mean is that the people you cast in your life have very little to do with how things turn out. If one of my patients wasn't married to Steve, the alcoholic womanizer with intimacy issues and a mean temper, she'd be married to Paul, the alcoholic womanizer with intimacy issues and a mean temper. Remember that movie with Gwyneth Paltrow where she gets on a train and you can see her life as it would have turned out if she got on one train instead of the one that came along five minutes later?"

"*Sliding Doors,*" I said.

"Well, this whole idea that one little thing like catching a later train would have changed the outcome of everything is utter nonsense."

"But Greta, ultimately she meets up with that same guy in the hospital," I reminded her. "So missing that train changed the course of her life, but only for a short while. She was destined to meet that guy somehow, some way."

"My point exactly," she said.

"I thought your point was that the message of the film was nonsense."

"Maybe that one's not a good example, but the idea that life could be dramatically different with such minor changes is a sham," she said.

"Is it? Because in one of the books you gave me it said that small changes make a big difference."

"Good for you," she dismissed. "You've been reading them. Anyway, I'd like to write an article, a short story or something where a married woman wonders what her life would look like if she had married someone else. Then she gets a visit from an angel who shows her what life would have looked like if she never married her creepy husband. Can you guess how it looks, Mona? Exactly the same, but with a different creepy husband. Her kids have different features, but they're still giving her the same problems. She has the same couch, the same paintings on the walls, and wears the same smile in her wedding portrait."

"*It's an Irrelevant Life?*" I suggested as a title.

"It's not her life that's irrelevant. What's useless is sitting around wondering what might have been, because what might have been is what *is*. The grass may look greener on the other side of the fence, but grass is basically grass."

"I think it needs work," I told Greta.

Snapping back to present day, I asked myself if perhaps I was suffering the same emotional immaturity that Greta described with her patients. Maybe life was just dull, and the important thing was not finding the right guy, but the right type of guy. And Adam was the right type. I'd invested quite a bit of energy into Adam, and persuaded myself to give our relationship one more month before deciding whether or not we had a future together. But to ensure that decision was even mine to make, I figured I'd better redeem myself for the disastrous zoo incident. If Adam took a moment to review our dates, he might realize they weren't the best he'd ever had after all. He could realize I'm a potential CPR killer with a shady past. But Mike was on to something with the sports jargon. If only I hadn't blown it with the Jim Boeheim blunder. The next image-enhancing stunt I'd pull would have less talking and more action— good, clean, nonviolent action devoid of a heavy metal soundtrack.

I called Tim to see if there was another actor in his company that could use extra cash. Not surprisingly, there was a guy more than happy to make a cameo appearance on my next date with Adam. His role: the purse snatcher. Mine:

the damsel with no distress. When Toby snatched my purse after Adam and I left the movie theatre Saturday night, I'd chase him, and reclaim my purse along with my dignity. Adam would see that I was a woman who really *could* save the day—or in this case, night.

That was the plan anyway.

I remember right before I graduated from high school, Grammy and I were walking down Ocean Boulevard when this scrappy-looking kid with an undersized denim jacket and a mess of black hair whipped by and snatched the purse right out of her hand. Without a moment's hesitation, she bolted after him. Grammy was sixty-eight years old and she didn't stop for a moment to think about the potential danger of pursuing a criminal, or the fact that in a race between an adolescent and a senior citizen, the geriatric usually loses. She just said, "No one takes *my* purse," and darted off after him. Not a particularly bright budding criminal, the kid looked back in disbelief that Grammy was chasing him and within seconds was flat on his back, knocked unconscious by the street lamp he ran into. Like some sort of madwoman, she put her foot on top of his limp body and held her purse over her head. Picture that snapshot joined by the cinematic spinning newspaper headline, reading, "Local Senior Helps Keep Coronado Crime-free." Within days, the news of Grammy's heroics spread across the island and everyone was calling her "Gray Lightning." Although the few news outlets that covered the story did their mandatory "Don't try this at home, kids" disclaimer, it was pretty clear that everyone thought Grammy was the coolest.

Even Grammy did her share of backpedaling after the adrenaline rush returned her to the reality that she'd just risked her life for a few hundred bucks and prescription shades. "Normally I wouldn't have done something as reckless as that, Mona," Grammy explained. "But this community means a great deal to me, and when that boy snatched my purse, it was as if he was trying to take away the Coronado I love. If I had been thinking straight, I would have let the boy take the purse, but at the moment, the thought of being robbed lit a fire under me." Apologies not withstanding, I could see that Grammy was also pretty pleased with her newfound status.

My staged purse snatching had the similar theme of someone falling; unfortunately that someone was me. I chased Toby for all of ten yards on the downtown San Diego sidewalk before my ankle snapped from under me and I was left watching Adam quickly gain on Toby. Unarmed and completely unprepared for Adam's chivalrous pursuit, Toby ran clumsily like the school nerd being chased by the bully. (Casting could have been a bit better on this one.) Soon Toby was flattened onto the sidewalk getting the living daylights beaten out of him. I hobbled toward them watching Adam's fist rise and plunge into poor Toby like an industrial sewing machine. "Stop!" I shouted. "He could have a gun." This admonition caused a gasp from passersby who quickly dove to the sidewalk to dodge Toby's imaginary bullets.

Toby was facedown on the sidewalk with Adam's knee on his back, his hands being masterfully bound by my boyfriend's necktie. When Adam tossed my purse to me and winked, he seemed kind of hot until I remembered he just beat the crap out of Coronado Playhouse's Clarence the angel. Again with the damned cell phone, Adam dialed 911 and waited for the police to arrive.

Toby shot me a terrified look, and I tried to nonverbally communicate that I would take care of everything, though honestly I had no idea how I'd do that. Within minutes we heard sirens and four officers jumped out of their car with batons poised for the whooping poor Toby had already received.

"You guys," I pleaded pitifully. "I really didn't have much in my purse. Why don't we give the guy a second chance? I don't want to press charges against him."

"Ma'am, it's not your choice," said a junior officer with slick brown hair and an oversized chin.

Toby looked at me with sheer panic. His beady eyes sat under vertically scrunched eyebrows, punctuating his face like exclamation points. Toby's entire face was covered in sweat, and regrettably there was a little blood from his lip. He was cuffed and shoved into a police car, crying that his lip was bleeding while Adam gave a statement to the police.

"Where are you taking him?" I whined.

"To the station?" reported an officer.

"Which station?" I cried as the passenger door slammed shut.

"The *police* station, lady."

I ran to the driver's window and rapped on it frantically. "Which police station?" Then in a muttered whisper, I told the officer, "Rss isn huh wy it rooks. R'll cuh dow huh huh statuh and hsplain reverything."

"What you saying, lady?" he shouted.

I leaned in about an inch away from his face and whispered, "I said this isn't how it looks. I'll come down to the station and explain everything, okay? He isn't really a purse snatcher. He's an actor."

"Come on, Mona!" Adam shouted. "Let the boys do their job and forget the bleeding heart routine. He'll get what he deserves."

*He'll get what he deserves. He'll get what he deserves,* haunted me like the ghost from the past. I couldn't remember where I'd heard this before, but the words struck me as cruel, punitive, and completely unforgiving. Maybe because they were, but there was something more to this phrase that crept into me and hurt in a place I wasn't aware existed. But not quite as much as Toby had been hurt, so I quickly refocused on getting myself out of this date and down to the police station before the actor had a criminal record.

"Adam, I'm a little shaken up by this whole thing. I think we should call it a night," I said.

"Okay, it's a night. I'll take you home and make you a cup of tea before you check in for the evening."

I wasn't particularly interested in having sex with Adam, but wondered why he wasn't pursuing a more physical relationship with me. So far, on these greatest dates of his life, he hadn't even tried to kiss me. I was in no hurry to kiss him, but it bothered me that the feeling seemed to be mutual.

# Chapter 27

"All right, lemme get this straight," an older pudgy police officer delivered entirely through the right side of his mouth. He sighed for effect and continued. "You say this guy snatched your purse 'cause you paid him to?"

"Yes, Officer Marman." I shook my head eagerly, hoping that my reading his name from his tag would help us connect.

"And you did this 'cause you wanted to show off for your new boyfriend?" I couldn't tell if he was baffled or amused or a little bit of both.

"Yes, yes, that's it." I craned my neck to see the officer who sat in a dispatcher box a few feet above me. The walls were the pale blue of a computer screen, almost gray. I felt as though I'd done something wrong just by the hard surroundings of metal desks and hardwood chairs set against the stark background of nothingness and gating. Three prostitutes and a drunk guy muttering about Bob Dylan being a murderer sat in the lobby waiting for their photo session and booking for the night. Slouching in her chair, one of the hookers sat with her arms folded across a red sequined tank top and a look on her face that was pure righteous indignation. "I don't know whatcho thinking,"

she repeated to the officers who brought her and her friends
in. "This bullshit. You undastand me, buuuull-sheeet, mother-
fuckon." I was amazed at her complete conviction that she
had been wronged by the police when I was on the brink
of peeing in my pants just for being there. However, from
the smell of things, I wasn't the only one who had that impulse. "You motherfuckers gonna be sorry," said another
prostitute in a green lamé prom dress hemmed to the upper
thighs. "Sorry-ass motherfuckers." I kept waiting for the
third to get up and start singing "She Works Hard for the
Money," realizing that I'd gotten far too used to the characters in my life being paid actors.

"Hold on a sec, toots," said Officer Marman. He picked
up a phone receiver. "You gotta get in here, Davy. Bring
Ernie and Burt, too. I'm definitely takin' the pot tonight."
Within seconds, I was surrounded by six uniforms. "All
right, tell them what you told me."

"Where is Toby?" I asked.

"Who?" Marman asked.

"Toby, Toby, the guy who snatched my purse." I panicked at the thought that they'd misplaced him—lost in the
criminal justice system after only forty-five minutes. Damn
that Adam and his tea!

"She means Weepy Boy," said Burt.

Oh no! "Weepy Boy?" I asked.

Marman smirked. "He ain't exactly a hardened criminal."

"Has he been crying?"

"Since the moment he got in the squad car," said another officer.

"I insist you let him out!" I stomped my foot.

"Oooow, child!" said hooker number three, laughing
through her bubblegum.

"You go girl!" said the green prom dress. "Don't take

that shit from these motherfuckers. Getcho man out this place."

"I'm sorry," I said. "I realize my foolishness caused you unnecessary work this evening, officers. I do apologize for that, but you must understand that the thought of my dear friend—a fragile soul at that—sobbing in a jail cell and not knowing his fate is simply unbearable to me. You must understand that."

"It's not like we beat him or anything," said Marman.

Red Sequins chimed in. "Don't believe that sheeeet, girl. We seen that boy and he got his ass kicked. Yo man is one ass-kicked motherfucker in jail."

"I'm sure you didn't harm him, officers. If anyone put him in harm's way, it was me, and I feel just awful about it. Can you please get him now, then I'll explain the whole story to your colleagues here?"

When they brought Toby out into the lobby, he looked as though he'd been released from a three-year sentence. His slouched body was topped with a head that weighed nearly a hundred pounds, or so it looked from the way he struggled to keep it up. His eyes were blotchy and red and the sight of his split bottom lip made me jolt with sympathy pain. "Oh God, Mona, you have no idea what this night has been like." He ran toward me with arms outstretched. For a moment, I thought he might just pretend to hug me so he could get close enough to grip my throat with his bare hands. Whether it was genuine goodness or fear of committing a crime in a police station, Toby hugged me with all his might and sobbed into my shoulder. "You have no idea what I've been through. Look at my lip!"

"All right, put the harmonica away, jailbird. G'head, Miss Warren."

"Well," I shifted my weight uncomfortably as the officers grew quiet. "Seven years ago, I met my grandmother's accountant. Well, actually he was her accountant's son who had just become a CPA and joined the family business. Anyway, he was just magnificent. Confident, sexy, and totally charming—everything I wasn't. I looked at him and thought *that* is the man I'm going to marry. Grammy told me she'd known Adam's family for years and they were as close knit as could be. And you could see it just by looking around the office, too. There were pictures of all of them together on a sailboat, smiling in the sun with their arms draped around each other's shoulders. There was one of Adam on a horse with his six-year-old niece who was missing both her front teeth and had the biggest, most beautiful smile you'd ever seen. There was another one of Adam's parents, and I don't know where they were or what they were doing, but they looked so happy, so in love with each other still.

"I thought, I want to be in those photos. I want to be part of them. And I looked around the office some more and there was all this stuff, souvenirs and paperweights and I didn't know where any of it came from, but I imagined there were stories behind everything. They had history. Texture. It was like Grammy and I were these two little drops of water and they were this big ocean and I wanted us to just drop right into it with them." I looked over and now the hookers were listening, too. "I don't know, Adam just seemed perfect. Like he'd be the ideal man to marry. I don't have a family." I choked on my words. "They, they . . . they all died a long time ago and it was just me and Grammy for the last fifteen years. Then she died last year and I, I . . ."

Marman pulled a chair and told me to sit down. Another brought me a glass of water. "I felt so . . . I was so alone. Then one day I walked into my office and they tell us that they're having financial troubles and asked who wanted to leave. At that point, I realized that nothing is permanent; everything is completely fluid, changing, and disappearing. And I was like, hey, I'm not getting any younger and my life is passing me by. If there is one thing I really want in this world it is the feeling of belonging somewhere, being a part of something. Love. I want to be part of a family again." I stopped to wipe away a tear that had escaped in my losing battle to hold them back.

"So, I thought, if I want to marry Adam, I'd better kick it into high gear and make it happen. Anyway, to make a long story short, I've been trying to impress him, to show him what an asset to his life I'd be, but everything I do turns out wrong. I hired some guy to pretend he was my cool forlorn ex-boyfriend and, well let's just say, that didn't go well. Then, I tried to save someone's life, but ended up getting some poor woman's driver's license taken away. And now, instead of looking like a woman who can take care of herself against a purse snatcher, poor Toby got beaten up and arrested." At this point, I buried my face into my hands and sobbed.

"Jeesh." Marman sighed. "I thought this was going to be a funny story."

"Yeah, that's really sad," said another.

"Didja ever think of maybe cooking your boyfriend a meal?" Marman offered.

"How 'bout sucking his dick?" the green prom dress offered.

Toby wiped his nose on his sleeve. "Or fall in love without engineering the whole thing."

I laughed.

"What?" a few asked.

"It's just that I used to be an engineer, that's all. I found it amusing."

"Owww, child, you can take the girl out of engineering,

but you can't take the engineering out the girl!" said a
hooker.

"All right, your story wasn't the track up I thought it
was gonna be, but I believe it. And I doubt Weepy Boy
over here is gonna snatch any more purses, that right?"
Toby shook his head emphatically. "You seem like a nice
enough girl. Can I give you a bit of advice? You don't have
to be Evil Knievel to get a guy to fall in love with you. My
wife didn't do squat to get me hooked. She still don't do
much, but I love her. It'll happen or it won't, and if it don't
it just means there's someone else." I felt like I was his
teenage daughter hearing that if a boy didn't like me it was
his loss. "You're a terrific little lady, you hear me?"

"What about some love for Ruby?" one of the hookers
taunted Marman.

"Owww, child," said her friend. "We ain't never gettin'
outta here tonight."

"Death row for three ho!" Ruby said as she laughed.

I leaned in closer to Marman and asked what would become of these women. He said they would likely be bailed
out by their pimp later that night and beaten for cutting
into his profits. Or, he might not show up and they would
be sent to Las Colinas Women's Detention Center. "Most
likely back out on the streets tomorrow night with a black
eye and a fat lip," he said far too casually.

"How much is their bail?" I asked.

"You're not thinkin'—"

"How much?" I said.

"Two grand a piece," he said. "You got that kind of
money?"

"Can I write you a check?"

Officer Marman laughed. "Miss Warren, you seem like
a good kid, but we don't take checks from anyone. Ever
heard of fraud?"

*Heard of it? I'm living it.*

"Give me an hour to get back here, okay? Come on, Toby. You're coming back to Coronado with me."

I gave Toby an extra couple hundred dollars for his trouble that evening, got him into a taxi, and returned to the police station, which looked like a warmer place than when I'd first passed through its doors an hour earlier. After taking care of Ruby, Tiffani, and Parfait's bail, I handed Marman an envelope with five hundred-dollar-bills in it. "Look," I whispered. "This is not a bribe, okay? You just gave me some very good advice and I want to thank you. In this envelope is the name of a woman who lost her driver's license because I asked her to pretend to pass out in the zoo so I could save her. Anyway, there's no reason she shouldn't drive so if you could—"

Marman grabbed the envelope and opened it. "This isn't a bribe?" he asked skeptically. "It's for my good advice?"

I shook my head. Marman took the slip of paper with Julie's name and tucked it in his shirt pocket, then handed the envelope full of cash back to me. "Miss Warren, this is a bribe in the first degree. You wouldn't pay Sigmund Freud himself this kind of money for his advice."

*My male consultant gets a lot more and he's a complete idiot.*

"But—" I attempted.

"Miss Warren, first off, we don't have any say in license suspension. Second, what I told you was 'cause you seem like a nice girl. A nice girl who's had a hard life and don't have anyone around to tell her that any guy would be crazy not to fall in love with her. Not 'cause she can do a backflip or jump through hoops to prove how great she is, but because she's good and kind and cares about people. 'Cause she's pretty, creative, clever, and a little bit nutty.

And she loves family. That counts, Miss Warren. All of this counts a hell of a lot more than you know. That's why I told you what I did, not 'cause I thought you were gonna *pay* me for it. People say nice things to each other without getting paid for it. I know some people at the DMV. I'll see what I can do for your friend. It don't seem right that she can't drive if you swear to me on your . . . just promise me that you're telling me the truth that she didn't really go out cold 'cause, if that's the case, she really shouldn't be driving."

"I promise," I said to my surrogate father for the evening.

"Free at last!" I heard Ruby's voice echo through the corridors. "Free at last, free at last. Good God Almighty, I'm free at last!"

# Chapter 28

When I returned home, my half cup of cold tea sat on the kitchen countertop. It had been nearly four hours since I'd been home, but that mug with its pressed Tetley tea bag sitting in a spoon beside it seemed like a relic from a former life. After leaving the station, I paid Ruby, Tiffani, and Parfait to be my bitches for the night. At first, they assumed I wanted to have sex with them, a great disappointment to Parfait, who quickly announced that she "hated eating punany." I didn't have any desire to have sex with any of these women—or women in general—but couldn't help wondering why the thought of me was so repelling to a hooker. Much to her relief, I took the three of them to a diner and asked them each what they would do if they didn't have to street walk. Parfait and Tiffani didn't know, but Ruby said she would be a dancer, a singer, a model, and the CEO of a recording label.

At times during my evening as Richard Gere in *Pretty Woman*, I felt like the benevolent john empowering Ruby by asking her to focus more on what she wanted from life. At other moments, I suspected my motives weren't as pure. Perhaps I was a voyeur peeking into the unseemly underworld of poor prostitutes, both repelled and intrigued by their plight. I felt guilty driving across the bridge that separated our island from the rest of the city, and returning to my life of clean granite countertops and crystal vases.

The number four blinked on my answering machine, letting me know I had messages.

Beep—*Hi, it's Greta, touching base about tomorrow morning. Don't forget we're having the team brunch at the Big Kitchen afterward.*

Beep—*Men are total dickheads,* Vicki launched without introduction. *I am so pissed off right now I could scream. Anyway, I found the most amazing stained glass window at Architectural Salvage. It's sacrilege to even describe it as just a window. It's a work of art. Anyway, I put it on hold for you to look at after the lunch thingy tomorrow. I hope you don't think I'm being pushy, it's just perfect with—"*

Beep—*Mona Lisa, Mona Lisa, men adore you,* a very drunk Mike sang into the phone with a backdrop of sports bar behind him. *I've been looking for love in all the wrong places, looking for love in too many faces—"* he switched before fumbling to hang up.

Beep—*Hello, Mona. It's Adam calling to see that you're okay after tonight's incident. I guess you're sleeping. I'll call you tomorrow. I had a terrific time tonight, aside from the mugging. You really are a lot of fun.*

Immediately, I picked up the phone and dialed, hoping it wasn't too late to call. "Hello," he said groggily.

"I woke you up didn't I?"

"Hey," he said, pleased. "No, it's okay. Is everything okay?"

"Fine, I just wanted to return your call. You sounded kind of, um, well, troubled."

"You mean drunk. Sorry about that." I heard a woman's sleepy voice call Mike's name.

"Oh, you're, um with someone. We can talk later."

Mike muffled the phone and then returned to me. "Don't worry about it. Hold on a sec," he said as I imagined him slipping on his sweatpants and leaving a mass of blond hair on a pillow beside him. "Let me get to the other room."

"No, that's okay, I don't want to interrupt your, um night," I stammered.

"I said not to worry about it. My friend is just sleeping."

"Good friend?" I asked, trying my hardest not to sound jealous.

"New friend," he said nonchalantly.

Too chipper, I said, "How great! This is a bad time to talk so why don't we—"

"Mona Lisa, it's one-thirty. You wouldn't've called if it wasn't important. What's up? I'm in another room now. I'm all yours."

*All mine?! All mine?! You just had sex with a stranger! How "all mine" could you be, you perma-trolling fuck-hound?!*

"Um, okay. I just wanted to tell you that you were right about the purse snatching thing. It didn't go the way I'd planned."

"I told you that one was a loser, Mona Lisa," Mike said. "Stick with the sports references. I'm telling you that's the best card we've played." I imagined him sinking into a denim La-Z-Boy, and wondered what his home looked like. Probably a huge flat screen television was the focal point of his otherwise bare living room. Maybe a small leather sofa right in front of it and a functionally ugly table to support beer bottles and chip bowls. "Guys aren't into this superhero shit. You know the only reason we dig Wonder Woman is 'cause of her rack and invisible plane, right? Catwoman, too. I don't even know what she does, but she sure looks good in that vinyl suit. Maybe that's what you need to do, Mona. Get into the whole costume thing."

"Mike, your sister bought my entire wardrobe. I am into the whole costume thing."

He laughed. "I remember that first time I met you with that smock thing and clogs. You looked like something out of a gardening magazine."

"Mike, focus. What am I going to do?" I hoped he'd tell me to forget about Adam, and promise that tonight's bar girl was his last one-night stand. I silently begged to hear something sweet. I'd even take the drunken serenade at this point, but he sounded completely sober and sung out.

"Okay, the way I see it, you've been making a lot of assumptions about what you think this guy wants in a woman. You've gotta figure out what really turns him on. What his hot buttons are. What are some of the things he does in his free time?"

"Mike!" I shouted. "*You* told me to have a sordid past. I pay you so I don't have to make assumptions about him. You're supposed to be the male consultant!"

"And *you* were supposed to be Claudia Schiffer," he said. "I never said I had any great inside track to the male mind. You chose me 'cause you thought I could help you. I never said I'd be any good at this."

"Well you're useless!" I shouted. Softening, I asked if he would still advise me if I weren't paying him.

"I wouldn't know you."

*You are such a guy!!!!!*

"Okay, but if you already knew me and we were friends, would you spend time with me on the phone listening to my problems and giving me advice? Or is this all just about the money for you? I mean if I fired you, would we still be friends?"

"You firing me?" he asked. Until that moment, I hadn't

considered it, but I wondered if Mike's interest in me was purely economic. There was only one way to ever find out for sure, and asking him wasn't it.

"Yes, Mike. I'm firing you."

"Whoa. Okay. I didn't know you weren't happy with the way things were going. You seemed okay with how things were. When did this come on?"

"It's not you, it's me," I told him. "I just don't want to feel like this is all about the money. Every time I talk to you, I wonder if it's only 'cause you're being paid."

"Oh. I didn't know you thought that. Okay then, I'm off the payroll, I guess," he said.

*Say it ain't so! Tell me you love talking to me and you'll still be a part of my life even after I fire you.*

"Are we still friends? Will I still see you?" I asked a bit too desperately.

"I'll see you tomorrow at the soccer game," he said.

"Are you going to the brunch afterward?"

"I don't know, maybe. I'll see how I feel tomorrow." He yawned. "Right now I'm thinking I'll be lucky to make it to the game. I'm gonna get back to bed, Mona Lisa."

*Back to bed. Back to bed. Back to bed with HER!*

I washed my face and watched the mascara stream from my eyes. I carefully wiped away black tears with the makeup remover Vicki suggested I use to avoid pulling my lids into a state of premature wrinkles. Stripping away my expertly applied makeup, I saw my real face, one that was depleted of life; siphoned.

I woke up in the middle of the night and decided to walk to the naval base in my slippers. Tonight, I would take the greatest risk of my life and scale the wall of North Island while the nation was just days away from declaring war on Iraq. I knew if I made it inside without being detected, everything would be okay. Perhaps I would just tip-toe into the commissary and steal a Chipwich, or maybe I'd sneak into the mess hall, peel and shred potatoes to surprise the cooks with ready-to-fry hash browns for break-fast. Whatever I did was really irrelevant. It was making it inside during a time of heightened security that was my primary goal.

The thud of my body landing on the grass inside the naval base set off a series of lights that scanned the ground until fixing on me. I saw myself, looking like a blinded sil-houette sitting beneath a UFO. "Put your hands in the air, Miss Warren," an unseen man blared from the base public announcement system. "Don't make a move or we'll have no choice but to shoot."

Next thing I knew, I was sitting in an interrogation room, wearing no underpants and smoking a cigarette like Sharon Stone in *Basic Instinct*. Except no one looked particularly titillated by me nor did I feel sexy wearing a patch of grass on my left arm. "Miss Warren, trespassing onto a U.S. mil-itary base is a capitol crime."

"Capitol crime?" I shuddered at the faceless captain. "As in death penalty?"

"Precisely," said another uniform.

"But I didn't do anything except try to come inside. I was just going to look around, I wasn't going to—"

"Silence!" the captain shouted. "Pay no attention to the man behind the curtain."

*What curtain?*

"Your intentions are irrelevant, Miss Warren. You have committed an act of treason against the homeland, and now you will get what you deserve." With these words, my hands were cuffed and my body yanked from the metal chair. I sat up and my eyes shot open, rescuing me back into a state of consciousness.

"Good God," I said to no one, wiping a layer of sweat from my forehead. My heart still raced as if I were about to be escorted to the naval death chamber. I turned on my light and scanned the room to assure myself that I was indeed safe in my own bed. I leaned back into my pillows, silently repeating that there was no place like home. I fell asleep to the sound of Officer Marman's voice: "You had your ruby slippers all along."

# Chapter 29

Greta and I drove to Vicki's house the next morning to pick her up for the game. Vicki's car had broken down and she had no means of transportation other than her friends and the less-than-efficient San Diego mass transit system. Most of the time, economic class was an intellectual concept, not something I got to see firsthand. Of course, I knew there were "those less fortunate," as Grammy used to call people with limited means, but they were these nameless, faceless people for whom we would collect food at Christmas. Or, removing ourselves even one step further, we would attend elegant garden luncheons or hat parties to benefit the "less fortunate." Vicki wasn't quite at the level of a canned food recipient, but driving through her neighborhood posed a stark contrast to the streets we'd driven to exit the island.

Although we were minimalists on the commune, I always knew that this was a matter of choice rather than deprivation. Never in my life had I met someone whose car broke down. Automotive death was not a part of the Coronado car life cycle. Everyone we knew always had relatively new cars that were quietly replaced every few years.

Greta and I passed two seemingly unattended young

children playing with remote control model cars on the sidewalk in front of Vicki's house. The apartment complex was a flat sea green concrete with wrought iron bars shielding every window. From one window hung a bright red planter box with a few rotted stems bent hopelessly.

Before we'd reached the second story of the apartment building, we heard shouting from Vicki's apartment. It was hard to hear exactly what she and her boyfriend were fighting about, though we could easily get the gist of the discussion. He was a loser; she was a bitch. When I knocked on the door, I half expected Marlon Brando in a sleeveless undershirt to answer. Unfortunately, I did not get the Hollywood sanitized version of the abusive lover.

In an instant, I understood why Vicki had never mentioned a boyfriend before. He was disgusting both to look at and to listen to. The man literally had a head in the shape of a papaya, gaining girth during the long journey north. His eyes were covered in crust at eleven in the morning and his face looked as if it hadn't been shaved in four days. The same time must've elapsed since his last tooth brushing as I could see scraps of food clinging to coffee and tobacco stains.

"What?!" he said.

"Shut up, you dickhead!" Vicki shouted. "These are my friends. I'm going to play soccer, remember?"

"How could I forget, Bruiser?" he snapped. His arm acted as a door chain, allowing us to see his limp black armpit hair draping from his undershirt. "You better not get any more marks, you hear me? People think I'm beating up on you." Vicki grabbed her cleats from the chair beside the door and brushed past him.

"Where's my kiss, Mia Hamm?" he called after her.

"Kiss my ass," she shouted.

The three of us were silent for the first ten minutes of

our car ride, then Greta and I simultaneously burst into questions about Vicki's boyfriend. "I'm sorry, Vicki, but that guy is gross. You have so much going for you, I can't understand why you're with that creep," I said.

"It's temporary," she said tersely. "Just until I get back on my feet."

Greta couldn't resist a little sarcasm. "He seems like just the guy to help you with that."

"Jimmy's not that bad," Vicki said.

"Compared to what?" I asked.

"Come on, you guys. We're not all on the same boat here. I've got an exit strategy. If I keep dancing, I'll be able to move out in another two or three months. Jimmy knows I'm leaving, which is why he's pissed at me. Ever since I started making money, he says I'm too big for my britches. Says I think I'm too good for him."

"You do, don't you?" I asked.

"Do what?" she knit her brows. Greta pulled into the soccer field parking lot and turned off her ignition, but none of us got out of the car just yet.

"You *do* think you're better than him, don't you?" I asked.

"I think he's a dickhead," she answered.

"And you know that you're better than a dickhead, right?"

Without thinking, I insisted that Vicki stay with me for a few months while she decorated the downstairs bedrooms. "Don't even go home tonight. We can go to your apartment Monday morning while Creepo's at work and pick up your stuff. You'll stay with me, do the downstairs rooms, and keep dancing until you get some cash reserves."

Vicki laughed.

"What?" Greta turned to her. "I think Mona's right. It never fails to amaze me how many beautiful young women with so much promise and talent wind up with men completely and totally unworthy of them. You need to get yourself out of there today. That guy is trouble."

I nodded, and without further discussion insisted that Vicki move in immediately. It was not without some guilt that I began to worry about Vicki's ability to decorate my home with her limited knowledge of interior design. I hated myself for such snobbery, but quietly fretted that she might make my grandparents' dated (but undeniably regal) estate look, well, cheap.

After the Kickin' Chicks' worst loss of the season, the team and friends gathered at the Big Kitchen for their end-of-season party. By one, most of Judy's other patrons had cleared out of the breakfast joint and went about their day. The gravel-voiced goddess emerged from the kitchen to personally serve coffee for everyone.

Mike looked surprisingly well-rested, though he didn't show up to the game until halftime. I tried to keep my eyes on the field and not allow my head to turn every few minutes, checking for his arrival, though I was not entirely able to control the impulse. His hair was still wet, which meant that while I was sitting in my fold-up fan chair, dutifully cheering for his sister, Mike was likely showering with HER. "Good morning?" I accidentally asked instead of stated when Mike arrived.

"Hey, morning to you, Mona Lisa." He leaned to kiss my cheek. *Just morning, ay? Not a necessarily good one for you? Or was it going well until you realized you had to show up to the game and tear yourself away from HER?*

"What's the score?" Mike asked.

*You everything; me squat.*

"Three, nothing, we're down," I said, keeping my eyes locked on the field for the first time.

"That sucks." He scoured his chair legs into the soil and plopped into his seat beside me.

*What sucks is that I've completely and totally fallen for you when you are unavailable to do anything other than break my heart. I cannot afford to fall in love with you. I simply do not have the emotional reserves to do it, and that is what sucks, not the Kickin' Chicks being three goals behind at halftime!*

"Yeah, totally sucks," I returned.

"Hey, it's a game, kiddo, don't sweat it." He punched my arm. "Don't take it so hard."

A game?! Kiddo?! Arm punching?! I wanted to kill him, then cry.

At the Big Kitchen, Mike sat his well-rested, clean-smelling self next to me. "What're'ya having, Mona Lisa?"

*Heartache.* "Um, probably the sautéed veggies with tofu and brown rice. How 'bout you?"

"Not sure yet," he said as he continued looking at the menu.

*The indecisive jerk doesn't even know what he wants for breakfast!*

After Judy took our breakfast orders, Brooke stood at the head of the table and toasted the end of a successful soccer season and awarded each player with a special designation. Greta won the "Brick House" award for allowing only ten goals to be scored against the team in twelve games. "Unfortunately, four of them were today," Brooke said as she winked. "But we still love our little Tokyo tomboy." Vicki won Rookie of the Year, which she accepted with a self-mocking round of blown kisses around the table. "And the reason I named these two last is because Greta and Vicki not only brought their love of soccer and their athletic prowess to the team, they also brought us our two most loyal fans." All heads turned toward Mike and me. "When we met Mona back in January, she played a scrimmage with us and let's just say she had a lot of spunk. We knew she'd be a valuable asset to any team as long as she stayed off the field." The group laughed good-naturedly as Mike patted me on the back.

"You're next, buddy," I muttered through my smile.

"Anyway, Mona has been to all twelve games, which tells us that she's either a true blue Chicks fan or," she paused for effect, "she's got a crush on one of the players."

Through the laughter of the crowd, Mike announced his sheer delight with this idea by patting his heart with his hand. "Lesbian soccer groupies, now we're talkin'."

"I'll get to you in a minute." Brooke held court with her hand on her waist and her head moving back and forth like a talk show panelist. "So it gives me great pleasure to give a special award for our number-one fan, Mona Warren, who, by unanimous decision, we name an honorary Kickin' Chick." The table erupted in a round of "awwww" and applause. Thankfully, before I could get mushy at the thought, Brooke quickly turned her attention toward Mike. "Now you, Dog," she placed her hand on her hip again. "We had our doubts about you when you showed up for Vicki's first game and started going off about this one's a lesbian and that one's a dyke. And God knows you don't do much to dispel that machismo image in that punk-ass column of yours. But Mike, I'll give you this. You show up at the games and you are a true blue fan." The team laughed and nodded in agreement. "The time you really won me over, though, was when you showed up with pink face paint to one of our games."

"Hey, it takes a secure man to wear pink," Mike heckled.

"It takes a loser to wear face paint," Vicki shouted from across the table.

"Hey, it shows commitment to the team." Mike laughed. "I'm a guy who's not afraid to commit. Or wear makeup. Or pink. Shit, I'm queer," he said, sliding into his seat and feigning embarrassment over his self-outing.

"Well, Mike," said Brooke with a tremendous lipstick smile, "so am I." She winked. "And as a special gift to our most dedicated male fan, I'm going to give you what you've been waiting for all season." Dramatically, she flipped her long black hair behind her back and strutted around the side of the table to Nadia, our angelic-looking brunette midfielder. She placed her hands on Nadia's full cheeks, turned to Mike and asked if he was ready. Before he finished nodding, Brooke leaned in and gave Nadia the most passionate, soulful kiss I'd ever witnessed—live or celluloid.

The group began clapping, but Mike just watched, agape with delight. Brooke emerged for air and winked at Mike. "My girlfriend," she said playfully. "So what'd'ya think?"

"I think women's sports are highly underrated," he said.

# Chapter 30

---

*Some lady wrote to the magazine and said I was a professional womanizer. I think she meant that as an insult, but it left me wondering, if that's true, are all of these bullshit dinner dates a tax write-off?*
*—The Dog House, April*

April was a whirlwind of dates with Adam and a complete overhaul of my two guest bedrooms and downstairs bathroom. Vicki chose warm summer tones for the walls that blended nicely with the floral bedspreads and curtains she chose. She had a remarkable gift for using every ray of natural light you never knew could find its way indoors. The rooms were bright but unimposing, like a garden. There was something more personal about them than your typical generic guest rooms.

We wound up buying the window Vicki found, but hadn't yet figured out where it would go. It was deep red and had malt stripes around the curved top with a beveled clear face—perfect for a plantation, which my home was not. Still, a piece like this comes along once in a lifetime, so we

snatched it up and stored it in the garage before we moved
Vicki out of her apartment that night in March.

Much as I hated to admit it, the *Psycho* theme for the
bathroom was so kitsch, it worked. Vicki framed a small
black-and-white photograph of Janet Leigh screaming in
the shower and matted it on a vortex print circled with a
pencil thin, blood red Lucite frame. Inside the deep frame,
Vicki mounted a kitchen knife. Vicki found another black-
and-white shot of Janet Leigh counting her embezzled
money—the scene before she takes her fateful shower—
and placed it on top of ten dollar bills scattered behind the
photo. Jagged edges of money erupted from every edge of
the photo until it met the same red frame that surrounded
the shower photo. Vicki had a shower curtain made that
was clear with a silhouette of Norman Bates with his arm
outstretched above his head, ready to attack. Vicki had
vortex toilet seat covers and a rug custom made, and a
hand-painted soap dish in the same pattern. Resting in the
dish were red soaps she'd carved into drops of blood.
Towels were plush deep red.

Adam would never fit in here, I thought. When he saw
the *Psycho* bathroom the following week he said it was
"disturbing." This is the same man who decorated his own
guest bathroom with Oklahoma Sooner football wallpaper, photos, and memorabilia. The toilet paper rolled
off the face mask of a Sooner helmet. The bathroom in his
bedroom was done in a rubber ducky motif. Unlike his living room, at least Adam's bathrooms reflected a little personality. Problem was, I wasn't particularly drawn to that
personality.

There was no doubt about it, Adam was a decent, kind
person, but so bland I could barely stand it. Once he actually asked if I'd like to take a "long, romantic sunset walk
on the beach." Sure, I'd like to take a walk on the beach

with someone I love. Sure, I'd like the conversation to be so smooth and effortless that we both look at our watches and wonder where two hours went. But who plans for this? It all sounded so trite and contrived, like a verse from the Pina Colada Song. The thought of replacing my new housemate for my intended husband was deflating. And yet, on autopilot, I continued dating him, afraid to create a void in the space I'd put him. This was unfair, I knew. But the doing nothing, the coasting, the status quo was so comfortable, I convinced myself that I just needed more time to let my heart catch up with my head.

When Vicki finished the *Psycho* bathroom, she was so eager for me to shower in it, I should have known she was up to something. Naively, I assumed she was just excited about my experiencing her new creation, and was shocked into cries of terror when red paint shot from the shower-head. She tore the curtain back and held a butcher knife, laughing psychotically. "My mommy made me do it!" she screeched.

"You're out of your mind!" I screamed, laughing at her. Vicki jumped around like a twelve year old, thrilled with her prank.

"Mona Warren, you're the best friend I've ever had."

After twenty minutes, I was back to my normal color, and walked out into the living room with a towel turban and robe to see Vicki and Mike sitting on the couch together. "Oh hey, I didn't expect you." I inadvertently touched my headpiece and wondered if my mascara was running under my eyes. "Did your psycho sister tell you what she just did to me?"

"How've you been, Mona Lisa?" Mike smiled.

"Good. How 'bout yourself?"

"Not bad."

Vicki took stock of the awkwardness in the room, looking at Mike, then examining me. Following the hysterical laughter from the shower scene minutes earlier, the silence was all-encompassing. Deafening quiet. Unending silence. After a full minute of this, Vicki finally had to say something. "The tension is so thick in here, you could cut it with a knife." She laughed as she made the screeching sound effects of Norman Bates.

Mike forced a chuckle. An "oh" escaped my socially inept lips. "I'm going to get some clothes on. I'll let you visit with your sister." As I ran upstairs, I heard Mike say that he had come by to see me, too. But I knew he was just being polite. It had been two weeks since our business arrangement had ended and I hadn't heard a word from him. No phone calls. No instant messages. The absence of cash led to the absence of Mike.

This was the night I decided to really throw myself into making things work with Adam. What he lacked in excitement, he made up for in stability, which was precisely what I needed for a happy future. While Mike was still in the house, I ran upstairs to my room and called Adam. We booked five dates for the following three weeks including a barbeque with his family on Easter Sunday. I knew if it was time for me to meet the family, Adam was getting serious about me.

Five dates without any public relations efforts to bolster my image made me feel like I was a raw grain sitting in a barrel at the health food store. I desperately needed packaging. A cute graphic on the box. At least a logo. But I decided to take Greta's advice and go organic.

Adam took me to see *Chipping Away,* an independent film being shown on the sail of the *Star of India.* I thought it was pretentious drivel. He said this was his fourth viewing and that in college, the film changed his life. I had to laugh when Adam said that he liked my candor. "A lot of women don't speak their minds in a relationship, but you always tell it like it is, Mona. It's important to be forthright. That's what I believe," he praised.

*Ah yes, the honest and forthright Mona Warren. Film critic. Total fraud.* Though it didn't bother Adam that I detested his favorite film, it definitely rubbed me the wrong way that Adam seemed so impressed with this irritating pseudo-psychological piece of shit of a movie. Who could enjoy a movie shot entirely from the perspective of the bottom of a bowl of chips at a cocktail party? For the first half hour of *Chipping Away,* the entire screen was covered in yellow and dark blue tortilla chips. We heard voices of party guests whispering their dirty little secrets, come-ons and gossip as they reached into the chip bowl. As people grabbed them, the chips would shift every now and then, but how exciting is that to watch? Then finally, the last obstructing chips were removed and the audience saw the faces of the voices we'd become familiar with. But our view was still from the bottom of that goddamn bowl of chips! Never once did the camera move. It was nauseating to watch huge hands reaching into the bowl and then look up at giant chins and nostrils. The ending was less than climactic. The hostess said, "Oh look, we've run low on chips," and refilled the bowl entirely with dark blue ones. And that was it. The end. She refilled the chips. What the hell does that even mean?

The next week, I took Adam to an art installation, which he said he "didn't get." He got deep meaning from the chip flick, but saw absolutely no beauty in sprawling mosaics made of the tiniest pieces of stained glass.

That weekend, Adam and I had a forced conversation over dinner about our life's ambitions. He asked where I saw myself in five years. *Married to you and in a committed relationship with any doctor who can hook me up with Zoloft.* "If there was one thing you could change about yourself, what would it be?" he continued. I felt like I was being interviewed for a job.

"Um, I don't know, I'm pretty happy with who I am," I lied. *If only I knew who that was.*

"That's refreshing!" Adam slapped the dinner table. "Everywhere I turn in this town, women are getting plastic surgery, taking self-improvement classes and the like. I think these ladies have it too easy. That's what's wrong with our culture, especially here. We don't have real problems so we have to make up silly little things to work on. Self-esteem, droopy eyelids, lactose intolerance. One woman at a meeting last week said her chi was out of balance." He laughed. "Can you imagine, her chi? She was getting acupuncture to get it all back where it should be. We're a very spoiled country, that's what I believe. You go to Iraq and I guarantee you, no one's complaining about their chi being out of whack. They've got real problems to deal with."

I felt guilty wondering if perhaps my chi was off balance and that was my problem. Maybe what I needed all along was better chi.

The next weekend I invited Adam over for a home-cooked Chinese meal at my place. My culinary skills blew him away until he saw the carryout containers in the garbage.

At his family's Easter barbeque, I was determined to show him how well I would fit in with the Ziegler clan. I got along well with his father, who shared my passion for music, but realized I had to start marketing myself not only as daughter-in-law material, but as a good mother. A gaggle of under-ten kids were playing Toss Across in the backyard. Instead of showing them what a great auntie I would be, I wound up getting really competitive and shouting at my team to "focus or we're going to get slaughtered!" My would-be cousin, Jeanette, really appreciated the opportunity to explain what slaughter was to her eight-year-old son.

I returned home that evening and decided to return to my original plan of figuring out what made Adam tick. I wondered why I was trying so hard to impress Adam, when frankly, I wasn't all that impressed with our compatibility. I definitely liked him, and there was a part of me that even loved him as a human being. He was a genuinely good and decent person, who would never intentionally hurt a soul. The connection just wasn't there with him, though.

I kicked myself at my next thought—that the connection wasn't there with Adam because it was already made with Mike. The coach in me took over. *Mike is a player. He will use you for sex, then discard you like an old newspaper. Look how he treats women. Read his column! You need someone who will stay the course with you. You need a long-term investment, not the impulse purchase of a novelty item.*

As my keys unlocked the front door, I heard voices from the television set. "Vicki?" I shouted in. "You home?"

"Mike's here, too," she returned.

The whole room stiffened. Leaves of plants tensed. Air ceased to flow. Flowers craned their petals to see what would happen next. Against the backdrop of stillness, I hoped my racing heart would go unnoticed.

"Hey." He waved.

"Hey." I tried to sound less enthused than him. "You guys have a good time at your picnic?"

"Our family's crazy," Vicki said, clicking the television off. "We were just talking about how fucked up they are. Dad's like this sergeant who has to be in charge of everything." She imitated his stern voice. "Don't press the burgers or you'll dry 'em out, Vicki. Mike, you need a haircut. Marion, you've had enough to drink today."

Mike shrugged. "I could use a haircut," he said. "Mom was drinking a bit more than usual."

"Whatever." Vicki sounded annoyed with him. "Two minutes ago you said this was the last holiday you were spending with them. Now you're fine with the freaks. What's up?"

Mike didn't have to answer Vicki's question. I knew what was up. The same thing that's always up when people complain about their families in front of me. They realize that I would love to have someone to bitch about. Mike and I had talked about my longing to be part of a family, or even a community of people with a shared interest. Hell, I'd join a book group if I thought it would give me the peace of truly belonging somewhere. I'd settle for being waved in at the naval base. Mike knew this about me, and felt guilty griping about a father who was overly controlling about grilling burgers when mine had driven seventeen people off the side of an icy cliff.

I'd planned to dart off to my room, but could not tear myself away from the place Mike was. I sat in a chair beside the couch where they sat, and tried not to pry into Mike's social life, though I was dying to ask if he was seeing anyone. More important, if he missed me. Thankfully, Vicki's presence kept me from blurting anything as stupid as that. If Mike missed me, he would have called, I reminded myself. Even if I asked him, he'd tell me he did just to avoid hurting my fragile, orphan feelings. Clearly the man was not carving my initials into his wrist with a fork. He was not joining any support groups for lonely guys. Mike was just going about his business, completely unfettered by the fact that I was essentially out of his life.

"So how's the Dog's life?" I tried my hardest not to fume.

"Pretty shitty, to tell you the truth," he said.

"Oh, poor baby." I was sounding far more sarcastic than appropriate. "Sorry. I just had a rough day with Adam."

"I don't even know why you're with that guy," Vicki jumped in. "He's so boring."

"Not like exciting Jimmy," I shot, now furious at both Doughertys in my home. I sighed and buried my face in my hands. "I'm sorry, you two. I don't know what's gotten into me today. I'm just not myself."

These awkward silences never seemed to bother Mike, but always set Vicki into automatic overdrive in peacemaker mode. Whenever there was tension, she made a joke or changed the topic to something less emotionally charged. "So Mike was telling me he loves what we've done with the place," Vicki beamed.

"Yeah." He nodded. "Nice of you to give Vicki a break like this, Mona Lisa."

"Well, it's long past due. She's got a lot of talent," I said as though she weren't sitting right there in the room with us. "In fact, I was going to ask her to do the whole house. As long as she's here, I may as well put her to work, right?"

"Ohmigod!" Vicki jumped from her chair and hugged me. "You are like my guardian angel or something." Like a wind-up doll, she started muttering about needing to get a license, hooking up with an experienced designer, and counting rooms on her fingers. "The whole house? The entire thing, right?"

I nodded, my eyes never leaving Mike's, who returned my gaze as intensely. We looked as though we could be facing off for a fight, or about to kiss.

"I'm glad my sister was more helpful to you than I was." Mike said, breaking our silence.

"You were plenty helpful," I said. "I just didn't need your help anymore."

"Done with me, huh?"

"Exactly." I clenched my jaw and forced back any tears that might have even been contemplating making an appearance.

# Chapter 31

Although I was hanging dead on a meat hook, I could hear every word the white-coated butchers said. I could feel the cold air of the refrigerated slaughterhouse. And I could smell the blood from my own body and the others around me. Adam's cousin Jeanette walked by my body and slapped my rump, commenting that I'd make a fine grill. She wore white stiletto heels and held a rolled-up copy of *Highlights* magazine in her jewel-speckled hand. Pointing at me, she said, "This one got what she deserved but what a shame for these innocent children."

A knock on the door startled me back to consciousness. Vicki was still in her pajamas and hopped onto my bed like a child on Christmas morning, unable to wait for the day to begin. She even looked like a child with her two low pigtails draping over her sleeveless pink tank top. The matching pink flannel pants were adorned with baby blue bows. "So, about decorating the house," she began. "I wanted to ask you a few things." I nodded for her to continue. "We could do the whole house in one style, like clean and modern, or rustic or whatever. Or we could mix things up a bit and have different themes for different rooms."

The thought that it was acceptable to do an entire house in a patchwork of different styles—and have it all come together beautifully—caused me to sigh aloud with relief, though Vicki had no idea how liberating her simple idea was. "Is it too early for this?" she asked.

"No." I laughed. "We should've talked about this awhile ago." Vicki looked puzzled, undoubtedly because she'd only been given the green light on redecorating less than twelve hours earlier. "Different themes would be okay. It'll be fun," I relieved her from the confusion my earlier comment had caused.

"Okay," she said, moving into excited decorator mode. Her posture changed as she grabbed the pencil and notepad on my nightstand. "I was thinking since you're such a fan of movies, we might do the living room in the style of your favorite old flick. What's your favorite?"

Without pause, I answered, *It's a Wonderful Life.* Vicki knit her brows trying to remember what the set looked like. "Weren't they kind of poor?" she asked.

"Middle class. George Bailey's dad wasn't much of a businessman," I told her. "Their home really wasn't anything to look at."

"Hmmm, okay, what's your second favorite? Think of a place with a little flare."

*"Gone With the Wind,"* I told her.

"Tara," we said simultaneously, as though a lightbulb lit between our heads at the exact same moment.

"Ohmigod! That window, that window!" Vicki fanned herself with her hand. "How perfect is that window we bought?! We'll do the whole downstairs common areas in Southern grandeur, marble floors, big palms, plush red chairs with satin rope tassels. Do you love it?"

"I love it!"

"You need to give me some time to get my license so I

can get the designer discount on stuff. Or I can hook up with someone who's already doing this and cut her in for a piece of my profit for use of her license," she thought aloud. "Oh well, you don't need to be bothered with these details. I'll work it out. This is so exciting. I'm going to create Tara. You are going to love this, Mona. Love, love, love," she rattled. She popped up toward the door. "Okay, I'm going to jot down some ideas. Tara," she said dreamily. "Tomorrow is another day." She held her hand to her head and exited the room in high drama.

I was able to close my eyes and enjoy a few more minutes of quiet before I heard the doorbell ring and female voices chattering downstairs. I'm sure Greta would keel over with shock if—just once—I was dressed and ready to run right when she showed up. "Be down in a sec!" I shouted downstairs.

As the familiar Pacific shoreline scrolled past us, I told Greta I was planning to take singing lessons. I'd always loved the times when my mother sat us kids around the piano and asked us to match the notes she played. It was like that scene in *The Sound of Music* where Julie Andrews is carting the von Trapp kids all over Salzburg, assigning each of them a note, belting that when you know the notes to sing, you can sing most anything. Mom would play six notes and we'd repeat them for her. Then she'd play longer sequences until I was the only one left singing alone with her. Within a half hour the other kids lost interest, but I always ultimately wore out my mother. In some ways, it was like musical *Survivor*, the only way to get one-on-one time with her. But I really truly loved it. The most at peace I've ever felt was sitting on the hand-loomed rug beside my mother's piano carefully maintaining a song's melody while she harmonized with me. Sometimes now, when I sing alone in the shower or in my car, my voice sounds hollow to me. My ear missed the fullness of my mother's accompaniment.

"I hope this isn't another way to Appeal to Adam," Greta said.

"Not really," I said as an ocean breeze washed across my body. "I've always loved singing, but never pursued it." Just saying those words brought a smile to my face. I felt like leaping as I ran. *I've always loved singing. I've never pursued it. But now I am.*

"Did you just skip?" Greta giggled.

"No." I laughed as if she were crazy. *Did I?*

"Mona, you just did this fairy skip thing," she teased. She leapt through the air and fluttered her hands, imitating me. "Do tell what's got you so giddy."

"I don't know," I playfully denied. "Vicki's redecorating the house, which is pretty exciting. I've got my first private boxing lesson this afternoon, which I must confess I'm a little more giddy about than I should be. And, I don't know, I'm feeling good about my decision to take singing lessons. I feel, um, hopeful, I guess. I don't remember the last time I felt this hopeful."

I lied twice. I remembered exactly the last time I'd felt like life was a clear road ahead of me. It was a week before the accident, the first time I ever beat Todd in chess after six months of straight defeat. Before I checkmated him, I looked at the dark wood grandfather clock in the corner of the common room. It was just before midnight and the sky was sparkling with stars and a thin slice of moon. I told myself to remember this moment. *The world is wide open for the girl who is about to take down the boy genius,* I said silently. I felt as though beating Todd at a game of strategy and intelligence initiated me into a secret club of high achievers. I smiled smugly, knowing that I could do anything.

The second lie was that my singing lessons weren't partly to impress Adam. I definitely wanted to learn how to sing, but I've wanted this for the past fifteen years without acting on it. It wasn't until I did another Internet search with Adam's name that I was reminded of his love of music. *Savings and Loan Magazine* did a two-page profile on Adam's impressive career, which I thought was odd since he was still fairly young. In any event, he told the reporter that his first love was Julie London, the sultry, bluesy singer who crooned "Cry Me a River" so soulfully, he actually did. There *was* more to Adam than I was seeing on our dates, I realized.

"Greta," I said as we switched from running to walking.

"Yes?"

"I'm a total fraud."

"Why do you say that?"

I sighed. "Part of the reason I want to learn to sing is to impress Adam. It's not the entire reason, but it's definitely a factor. It's just that you've been so opposed to this whole thing with Adam, I'm almost afraid to tell you anything anymore because I feel like you're going to judge me as some shallow, manipulative little twit."

"Wow," she said sadly. "I wonder if my patients ever feel like that."

"I'm sure they don't," I quickly apologized. "I'm sure it's just me, and like I said, it's 'cause I feel like a total fraud."

Greta stretched her leg in front of her and leaned into it. Not looking at me, she said, "We're all frauds to a certain degree."

"Why would you say that?"

"Because it's true. Listen, Mona. I'm sorry if you feel judged by me. I really don't mean to come off that way. I think it's great that you're taking singing lessons, and the boxing is cool, too. It's a great way to work through some of your rage."

"My rage?"

"Yeah, Mona. It's natural that you've got a lot of anger. My God, your whole family was taken away from you in a moment. Of course, you're angry."

"No I'm not! How could I be angry at them for that? They were killed, how could I be angry at them?"

"For leaving you," Greta said.

"They didn't leave me, they were killed."

"Maybe not angry at them, but you've got to be angry about what happened. You've spent half of your life without them."

"I've never been without them," I gulped, guilty for surviving. Guilty for not being where I should have been that day. I've never spent a day without them. Their absence has always been a presence.

Grammy's friend, Captain John, jogged toward us, waving his hands to fan his sweating face. He stopped to catch his breath. "Morning, ladies."

"Good morning, sir," I said.

"Morning, Captain." Greta smiled.

"Fine morning for a run, wouldn't you say?" John panted.

"Yes, sir. A fine morning indeed." I stood at near attention.

"I'd better keep moving. Keep the old heart rate up," he said, awkwardly catching himself remembering that Grammy died of heart failure. "I'm sorry, Mona. What a terrible thing for me to say."

"Please." I tried to recast myself from the old role as the world's eggshell. "I'm sure Grammy would've wanted to keep her rate up, too, if given the choice. And I'm sure she'd be happy you're in good health, sir. Really, no offense taken."

"Good day to you, ladies." John ran off, still repentant of his non-faux pas.

A flock of seagulls flew against a clear blue backdrop, swooping down to the beach to sip crabs from their shells and leave tiny prints along the shoreline. How could Adam not love San Diego? And now that I finally had a life, did I really want to uproot it?

# Chapter 32

"Clarence! Clarence! Help me, Clarence," shouted Tim as he stood on stage holding a soft book in one hand, shaking the other fisted one toward the sky. "Get me back. Get me back. I don't care what happens to me. Get me back to my wife and kids. Help me, Clarence, please. Please! I want to live again! I want to live again. Please, God, let me live again." My fictitious ex-boyfriend, Poison, was begging God for life.

"A bit overdone," said a male voice from the audience. "Same level of passion without all the hype." *At least he hasn't destroyed any property,* I thought. "Try it one more time."

Toby, my would-be purse snatcher, was perfectly cast as the timid angel second class. "You see, George, it really has been a wonderful life," he said.

As much as I loved *It's a Wonderful Life,* these two were killing it for me with their stilted delivery of lines and stiff bodies. And why was Clarence even on stage at this point?! By the time George Bailey wakes up by the bridge, Clarence is back in heaven.

"Where's the goddamned bell?!" the director rose from his chair and shouted backstage. Suddenly a gong sounded from backstage. "Why am I waiting an eternity for the bell to chime?!" Some small independent theatre companies are too hip and cutting edge to be appreciated by the mainstream. This one just sucked.

From the back of the theatre, I offered that Clarence doesn't earn his wings until George is home with his family and friends—not at the bridge. "He needs to be with all of those people whose lives he changed. That's when it all comes together and the angel earns his wings," I said as though I were part of Frank Capra's personal accuracy enforcement squad.

"It's the very last moment of the movie," I continued. "A bell from the Christmas tree jingles and Zuzu says that her teacher told her that every time a bell rings it means an angel just earned his wings. Then George winks and says, 'Atta boy, Clarence. Atta boy,' and that's the end. After the bridge scene, they still have all that whole part when George comes home and everyone starts coming over with all the money they collected." As all eyes focused on me, I felt acutely aware of my appearance. Not embarrassed of my mere existence as I was just a few months ago. Not showcasing myself as Vicki often does. Just aware of my bohemian embroidered crepe blouse topping my denim skirt and blue canvas wedge sandals. I held a simple brown leather knapsack in my right hand and clutched my amber square sunglasses in my left hand. For the first time I could remember, I felt no discomfort from people looking at me. I felt no need to apologize or explain why I was there. I brushed a loose strand of hair from my face and stood quietly as the director wondered who I was. "I mean, you can do it any way you want, of course, but if you're going to be true to the original script, you should wait till he gets home before you ring the bell."

Twisted in his red velvet theatre chair, the director stared at me for a full minute. He had pointy features, which would have made him a perfectly cast Potter. (Not until opening night of the show did I learn that the director actually did cast himself in this small role.) I stared back and folded my arms. "I'd also rethink the gong," I said in a momentary lapse in comfort, a need to fill the dead air.

"You would?" he asked, raising a brow as if to ask who the hell I thought I was anyway. I nodded. "Are there any other suggestions you have for me, Miss, Miss—"

"Mona. Mona Warren. Please excuse the interruption. I didn't realize you were rehearsing. Toby said you take a lunch break at this time."

"May I ask who you are, and how it is that you think you're so important that you can come into my rehearsal and inject your unsolicited opinion about my directing choices," he smarted. I couldn't contain my grin. *I*, Mona Warren, was being accused of arrogance.

"My apologies." I smiled. "It's just that this is my absolute favorite film of all time and when you snapped at your stage crew that they were supposed to ring a bell right then, I couldn't help correcting you."

If silence could make the sound "uh oh," it did. A hush fell over the theatre as though I'd just committed a grave offense and was about to be drawn and quartered. "I am perfectly aware of when Mr. Capra chose to sound the bell," the director returned. "I've made a different one."

"Oh hey, Mona." Julie scurried from backstage in a black-and-white party dress, her hair rolled like Mary Bailey. "I thought I heard you." She shielded her eyes from the lights with her hand and thanked me for removing the fainting spell from her driving record.

"Please, it was the least I could do," I shouted back from the aisle.

The director bonked himself on the head as though he

were thinking he could've had a V8. "Is this the crazy woman who hired you kids to do all those stunts?" From onstage, three retro-dressed actors nodded affirmatively. "Well, why didn't you say so?" He stood extending his hand for me to come and shake. "Why don't we take a break now? I'm busting with curiosity to see what Ms. Warren wants from our merry little band of players this time. Sit, sit." He patted the seat beside him.

Julie, Toby, and even Tim took the seats around us and leaned in to hear why I'd stopped by. "Really, I just wanted to see that Julie's driving record was taken care of."

In his repulsive, sliding accent, Tim asked, "Still not budging on paying for the window, ay love?"

"Absolutely not!" I laughed. "I never told you to throw a brick through the diner window. There was no reason for you to do that." I turned to the director. "Did you know he threw a brick through the window of a diner 'cause that's what rock stars do?"

Julie gasped then laughed. "Tim! You said her boyfriend threw the brick."

"He *did* beat the stuffing out of me," Toby said, defending any upcoming charges of exaggeration that might come his way.

"That is true," I said, looking at Toby's healed face, remembering the fresh pink bruises christened by his tears.

"That's your problem in this show, too," the director said to Tim. "He flies off half-cocked, spewing dialogue without any understanding of what the character has been through. Did you write up his life story like I told you to do? No. Did you think about how angry he was to be stuck in Bedford Falls when all of his childhood he dreamt of exploring the world? No. Do you have any idea who the people who shaped his life were? No. You're a lazy actor, Tim, and that's why rehearsals have been going so abominably poor."

"Wow," I said to the director. "You really think an actor needs to do all that?"

"I know so," he said. "How is Tim going to really understand his character if he doesn't spend time examining where he came from?"

"You should meet my friend, Greta," I said.

"Why?" he asked.

"Oh, she's a therapist. She's always talking about this kind of stuff."

He unwrapped a sandwich and took a dainty bite. "Sometimes I feel like one," he said, winking at Julie. "Was there anything else?" he asked hopefully.

"Well, I just realized that you could probably steer me in the right direction. I want to take singing lessons. Do you know anyone who could work with me? I'm a real beginner, but—"

They all laughed aloud for reasons I did not understand. "Ollie is *the* man," said Tim. "If you can get him, that is. He's not like us peasants, desperate for cash."

"Wonderful! How can I get in touch with this Ollie person?"

"You are in touch with him," the director said as he leaned toward me and placed his hand on my forearm.

"You do voice lessons?" I sounded surprised, then realized I shouldn't be. A theatre director who also taught singing. Logical enough.

"Well—" He hesitated. "My schedule is pretty packed, but let me see what I can do." As he spoke, he moved himself to a piano offstage and played the opening notes of "Can't Help Lovin' Dat Man" from *Showboat*. "Let me hear a few bars, sweetheart."

After my first few notes, I noticed my voice was quivering so I closed my eyes and pretended I was alone in my car. I imagined this was what a bird must feel like gliding through the air, the thrill of falling, then soaring freely back to the sky. I swear I actually felt my hair blow back. I remember feeling like I could keep singing this song long after the music ended. But we never got that far.

The theatre was silent as Ollie stopped playing abruptly. "Okay, I've heard enough," he said, standing to return to his rehearsal.

"That bad?" I masked my tears.

On cue, they all laughed again. "That bad?" Julie asked. "Are you joking? What's Ollie supposed to teach you?"

"There's plenty to teach," added the harsh director's voice. "Mona, you are gifted, please don't misunderstand. You have one of the loveliest natural female voices I've ever heard, to be frank with you. With training, you're going to be amazing."

"Amazing?" I blushed with my voice.

"I think she already is amazing," Julie said. "Hasn't anyone ever told you that you have a great singing voice, Mona?"

"Um, no," I said.

"Cold fucking world," Ollie quipped.

I laughed. "No, it's not that. I guess no one has ever, um, heard my voice before. Heard me sing, I mean. Just a few people, I guess."

Ollie unceremoniously handed me his business card and told me that the only times he was available were Monday evenings. I paused to check my calendar. "That'll work," I said, noting that for the first time in my life I actually might have had conflicting plans.

# Chapter 33

*Women say they want a sensitive guy. They also say they want a guy who's honest about his feelings. News flash, ladies: You can't have it both ways.*
—The Dog House, May

I hated myself for circling the gym parking lot to check for Mike's car, but I did. Twice. It seemed for the past few weeks, Mike and I were on entirely different workout schedules. I'd only seen him the two times he was visiting Vicki, and other than that, zero contact. He was, without question, a whore—a friend available to me only for a fee. What infuriated me was that I began to trust him. I started to believe that the conversations we had about his life and his rarely acknowledged feelings were genuine. I fumed, enraged at us both. At him for being smooth. And at me for thinking our friendship was solid enough to skate on.

It was like skating, too. It's humiliating to admit that I was starting to feel that exhilarating freedom of speed skating with a partner, having him whip you around the curve fast enough to make your heart race. Still, you feel you're safe because your gloved hand is tightly grasping his. But the reality is that just inches past most frozen parts of most ponds are thin areas where ice breaks and people fall in.

I despised Mike, which was a perfect frame of mind to be in for my boxing lesson. Changing in the locker room, I caught a peek at my reflection in the mirror. At first, I thought it was someone else and told myself that if I continued to workout, I could get in that good shape pretty soon. Then I noticed that she and I wore the same underwear and we both snapped toward each other at the exact same moment. I smiled at myself, and I smiled back.

I walked to the exercise room where my teacher, Tio, was jabbing at bags as he waited for me. "Hey, girl." He smiled. "Ready to kick some ass?"

"Born ready," I lied. Or maybe I was born ready, but that readiness took a detour, only now rounding the corner back to me.

As I punched and ducked at the bag, Tio asked me if I was ready to start fighting real people instead of just punching the bag. "You've been getting pretty tough here, Mona. Don't you think you should find out what you're really made of? Unarmed combat is the ultimate test, girl."

Sure, I could beat the crap out of a defenseless sack of sand, but another person—a person with her own set of fists and ability to duck—was another story. Continuing my jabs, I told Tio I'd had enough of getting my ass kicked to last a lifetime. "Why you think you'd be the one getting your ass kicked?" he asked. "Maybe it'll be you knocking some teeth loose." The thought of knocking someone's teeth loose held no appeal. I did get a bit puffed at the thought that Tio might put his money on me in a fight, though. "It could happen. You're a natural fighter, girl." I laughed in the absence of anything to say. I punched a little harder, determined to maintain my fighter image with

Tio. "Hey, you know who was asking about you?" he said, smiling.

*Mike?!*

"Oh, who?" I tried to sound casual, but silently, motionlessly shaking his collar shouting, "Who, who?! Tell me now!" It could only have been Mike because I didn't know anyone else here but the people at the front desk who scan my membership card.

"That Dog guy," Tio said.

A choir of angels sang Hallelujah. Really they did. It's just no one but me heard them.

*Casual, casual. Everything you say will get back to Mike.*

"Oh, how's he doing?"

*Excellent. Inhale, exhale.*

"He's lookin' fit. Asked if you were still boxing here. I told him you were my lunchtime gig every Monday and Thursday."

"Lunchtime gig?!" I shouted. "My lesson is at two o'clock, Tio! That's not lunchtime!"

"Settle, girl. It's when I eat lunch. What's your problem?"

"No problem." I took it down a notch after catching my reflection, looking like something out of a Paxil commercial. "It's just that you shouldn't wait till so late to eat lunch. You could get, um, hungry."

Tio scrunched his face, looking at me like the crazy white chick I was. He pointed at the punching bag, urging me to continue.

"Did he say anything else?"

"Who?" Tio asked. *Seriously, there must be a brain leak from all penises.*

"Mike. Dog. Did he say anything else about me?"

"He said he doesn't see much of you anymore and was wondering how you were doing." So he asked my boxing teacher? If Mike was wondering how I was doing, why didn't he pick up the phone and ask me? Why didn't he send an e-mail? Why didn't he ask his sister, who lived under my roof? What is wrong with this imbecile of a man? And more important, what was wrong with me for caring?!

"Whew, you really kickin' ass now, girl," Tio said as I continued punching. "Watch your face. Protect yourself," he commanded. "You're hitting good, but you keep leaving yourself wide open. Put your hands up, girl. Hands up."

Driving home, I dialed Mike's number, but hung up after the third ring. What was I going to say to him anyway? I dialed Adam's office and the honker put me through to him right away.

"Hello there, Mona," Adam said with a formal friendliness we hadn't gotten past. And I'm not just talking about our conversations either. We had been dating ten weeks with absolutely no sign of advancing our relationship to a sexual one. I can't say I was overwhelmingly drawn to him physically, but it was so damned insulting to be respectfully pecked on the cheek after each of our dates. I invited him in for coffee on Saturday night. He said he never drank caffeine after seven. I told him I had decaf, but he said he had an early meeting—with Jesus. Yes, Adam Ziegler was born Jewish but was baptized three years ago after he was born again.

Of course, I found out about his newfound relationship with the Lord at the worst possible time. On Saturday night, I idiotically followed one of Mike's last ridiculous pieces of advice and tried to sexually titillate Adam by giving him the impression that I once had a relationship with a woman. Melanie was actually a Venus Swimwear model trying to break into acting, and was hired to play Violet, the Bedford Falls flirt who would've become a bar brawling tart if George Bailey had never been born.

Far more subtle than toxic Tim, Melanie slinked into the restaurant where Adam and I were having dinner, and illuminated our table with her astounding sex appeal. She should've had film noir damsel entrance music. Melanie alluded to our relationship, and for a moment, I wished someone this good-looking—male or female—was ever interested in me.

"She broke my heart, you know?" Melanie told Adam. "She's ruined me for all other women." All male heads turned toward our table with such speed, I actually heard a swish. "I'll let you enjoy your dinner, Mona, but I want you to know my life hasn't been the same without you."

In her clingy red silk dress, Melanie wished me well with a luscious pout and warned Adam he'd better take good care of me. As she strutted away, her body was a visual smorgasbord—her flowing platinum hair, her muscular tan back, her perfect scoops of ass cheeks, larger models of her perfectly scooped breasts. Everyone within a six table radius was sexually charged. Men were ordering oysters. Women were lustily looking at their companions, changing their dinner orders to T-bone steak. The front window of the restaurant fogged up. If my chair had an armrest, I would've humped it. Everyone seemed infused with hormones. Everyone, that is, except Adam, who said that I should be deeply ashamed of my past.

"Mona, I've grown very attached to you, but clearly the person you are today is not who you were years ago," he said, like Ward Cleaver reprimanding Beaver. "Can you assure me that the lesbians and drug addicts are youthful indiscretions?" I nodded my head, wondering who, other than Adam Ziegler and Congressman Henry Hyde, used the term "youthful indiscretion."

"Okeydokey. I can live with that. After all, if I were perfect, I would've never come to know Jesus. Everything happens for a reason. That's what I believe."

At first I laughed, thinking he must be kidding. I realized he wasn't joking about four minutes into his excruciatingly detailed account of how Jesus paid him a personal visit and served as his spiritual obstetrician, delivering him to the world of Christianity.

"Hello, Adam." I spoke loudly into my car phone. "I just got out of boxing class and wanted to say hello, and see how you're doing."

"Doing well, but I'm going to have to get back to you in a few, okay? Is this an emergency? Can it wait?"

"Of course," I said. "I'll be home in a few minutes." I hung up wondering why I was still even in this relationship. The few times I started to break up with him, I panicked at the thought that he was my last chance for a stable, happy married life. As long as he was still interested in me, I was immobilized by the fear that Adam was as good as it got, and that if I gave him up now, I'd only regret it.

As I turned onto Alameda Avenue, I saw the familiar sight of navy guys waving certain cars in to the base. They scanned my car, then moved on to the next.

I returned to what I thought was an empty home, but saw that Vicki had left fabric swatches and paint samples sitting beside printouts from movie Web sites. In Vicki's handwriting, notes about Tara blocked entire pages with notes along the margins and asterisks on every page. At the bottom of each page, Vicki listed upcoming art auctions, estate sales, and art dealers.

She breezed by in a pair of red go-go boots and a knapsack, dashing madly out the door, saying she was late for work. "If I'm late one more time, I'm seriously fired," said my blur of a roommate.

"Who's at a strip joint at quarter to four on a Monday?" I asked her exiting body.

"Guys with dicks." The door slammed.

The answering machine taunted me with no messages, so I played the old ones to fill the silence. I sat at the piano, and sounded out a few notes. I stared at the silent phone. *Fine, don't call. I don't give a rat's ass.*

"Dog was asking about you." I heard Tio's voice. "I told him you were my lunchtime gig."

I picked up the phone and dialed without pausing to remember the number.

"Talk to me," Mike said casually. How could he be so happy-go-lucky when I missed him so desperately? I hung up the phone, which rang just seconds after I placed the receiver back in its cradle.

"Mona?" he said. "Why'd you hang up on me?"

*Fucking caller ID!*

"Oh, hey Dog. Sorry 'bout that. There was someone at the door so I had to hang up."

"Who was it?" Mike asked. I wasn't sure if he was just making conversation or trying to catch me in a lie.

"The postman," I said.

"The postman rings the doorbell?"

"Sometimes twice," I said. By the lack of acknowledgment, I could tell he didn't get the reference. *Dumb shit.*

"So what'd'ya call for?"

"Oh, nothing. I was just at the gym today and Tio said you were asking about me so I figured I'd give you a buzz and catch up. It's been awhile. What's going on with you?"

He hesitated, embarrassed that Tio had turned him in, I suppose. "Not too much. You know, same shit, different day."

*Thank you, Cliché Man.*

"So how's it going with your boy?" Mike asked. "What's his name, Aaron?"

Just hearing the sound of Mike's voice made me want to cry. Why hadn't he called me? Why didn't he care that we were no longer friends? I'll bet if I really was Claudia Schiffer he would've been back at my doorstep the next day—bullshit Dog Rules be damned.

"Adam. His name is Adam," I said through clenched teeth. "Mike, can you give me an honest answer to a question?"

"Shoot."

"Have you ever really been in love with a woman?" I asked. "Never mind, never mind. We don't have to talk about this kind of stuff now that I'm not paying you. It's just that I'm not really sure it's Adam I'm in love with, or the idea of Adam. Or someone like Adam. Or someone like who I thought Adam was. By the way, he's a born-again Christian and was totally wigged out by the whole hot-lesbian-in-my-past thing."

Mike laughed and I saw him sitting back into the blue chair I imagined he had. "A born-again Christian who goes to Ozzfest?"

"I know, bizarre." I laughed. "It's just that every time I try to break up with him, I get this anxiety like he's my last chance. Is that crazy?"

*Tell me it is crazy and that you are my last chance. Tell me that the only time you've ever really known love was with me.*

"Mona, I thought the whole thing was whacked from the start. He's not your last chance and even if he was, you'd have to spend your whole life married to a freak."

"Just because he's religious doesn't mean he's a freak," I defended my dud beau.

"Fuck that, I mean that he's not into the whole chick-on-chick thing. That should've been a lock."

"Be serious with me, Mike. How do I tell if I'm in love with someone?" I asked.

"You're definitely not in love with this guy, Mona Lisa."

"Why not?"

"You have too many questions. You're either in love or you're not and if you're second-guessing it, you're not."

"But you're a guy. You're less complicated than women."

"And thank God for that, really." He laughed. "Mona, you've been trying to force his square peg into your round hole for nearly three months now."

"Don't be a pig!"

"You and Adam getting married and living the Hollywood ending just ain't in the cards. I don't think you even like the guy, much less love him. If he disappeared tomorrow, you'd never give him a second thought."

"Do you ever miss your ex-wife?" I asked, really wondering if he'd missed me over the past weeks.

He sighed audibly. "Not really. Not much, I guess. I used to, but what're you gonna do, she made her decision and moved on. You know, she called me about a year ago and told me she and Mr. Sensitive broke up and asked if we could give it another shot."

"Wow. What'd you say?"

"We're not together, are we?"

"You might've given it a shot then split up again."

"Nah, we didn't give it another shot. Once a chick cheats on you, that's it. She made her choice, now she got what she deserves."

"Not everything's so black and white, Mike."

"Sometimes it is, Mona Lisa."

I found Mike's unforgiving attitude toward his ex-wife so thoroughly depressing, I didn't even have the energy to lift Greta's latest reading selection for me—*Canned Chicken Soup for the Soul: Why Women Accept Prepackaged Notions of Femininity.* Adam was definitely not the man for me, but Mike terrified me. An internal voice—that sounded an awful lot like Greta's—asked why I was on such a frenzied hunt for a man anyway. Would it be such a tragedy if I ended up alone? Alone?! The word was like being stabbed with an icicle. Alone. The Ahhhh sound was like a ghost taunting; loooooow felt like the hollowed bottom of a dungeon; the nuh finish was like a door slamming shut, followed by silence. Alone. I was terrified of being alone, though it's precisely how I'd felt for my entire adult life.

# Chapter 34

The high school gymnasium was decorated with black, gray, and white balloons and colorless streamers hanging from the ceiling. A donkey piñata swung as the jocks struck it violently with their bats. A band wearing velveteen tuxedos awkwardly played Billy Idol and Adam Ant while a hyper-productive bubble machine filled the gym with thousands of soapy little balls. Todd came back from Yale to take me to the prom and told me he would lasso the biggest bubble for me. "Silly, boy," I teased. "You'll pop the bubbles that way. Besides, I prefer you without a cowboy lasso, my little Indian boy."

Vicki slapped my hand with a whip of fabric swatches. "No touching," she snapped.

"Hit her back," urged Tio.

"Come on, Mona, we'll be late," urged fifteen-year-old Jessica, tugging at the red silk dress I borrowed from Melanie, my imaginary lesbian lover. "We're going to change the world. We need to leave now. Come on, we'll be late."

"Where are we going?" I asked Jessica.

"To the rally. Come on, Mona, I know you're not really sick. You never want to do anything with me anymore now that you're going out with Todd. At least come to the rally. We can make a difference. You know what they say, one person can change the world. Are you listening to me? Are you awake? Are you asleep?" Then Vicki asked me the same thing. "Mona, do you want to sleep down here or go up to your room?"

My eyes opened to the sight of Vicki's black leather jacket bent over me, her arm gently nudging my body. "Are you okay?" Vicki asked when she saw the look of panic on my face. "Nightmare?"

"Freaky dream, that's all," I assured her. I washed my face in the *Psycho* bathroom, which was a bit unsettling in the middle of the night, I must confess. I heard nothing but running water from the faucet and wondered if I did ditch Jessica for Todd. Should I have gone to the rally that day? Might Francesca or I have seen the oncoming truck a second before my father did, and shouted a warning that would have changed the outcome? Whatever happened to Francesca anyway?

I drifted to sleep that night knowing there was only one of those questions I could answer. Whatever happened to Francesca Greenwood? One day we were consoling each other in the kitchen. A few days later, I was living in Coronado. I don't even remember saying good-bye to her.

Francesca came back to me in my sleep and asked if she could braid my hair again. I sat on my floor as she sat at the edge of my bed combing my hair with her fingers. "This was a long trip for me, Mona. You should have come to see me before making an old woman travel cross the Western states," she scolded lovingly. "I miss you, dear. I miss hearing you and your mother singing together. I miss them all so much."

On that, I snapped awake. Though I knew it was absurd, I scanned the bedroom for Francesca and felt my loose hair. I drifted back to sleep and dreamt I was part of

the human chain saving George Bailey's little brother, Harry,
when he fell into the ice pond.

My morning rooster was Greta knocking on the door
for our run. I ran downstairs in my pajamas with my black
sleep mask pushed up to my forehead. "Do you have any
idea how long I've been knocking?"

"Sorry, sorry." I was still fixed on Francesca. She was
probably still alive and living in Montana. "Let's get running.
Do you want me to make some vegetable juice for you when
we're done?" My peace offering with Greta was always
healthy food or drink. With Vicki, it was just the opposite.

Most of the time I didn't even notice the smell of
Coronado because I was on the island every day, but on
our run I was acutely aware of the clean ocean scent. It
was such a well-scrubbed community, I can't remember
the last time I saw a piece of garbage on the ground or a
crushed beer can tossed on the sand. When people close
their eyes and imagine paradise, Coronado is what they
see. I didn't always think so, though. When Grammy's car
crossed the bridge for the first time, I found the place
grotesquely surreal. First of all, the entire county of San
Diego seemed insanely bright. There were no clouds or
even groves of trees to filter the sun. Every home gleamed
with care. Lawns looked like Astroturf. The few people
walking on the streets looked so well-rested and friendly.
It was like driving onto the set of a laundry detergent commercial. I expected to see women in lemon yellow sun-
dresses humming as they hung cool, clean clothes on the
line. Then I realized that their maids were inside ironing
men's shirts fresh from the dryer.

"Greta, do you think Coronado is the most wonderful
place on the planet?" I asked as we passed the Cape Cod
home I came to know as the half-mile marker.

"Beats Texas, I'll tell you that," she said, laughing. "You know I could actually be lynched for saying that in Dallas? Legally, too. I think they'd call it treason."

"Treason against Texas?"

"Buying a fuel-efficient car is treason in Texas."

"Was it really all that bad?" I asked. "You did stay for eight years. I think it's because your heart was broken there."

She sighed as if to say maybe. "I don't know if my heart was broken there or if I was merely grossly disappointed by the way things turned out." I was silent, hoping she'd continue. "I really wanted things to work out with Terry, but, well, there was such a lack of core compatibility, I guess. I wanted to do things and go places and Terry was kind of a dud. At first, I thought our differences complemented each other, but then the complacency with life, the complete lack of drive, started to drive me crazy." Greta's voice filled with frustration and a shake of anger.

"Guys are like that. They just want to sit on the couch all day and watch sports. Women are always the ones driving the social calendar."

Greta laughed. "Yeah, well, I wouldn't be so quick to write it off as a gender thing. Plus, when we had that scare with Mom's tumor, I realized I wanted—"

"What tumor?!" I stopped running.

"Keep moving, honey. It's not good to stop suddenly like that," she coaxed. "It was no big deal. Turned out to be benign, but it got me thinking that if I'm not serious about settling down and starting a family in Texas, I should get back to the homestead and be near the people I really love."

"I can't believe you didn't tell me your mom had a cancer scare. Why wouldn't you tell me something so important?!"

"Mom said she didn't want anyone to know because they start treating you differently," Greta explained. "They talk softer, put their hand on your shoulder, turn their heads to the side and ask, 'How *are* you?'" She laughed. "I can understand. She didn't want to go from Brenda, the person, to Brenda, the cancer patient. Or Brenda, the tumor."

"I wouldn't have done that," I said.

"You wouldn't have wanted to, but you might have. Anyway, she's fine now so there's no need to mention this to her."

We ran in silence for the next few miles until Greta asked if I wanted to get a cup of coffee. I told her I'd walk to Starbucks with her, but that I'd pass on the coffee. I wanted to start making plans to visit Missoula. "Tell me if you think this is a crazy idea," I began.

"There are no crazy ideas, only crazy people."

"Seriously," I said as we walked briskly. "I was thinking that I've never been back to Missoula since the accident. Really, I never saw Francesca after. I don't even think I got to say good-bye to her. I don't remember. Anyway, I want to get on the net and see if she's still there, and if she is, I want to go back for a visit. Do you think that's crazy?"

Greta said she thought it was an excellent idea. "I don't know why you haven't done it sooner, but I guess we're all ready when we're ready." She swung the door of the Starbucks open and greeted a fresh-faced boy with jet-black hair and an eyebrow piercing.

"Morning Texas Tea." He smiled. "Morning Skinny Chai," he said to me.

I smiled, incredulous that anyone could be so happy to be serving coffee. "Mona's fine. What happened to the other guy?"

"What other guy?" he asked. "I'm the only guy here." He winked.

On my walk back to the house, I saw Captain John in one of his usual crisp short-sleeved oxford shirts. Today's selection was burnt orange, which went nicely with his white hair and beige shorts.

"Morning, sir," I said.

"Morning, Mona," he said, more chipper than I'd ever seen him. "I spoke to my brother in New York and it hit freezing last night. Got a layer of frost on his windshield even, ha!"

"In May?" I was astounded.

"Hard to believe, isn't it?"

"You seem very happy this morning, sir." I think he may have actually blushed when I said that. "New girlfriend?" I pushed the envelope.

John was clearly taken aback by my comment, for which I quickly apologized. "That was inappropriate, please forgive me. Grammy would have had my head for talking to you that way, sir."

"That's fine, dear. I'm sorry I reacted that way."

"No, no, it's my fault, please. You deserve every happiness after losing your wife."

John sighed as though I'd deflated his new helium balloon. I'm such a socially inept moron. Here was a kindly old widower enjoying possibly the first morning of the year and I come and stick a pin in it. The captain put his hand over his heart and lowered his head. *Is there a doctor around?!*

"Are you okay, sir?!" I panicked.

"I'm fine," he said sadly. "It seems you have no idea how much . . . I should keep my trap shut."

"No idea how much what?" I asked. "Do you want to sit down somewhere? Let me make you a glass of carrot juice. We're a half block from the house." I put my arm around him and we walked at his elderly pace. I watched his white soft sole shoes shuffle in front of each other and noticed for the first time how large his earlobes were.

Captain John was one of the few men who actually accepted my offer for carrot juice. He excused himself to "wash up" before I remembered that he was going into Victoria Hitchcock's warped little creation. "Good Lord in heaven!" I heard him gasp through the closed door. "That's quite a unique latrine," he said upon his return.

"You don't like it?"

"I love it. I'm quite a fan of picture shows," he said. "Your grandmother and I used to drive to the city and see movies together quite a bit."

"Hmm," I said suspiciously. "Why not here on the island?"

"You know how people talk." He shooed his hand. "Men and women weren't friends like they are today. If a gentleman and lady were friends, there was most certainly some hanky-panky."

I inhaled and asked the question that everyone on the island had silently wondered at one point or another. I felt guilty because I would have never interrogated the captain this way if Grammy were still alive. But I felt like he came here to tell me something, and this was it. "So was there any, um hanky-panky going on with you two?"

"With Caroline?" he said her name in such a way that there had to be. It was like he was holding a fragile collectible. *With Caroline?* It was too precious not to be love. I wondered how the captain would deal with the "don't ask, don't tell" policy now that I was most definitely, indelicately asking. "Absolutely not," he said, almost self-righteously as he watched me sacrifice carrots into the vicious juicer. He paused for a beat. "Though I loved her deeply." His eyes welled with tears. "I believe the feeling was mutual."

His words took me back to a time before I lived here, but I could see Grammy applying her lipstick and checking her teeth the way she would before an important outing. He would never know her private idiosyncrasies the way a husband would, and yet he was probably the cause of so many of her mirror rituals.

I handed him a tall glass of carrot juice and sat by him at the kitchen counter. "Tell me everything. Isn't that why you're here, John? Don't you want to tell someone how much you miss Grammy? Aren't you feeling a little guilty that everyone is asking you about how you're getting along without Anne when you were in love with Grammy? You can tell me. I loved her, too. I promise I won't judge the two of you. It's not like the two of you would've been the first to have an affair."

"An affair?!" John barked. "We certainly did *not* have an affair. I knew your grandfather. Caroline and Anne were friends. We never so much as held hands, I'll have you know. It was a friendship, young lady."

"A friendship that would have been more if you both weren't married?"

With that, his eyes welled with tears.

# Chapter 35

Captain John stayed at the house for two hours that morning telling me more about Grammy than I'd ever known. It was the first time I'd ever considered Grammy as a woman with a need to emotionally and physically connect with a man. It's not just that she was my elderly grandmother; she had an icy fortress that was tough to see through. I got to see her fun side, but I also saw the chilly front she presented to the world.

"Your grandfather was a good man," John prefaced. "He built that business from nothing, you know. By the time he passed on, he employed nearly five hundred people," John said like a man who felt guilty. "He was at the office constantly, though, and Caroline was very lonely. One day she came by to give Anne something or other for a charity luncheon they were cohosting and, well, Anne must've forgotten about it or got caught up somewhere else, I don't even remember. Anyway, we started talking and it was the first time I'd ever seen your grandmother smile, and though it was inappropriate I told her she had the prettiest smile.

"It was every bit awkward; the spark was undeniable. We both tried to kill it, but one day we ran into each other and I just told her it was high time we cleared the air. We took a long drive and let everything out, and I can't tell you what a relief that was. For the both of us, I think. Anyway, we knew we couldn't act on it, which was very difficult, and I hate to say this, but I think it was harder on her than it was on me because I still loved Anne very much. Your grandfather was a good man, but he was never around. Caroline and I went on our drives and snuck downtown to the picture shows every now and again, which was perfect for me, but made your grandmother very unhappy. When we returned to the island, I came home to Anne. Caroline didn't have that. When she came home, it was to an empty house where your grandfather wouldn't return until ten, eleven o'clock at night, sometimes later.

"Caroline was very, very depressed. On several occasions, she told me not to call her anymore because it was too hard seeing me, being in love with me, and not being able to be with me for any more than a few hours. Remaining platonic was difficult for both of us. She was always kind to Anne, but I could tell that she was jealous. I know that must sound awfully egotistical, but it's what she said." John sighed and asked me if he should go on.

I nodded.

"She was horribly depressed. Caroline even started taking those mood elevators to help her get through her crying spells. The poor woman used to spend days on end in bed. I didn't know what to do. Mona, I hated myself for being the cause of her pain. I wanted to spend more time with her, but I was married. She was married. I promise you we never even kissed."

I couldn't understand why it was so important for John to clarify that he and Grammy never had a physical relationship when clearly what they had was a love affair. Why not kiss? Why not have sex? Several times, he assured me that he had not defiled my grandmother, though I wonder if his repeated denials of an accusation that hadn't been made were simply a chivalrous attempt to protect her reputation with me. He said he tried to respect Grammy's wishes to end their relationship, but after a few weeks, she always wound up calling him, saying she'd try to compartmentalize better.

"Caroline was a mess until you came along, Mona," he continued. "Honestly, I think you saved her. About a week after you moved in, she called and asked me not to call her anymore. Anne and I were on a cruise over the holidays so I hadn't heard about the accident or your moving in, so I laughed and asked her how long this New Year's resolution was going to last. She was icy like she hadn't been before, and said this was really it. She had a teenage granddaughter living with her, and that if this all blew up, she could never be an appropriate role model for you. And that was it. Caroline never called again. We never saw another movie or took another drive. We saw each other and she was always cordial. A few times, there were moments when that chemistry sparked between us, but your grandmother always looked away or ended the conversation. Then she was completely immersed in Coronado Clean, which was her life until that whole matter was worked out."

John stopped at my perplexed expression. "Coronado Clean?" I asked.

"I'm surprised you don't remember. About a year after you moved in with Caroline, there was a plan to open a strip club right on Orange Avenue near the base. People were so upset about the element such a place would bring to our island, but Caroline did the lion's share of lobbying to keep those people out of Coronado."

As if·on a director's cue, Vicki walked into the kitchen in her silk pajamas. "Ohmigod!" she gasped at the sight of the captain. "I didn't think anyone was here."

I introduced the two, John as an old family friend and Vicki as my favorite live-in decorator. *Vicki, this is John, who had an affair of the heart with my Grammy. John, this is Vicki. She gives lap dances.*

"You're a very creative young lady," John said. "Interesting bathroom decor."

Vicki promptly announced that she had decorated the two downstairs guest rooms and was getting ready to "Tarafy" the living room. Her cadence sped with excitement. "Do you want a tour of what I'm going to do? Mona wants it to be a surprise, but I'd love to show someone who knows her how it's all going to look. Well, my brother has been on the tour and he knows Mona, but anyway that doesn't count 'cause he wasn't really into it, so I didn't get the type of validation I so need and deserve." She giggled. John politely nodded, prompting Vicki to outstretch her hand for his as though he'd just accepted her invitation to the VIP room.

I rinsed John's empty glass and thought about what he'd shared with me about Grammy. Caroline. I couldn't imagine why I wasn't appalled that my grandmother may have very well had an extramarital affair, though I did feel a certain heaviness that she'd been so unhappy for all of those years. I'm not sure if I was angry with John for causing Grammy so much pain, or grateful to him for the happiness he brought her if only in thrifty spoonfuls.

"Oh, this is great!" exclaimed John from the guest bedroom.

"Do you like it?" Vicki fished for more.

"I love it. You have the magic touch, Vicki. You sure know how to add new life to a bedroom."

I shuddered. Though I knew they were talking interior design, the soundtrack was unsettling.

# Chapter 36

When I entered Francesca's name in my computer search engine, I hoped to find that she was still alive. This, as it turns out, was a grotesque understatement as Francesca's name turned up more than 700 results. I had to wonder if there were other Francesca Greenwoods, which there were, but mine occupied most of the cyberspace with articles she authored opposing the war against Iraq, meditation for senior citizens, and a feature on Missoula's upcoming bicentennial celebration of Lewis and Clark's expedition. Francesca was on the board of directors at Hunter's Glen retirement community, past president of the Older Women's League, and even ran in a close race for city council in 1992, Clinton's Year of the Woman. Her most recent rants were defending the Dixie Chicks' condemnation of President Bush, and a call for the city of Missoula to prominently feature Sacagawea, the sixteen-year-old mother who guided the expedition, in its celebration. "If there's anyone who gets less recognition than women, it's Native Americans. I know we're supposed to feel grateful that they put Sacagawea on the new dollar coin, but since that is used only slightly more than the Susan B. Anthony silver dollar, I'd say we still owe the gal something more meaningful, Missoula," Francesca mused. She was so much more alive than I'd ever hoped.

I sat back in my chair and opened more Web sites that contained her name, hoping to find her e-mail address. I couldn't find her contact information, but learned more about how Francesca had been spending her time since the accident. Two years ago, she was part of a committee that led 4,000 volunteers to create the Dragon Hollow Play Area next to the new hand-carved carousel. Her city council campaign focused on slowing the commercial and residential development of Missoula and beautifying the walkway along the Clark Fork River. "There are too many homes in South Hills and Miller Creek," she told a reporter. The Clark Fork River. South Hills and Miller Creek. The words I hadn't heard, uttered, or read in fifteen years caused thunder in my heart. My eyes scanned to the bottom of the article, where Francesca was described as the sole survivor from the "Magic Bus Accident of 1987." Sole survivor? Not since Jayson Blair's articles in the *New York Times* had a two-line characterization been so inaccurate. For a split second, I wondered if I'd imagined my entire life on the commune. If life other than Coronado ever really existed.

I heard the familiar chime of someone sending me an Instant Message.

*Surfing porn on the net again, Mona Lisa?*

And with that simple tease, I knew that my life had gone exactly as I remembered it, as unmemorable as major chunks of it were. Mona Lisa, my existential affirmation that I was indeed really here. I swooned so at the sight of his e-mail address I was grateful for the electronic shield Internet communication provides. The last thing I needed was a male chauvinist dog seeing me twirl my hair around my index finger and bring my knees to my chest. I thanked the technological lag that kept my giggle from reaching Mike's ears.

*Hey stranger,* I wrote then erased. Too accusing. *Oh, hey what's up?* Trying too hard to be casual. I opted for a simple *Hi* once I realized that my response time was taking way too long.

*What are you doing up so late?* Mike asked. I looked at the clock to see it was two-thirty in the morning.

> *I'm looking for a woman in Missoula. I'm thinking I want to go back and visit her. I haven't been back since I left.*
>
> *The same could be said about anywhere.*
>
> *How very clever for these wee hours. What are you doing up? Don't you have to lead the good men of America astray with your musings on the power of the penis?*
>
> *Thinking about stuff. Life and shit and all the crap that you wish you could do over if you had a second chance.*
>
> *Who are you and what have you done with my friend, Mike?!*
>
> *Cute.*
>
> *Am I?* I flirted.
>
> *Who are you and what have you done with my friend, Mona?*
>
> *You're not much of a friend these days.*
>
> *Sorry. I've been busy with work.*
>
> *Who cares?*
>
> *I thought you did.*
>
> *No, I mean who cares what your excuses are.*

*If you wanted to call me, you would have,* I erased then replaced this with *Nope.*

*That was a lot of typing for "nope."*
*Sorry, I had to grab a glass of water.*
*The IM screen said you were typing.*
*It was wrong! Anyway, tell me something.*
*What?*
*No, I mean just tell me something that's been*
*going on with you. Tell me anything you want.*

And I meant it. I didn't have an agenda, scripted lines of
what he was supposed to tell me. He could've told me
about his new spark plugs and I would've hung out online
with him till sunrise. When Adam shared his hopes for the
future, I silently made lists of things I needed to pick up at
Target.

*I'm not sure what to say,* he wrote.

*Do you ever miss me?* I risked. I saw the tiny print telling
me that he was writing. And writing. Then writing some
more. This could be brutal. How long does it take to
type—

*Yes.*

I collapsed into my chair, now even more grateful that
he could not see me. I wanted to ask why Mike let our
friendship lapse to the point where he had to miss me, but
I refrained for fear of looking like the lunatic I really was.
Searching my mental files for something coy to say, I came
up with nothing.

*I miss you, too,* I confessed. *But you wouldn't've*
*had to miss me if you picked up the damned*
*phone and called me!*

*Sorry. It's been a crazy month with work.*
*Plus, you dumped me, remember?*

*I discontinued our business relationship, I didn't*
*dump you. Big difference.*

*So tell me about this woman in Missoula you're
going to visit. Is she cute?*

*She's nearly eighty. Speaking of which, I think
your sister got my grandmother's old boyfriend
all hot and bothered this morning. Does this sort
of thing run in the family?*

*When are you going to visit her?*

*I'm not sure. Why?*

*Wondering if you'd like company.*

*You?*

*No, Adam. You should bring him to see how
he'll take to your past life and Grandmother Jones
in Missoula.*

*Oh, I don't think he'd care for it there. Too
earthy.*

*I'm kidding, loser! Of course I meant me.*

The last time I went out with Adam, he told me I was
amazing. Amazing. I'd never amazed anyone before in my
entirely unamazing life. And here was a good-looking, solid
man—a man I had orchestrated my life around impressing—telling me that I was amazing and I could barely
muster the enthusiasm to thank him. Mike, on the other
hand—a man I chose specifically because he was the lowest specimen of male life forms—calling me a loser made
me blush.

I desperately wanted to tell him that he could come with
me to Missoula, but I strained to type the words. Perhaps
it would be better if I made the journey on my own. I didn't
need the added pressure of Mike making wisecracks about
the peace sign on Waterworks Hill or the distinctly granola
feel of Missoula. Nor did I want Francesca to think Mike
was my boyfriend and silently wonder at what point I became part of the mainstream our family disdained. Plus,

visiting Missoula might be emotionally overwhelming for me, not the rock climbing adventure camp Mike probably imagined. Going alone was definitely the wiser choice.

*Okay,* I typed, poised my finger over the Send key for a few seconds, then pressed it. *I shouldn't have written that. Where's unsend? Is there an unsend on Instant Messages? This man can't just walk out of my life then reappear whenever it's convenient for him. There is no way I should share this intensely personal trip with a dog like Mike Dougherty. This rat bastard is probably going to write a column about all the hippie chicks he "banged" in Missoula. Why do I waste my energy on a guy like Mike when I am so close to the happily-ever-after ending with Adam?*

*When do we take off?* he asked.

I made reservations for a visit in mid-May, leaving Missoula before its bicentennial celebration. I wanted to see Missoula in its normal state, not with tourists dressed in nineteenth-century outfits, coon skin hats and Indian headdresses. It would be like someone from New Orleans making a homecoming during Mardi Gras. I wanted to see Missoula the way I remembered it, if that could be done from a suite at the Sacagawea Inn.

When I called Francesca a few days later, she cried as soon as I told her it was me. I'd planned on reminding her of how she knew me, though now the notion seems quite absurd. "I knew you'd find me," she sobbed at the sound of my voice. Until she said that, I'd never considered asking why she hadn't been in touch with me after all these years. Surely she knew Grammy's address and phone number. Our first conversation in fifteen years didn't seem like the right time to ask, though. "Tell me about your life, Mona," Francesca asked as I grew terrified at my nonexistent list of accomplishments. I knew she expected me to tell her I'd served in the peace corps or started a school for homeless quadriplegics. I regretted calling her. I regretted telling her that I would come to visit her. I loved her, of course. So much so that I couldn't stand the inevitable look of disappointment she'd have when learning I hadn't left so much as a door ding on the world, much less a dent. I was terrified to see Francesca because, though I had never really grasped this before, the unspoken truth for both of us is that we were supposed to do the good work that others never could.

# Chapter 37

*Why do women ask what guys' facial expressions mean? They don't mean anything. Women. First they complain they don't see enough of us, then when they do see us, they're hell bent on making you wish you were somewhere else.*
—*The Dog House, June*

Weeks passed with no earth-shaking, life-altering events. I started my singing lessons with Ollie, trained for my first boxing match, which was scheduled against another rookie bantam weight, and watched Vicki buzz around the house with fabric swatches, flooring samples, and lighting catalogs. I consulted with her on my stylistic preferences, but it was kind of like watching someone plan a surprise party for me. She was so completely lost in the planning, there were times when she didn't hear me come into the house. I watched her strut around the house with her telephone headset on chatting with Fredrique, a designer she collaborated with. Listening to her talk on the phone, it was clear Vicki was angling to be Fredrique's next protégé. I could only hear Vicki's reaction to the designer's feedback, but it seemed she'd won Fredrique's respect and was well on the way to being taken under the well-plumed wing.

I had a series of flat-lining dates with Adam. I couldn't understand why I was still dating him, but every time he asked to see me again, I feigned excitement and accepted the invitation. Greta's analysis was that I was afraid to let go of what I thought I wanted because I'm not quite sure what I do want. My take on it was a bit simpler. Our roles had reversed completely. Last year, he had little cognizance of my existence. I was an appendage to Grammy, a client from his father's handful of wealthy clients. Even professionally, I wasn't of much interest to Adam because he wanted to take the firm in the direction of serving growing businesses. Technology at that. How fascinated could he have been by our filings? Now all that changed. He was the one who seemed smitten, thrilled to be with me. Some nights he gazed into my eyes with that look of forever that I worked so hard to get from him, and it terrified me. Partly because I knew he was falling in love with a woman who likes Ozzfest and would reportedly "kill for playoff tickets." Another part knew that sooner or later, Adam would want to take our relationship to the next level and I was not entirely sure I'd have the ability to say no to whatever he offered. Having been powerless for my entire life has had its benefits. I've never had to break anyone's heart. I've never had to reject offers. I couldn't bear to be the one to bring down the ax on Adam because Adam was me. Sure, he wasn't staging public relations events for my benefit—unless he thought getting a speeding ticket last weekend would impress me—but he clearly wanted the relationship to blossom. I couldn't kill it with a clear conscience. I read a novel once where a woman found a new wife for her husband, so she could leave him for another man without feeling too guilty about it. Maybe that's what I'd do—find someone new for Adam. Nah.

Of course, I realize this sounds terribly self-important. Men have been dumped before and they seem to recover just fine. Generally they bounce back within hours. Minutes if they live within walking distance to a babe-packed bar. I realize that this was—as Greta would say—more about me than Adam. Still, knowing this didn't help me over-come the paralysis that kept me in this stagnant, stale, and thoroughly boring relationship.

A lesser part of me knew that I was keeping Adam around because it was nice to have someone who adored me. Mike and I flirted, but I knew what would happen if we started dating. It would be wonderfully exciting for about two weeks before Mike emotionally mounted my head on his wall like a chick-hunting trophy, and moved on to the next woman. I read all about this type of guy in an early draft of Greta's new book, *Hey, You're My Ex in Different Pants!*

When I met Mike at the airport, I wondered if he wasn't the dog he tried to be. Dressed in a tie-dyed T-shirt and well-worn jeans, he held a backpack and a suede jacket in one hand, looking like he was trying to fit in with Missoula. "Hey brother, peace and love and all that jazz." I leaned in to kiss his cheek. In a moment, I felt he was my best friend.

"Do I look dumb?" he asked as we looked for seats in the waiting area at the gate.

"Sweetie, you *are* dumb." I smiled. "But you couldn't tell from looking at you. You look good." I took a chance. "You look cute."

When we started to descend into Missoula, I felt like my insides were plastics in an oven. Everything melted, shriv-eling, stinking of fear as I remembered the last time I saw this landscape. It was different, though. More roads. More cars buzzing around on them. More buildings and homes, but it was still Montana. The mountains jagged toward the sky looking fierce, almost like they could tear you to pieces unlike the soft dry hills of San Diego.

"Are you ready for this, Mona Lisa?" Mike asked.

"I don't know," I said, wishing I could come up with something more insightful to say. But I didn't know. And insight was nowhere in sight.

Driving to Francesca's retirement community, I welled at the sight of the plush maples, oaks, pines, and cottonwood trees. These were the things that stayed the same, the characteristics that marked the area through time. It was like looking at a friend's baby pictures and recognizing her features. When I see Greta's photos with Santa Claus, I always think, *I know that little nose, I see those little eyes. I can see her in there.* I can see my Missoula here, but it had grown. Reserve Street widened like a middle-aged gut. Costco, Home Depot and Wal-Mart covered the earth I rolled a wheelbarrow over on the way to the Farmer's Market on weekends.

Hippie students from the university shuffled the streets, earnestly talking about politics from left to lefter. Boys in dreadlocks played Hacky Sack while girlfriends with babies in slings sat on wool blankets on the grass. I sighed with relief at the sight of a park with more guitars and kites than shoes. Some things never change. The Loose Caboose coffee shop modeled after a railroad train hadn't been swallowed by Starbucks (which I later learned was relegated to the back of the Missoula Barnes & Noble).

For me, though, all Hacky Sacks dropped to the ground, all kites plummeted, and the Loose Caboose came to a screeching halt when I saw that the peace sign had been removed from Waterworks Hill. Much like what the sign represented, the symbol was constantly being torn down, then mysteriously reappeared a few days later. The city council thought peace looked ugly on the side of the mountain. The hippies thought it looked good anywhere. But Francesca later told us that the peace sign hadn't been on the hill for years now.

Francesca was waiting at the entrance to Hunter's Glen in a crocheted orange and brown poncho resting over her like a table cloth. The centerpiece was long white hair tamed into a low ponytail. I wasn't prepared for how frail Francesca would appear at first sight, though the effects of her knobby elbows and flaking cheeks diminished once she opened her mouth and released a hearty shout of pure joy. "Baby girl, my baby girl!" Her arms reached to the sky like Moses parting the Red Sea. She held my face in her hands and kissed my forehead, my chin, my cheeks, and my lips. "Let me look at my baby girl," she said, examining my face. If she was a lipstick-wearing grandmother, there wouldn't have been much face left for her to look at, but as it was, Francesca lightly glazed me with a mint-smelling lip balm. "I knew you'd find me someday." She grasped my hands. "Let's go upstairs to my apartment. You must be Mike." She extended her leaf of a hand to him.

"It's a pleasure to meet you, Francesca. Mona's told me a lot of great stories about when you lived together."

*Oh my God. He sounds nervous.*

Francesca sighed sadly, then motioned us toward her apartment with her hand. She walked slowly, like the captain, lifting her feet off the floor only slightly. Elder-skating. "We had beautiful times at the house. It was paradise," she said, shaking her head at the unsaid.

For the entire week Mike and I were in Missoula, we spent most of our time with Francesca, who still drove. I nearly cried with joy when I saw she still had the VW minibus complete with our paintings along the sides. The odometer read just over 189,000 miles, but it may have broken like much of the rest of the bus. I gravitated toward the rainbow and hearts section that Jessica and I made by dotting paint with Q-Tips. I could see Jessica with her flowing, tangled red hair and face of freckles standing beside me asking who even drove these goofy vans anymore. "This was our shuttle bus," Francesca told Mike. "Small groups, trips to the cinema and such," she trailed.

"We never went to the movies!" I protested.

"Oh, you break my heart with your forgetfulness," Francesca said. "We only saw *It's a Wonderful Life* together four thousand times at the cinema. Why do you think your mother embroidered that moon on your ceiling sheet?" *Moon? I thought it was a sun.* "You were constantly talking about lassoing the moon. Such a sweet child. You said you loved us so much you'd lasso the moon." She turned to Mike, "Very high-drama child, you know? Anyway, that was the only film that played at the cinema for the first year we lived here. God knows why they picked that movie. Probably all they could get out here back then, but every weekend, come hell or high water, Mona would pile into the bus and join whoever was going to the movies."

I knew what was on the back of the minibus so I avoided looking at it for the first three days of our visit, but finally I couldn't resist a peek. I sat on the gravel of her driveway and faced what we never realized would wind up a graveyard of handprints. After we'd all decorated the bus, everyone dipped his or her hands in a bucket of green paint and left a print on the back of the minibus. "Which one is yours?" Mike asked me as he sat beside me. I answered by holding my hand over my slightly smaller green hand. "This was my best friend Jessica's." I glided over hers. "There was this boy who was going to—" I couldn't finish. My face was striped with mascara and I wiped my nose on my sleeve. After a few minutes, I tried to remember which handprints belonged to my parents, my tiny brothers Oscar and David, Francesca, Freddy, Jacqueline, Asia, Morgan, Scott, Lana, Leah, Maya, Karah, Lilac, and Teddy.

The crunching on gravel announced Francesca's arrival. "You have no idea how hard I had to work to get this bus, Mona. I don't drive it very much so I'll never see it go on me." She stood beside Mike and I, contemplating sitting on the gravel. "You'll help an old lady get back up again, won't you, Mr. Manly Man?" she teased Mike.

By the second hour of our visit, Francesca and Mike had roots and history together. She told him she'd read his columns and he didn't fool her for a minute. "You're a very lost young man, hiding behind a lot of bravado, you know that?"

"That pretty much sums it up," he conceded with a shrug of laughter.

Francesca spread her skirt across the gravel and continued her story about the VW minibus. "It was registered in your father's name, but he left everything to you and, well, to you. You were a minor, so you couldn't drive the thing so I had to buy it from your grandmother, who did not make things easy for me. Anyway, after nine months, she finally transferred the title to my name, but not without a lot of hassles. She was so angry at your father because of the accident. And she was angry at me. But I loved that bus with all of the kids' scribble paintings and handprints. That bus is my Vietnam wall."

"Why was she angry at you?" I asked Francesca. "Why was she mad at Daddy?" The word Daddy hadn't passed my lips since the day of the accident. "Give 'em hell, Daddy," I said, almost mocking their futile antinukes effort. He gave me a thumbs-up and told me he loved me before closing the door to the school bus. I had used the word "father," referring to someone else's. I'd even used "dad," though always prefaced by "your." "Daddy" hadn't been spoken in so many years, I half expected the word to get stuck like an old machine being turned on for the first time in years. Or an old faucet shooting out rusty water.

"She was just angry, Mona," Francesca said. "She had no cause to be angry with me, and despite what anyone says, that accident was not your father's fault. The road conditions were awful that day, but by the time it got too bad to drive, they were halfway there."

"Who said the accident was Daddy's fault?"

Francesca waved her hand like there were slow flies in front of her. "Some people want to find someone to blame when there's a tragedy like this. They think a bunch of hippies living on a commune, there must be drugs involved. There was a lot of gossip about town, was he stoned, was he not stoned, you know the sort of chatter that people without a purpose engage in."

I pushed my foot over a patch of gravel to interrupt the dead silence. Mike stood up, brushed the loose dirt from his jeans, and said he was going to go take a walk. "You two should probably talk without me around," he told us.

# Chapter 38

Part of me wanted Mike to stick around to hear Francesca deny the claim that my father may have bore some responsibility for the accident. Another part was relieved that he was taking off because I was terrified that the story got worse. That she would confirm these charges. A small aching part of me feared that Mike was leaving because he didn't want to know this much about me. The strip class, air hockey, and late-night e-mails were within Mike's emotional comfort zone, but when faced with my real life—the stuff that no one is supposed to see—he was not up for it. As much as the thought of Mike's evaporation troubled me, I was more drawn in by what Francesca had revealed, if only partially.

"Was he?" I asked tentatively. "Stoned, I mean?"

"He was fine, Mona." Francesca moved in closer, and brushed my hair from my eyes with her twiggy fingers. "Are you going to be able to lift me up now that we haven't got Mr. Muscles to help?"

"I can manage," I said. "Was he really, Francesca, or are you just telling me what I want to hear?"

"Mona, when have I ever told anyone something because it was what they wanted to hear? We smoked a lot of grass at the house, but we had a couple of ground rules. We never smoked in front of you kids and we didn't drive or use any of the farm equipment stoned. Most of us thought the rules were pretty silly because we'd all driven a thousand times stoned off our asses and we were fine, and a few of us thought that if we were smoking grass, we shouldn't hide it from you kids. Your mother felt strongly about it though, so we all went along with it because we respected her and wanted to create a space where everyone's voice was heard."

I heard seventeen voices screaming in terror.

"Anyway, I was up with everyone at six that morning and no one was lighting up, and I know Andy wasn't sparking up a joint on the school bus with you kids in it, but that didn't stop people from speculating. It was maddening. The newspapers were a trip. They immediately came up with some catchy little headline, the Magic Bus, for our school bus. They were real careful to write that the allegations of driving under the influence were still just that—allegations. But they made that story into a national sensation with all their hoopla over our social action, pot smoking, and living on a commune. It was like the death of seventeen human beings wasn't enough."

Francesca realized this was the first time I was hearing any of this and stopped. "Your grandmother didn't tell you any of this?"

I shook my head.

"I can't say that surprises me much the way she carried on when she was here," she continued. "I figured everyone reacts to tragedy in different ways, and your grandmother's was obviously to lash out, but I hoped one day she'd tell you that all those news reports weren't true."

"I never even knew about the news stories," I said.

"I'll never forget that woman. She came into our home

like she owned the place, which, truth be told, wasn't too far off since she'd lent us a hundred thousand for construction. She was furious at me for simply being alive. She didn't say much to me, but her rage was definitely there. She was like carbon monoxide. You couldn't see her, couldn't hear her, but she was there to kill. She was like this for about forty minutes before she went hysterical. She tore through the house, screaming about how filthy it was and how it was a wonder we all survived as long as we did. Then she picked up a picture of your father and mother and—I'll never forget this—she spat 'I told you not to marry this bum!' then threw the frame across the room and cried, 'He got what he deserved, but those kids were innocent.' She fell to the floor crying and I went to put my arms around her, to comfort her, but she started screaming at me, too, telling me I thought I could be a better mother to all of you, but look what I'd let happen."

"Oh my God," I interrupted. "How awful of her! I'm so sorry she said that to you. You know she didn't mean it, right? She was just overcome with grief. Grammy was really the most wonderful person, Francesca. I know if she were alive, she would apologize to you now. Really. I know she would."

Francesca sighed apologetically, not knowing until then that Grammy died. Softer, she continued, "I called you about a dozen times, Mona. I so wanted for us to keep in touch. The first few times, she just hung up on me as soon as she heard my name. Then I had to start communicating through lawyers about the van and some of the property at the house. After a while, she came around on that. I guess she had no use for this silly old thing." She motioned to the minibus. "The last time I called was about a year after you left Montana, and she was pretty pleasant. Well, she was cordial, at least. But she explained that you were starting a new life and that my presence in it would be a constant painful reminder of the past."

This was a lot to take in. Where was I during Grammy's stormy ravaging of our commune? Why hadn't I heard a single news report about the so-called Magic Bus? Where was I when Francesca called?

Then I realized that the most important moments of life are just that. Moments. And if you're at the beach while the phone's ringing, you're going to miss the call. But my life, up until the past few months, has been spent waiting by the phone and not at the beach. How had I missed so much while nothing else was going on?

Before we left Montana, Francesca said she had a few things of mine she'd been waiting to return. "Should I go?" Mike asked.

"Stay," I said and refrained from elaborating.

*If you want,* I didn't say.

*Stay forever,* I'd've killed myself if it slipped.

*If he stays he loves me, if he goes we're just friends.* I plucked imaginary petals.

"Okay," he shrugged. *Why did he have to shrug?* I wondered but didn't ask.

*Fine, shrug all you want. I don't even notice because I am not one of your column girls!*

"Why'd you shrug?" slipped out.

"Huh?" Mike asked. "Why'd I what?"

"Shrug? You just said 'okay,' then shrugged like maybe you weren't so sure or something, or that—"

Francesca jumped in, undoubtedly pitying what a social dolt I'd become. "Why doesn't Michael help me bring your box up from storage?"

Twenty minutes later, I heard Francesca and Mike's voices as they approached the apartment door, and was struck by the next image I saw. Francesca's arm held the door open for Mike, whose bare arms were strapped around a dusty taped box with my name scribbled on it. My past giving way to my future, which embraced my past.

Mike placed the box on Francesca's kitchen table and reached into his jeans pocket for a Swiss Army knife to slit the packing tape. As he peeled the cardboard flaps back, I smelled the familiar scent of smoke from our fireplace fighting through fifteen years of dust collecting on the box top.

A yellowed linen table cloth with red flowers embroidered along the periphery. I remember watching my mother hand stitch the flowers on the white cloth.

A rainbow colored yarn God's-eye I remember making with Jessica the first week we moved into the house.

My mother's journal.

My parents' wedding album, which was so old it actually cracked open to a photo of them, holding hands facing each other against the backdrop of a lake. I realized I never knew where they were married, though I was aware that it was an outdoor ceremony performed by one of their friends who had obtained a ministerial license. It looked like Montana, but I supposed it could have been anywhere. I turned to Francesca in a moment of panic realizing that she was probably the last person on earth that could answer that question readily. "Here in Butte," she told me when I asked.

The blue sheet with gold embroidered stars and the moon brought tears to my eyes. "Your evening sky," I said softly, remembering for the first time that this was how my mother presented the sheet to us kids. "Ceilings keep you trapped," she said. "But you'll always feel free looking up at your evening sky." Her billowy ceiling decor never made me feel particularly liberated, but not needing to pretend it did back then, did now. "My mother made this," I told Mike. "It hung on the kids' dorm ceiling all puffy, so we'd feel like we were in a cloud or something." He nodded.

Mike asked to see the whole thing and began to unroll the sheet by lifting the edge and shaking it out. With one firm snap, Mike ended fifteen years of the sheet's bound inertia. But with that same freeing movement, he also sent flying across the room the ceramic mug I made for Todd our last winter at the house. Francesca had packed the fragile mug in the heart of the tapestry to insulate it from other items in the box. Ironically, this protective measure was the very thing that broke it.

"Holy shit!" Mike gasped as he saw the white glazed mug shoot across the room and hit the floor. "I'm sorry. I didn't know that was in there." He picked up the five pieces it had broken into and examined them sitting in the palm of his hand. "I can fix this," he promised. "I'll take it to one of those pottery places where they can make it like new. You won't even see the cracks when I patch it up."

"It's okay," I told him, not explaining the significance of the mug. Mike felt bad enough as is. I told him I'd prefer he just glued the pieces back together on his own. I didn't want it to look new. I wanted to see the cracks where my brushstrokes of bitterroot had been broken by my clumsy, well-meaning dog.

"No, let me fix it right," he insisted.

"Believe me, if you glue it back together, you'll fix it right," I said. "I'm not going to drink from this cup." What I didn't tell him—for fear of seeming overly attached—was that I liked that Mike had made his mark on the relics of my past. Sure, the marks were cracks, but these fine fissures would represent the labor of his thick fingers gluing together pieces of my broken mug, and that charmed me to pieces.

"Shit, Mona. I feel terrible. Is there anything I can do to make it up to you?"

With that, a mischievous old woman chimed in. "There's something you both can do for me," Francesca said with a smile.

# Chapter 39

"Could we get arrested for this?" Mike whispered as we crawled over rocks and began scaling the rough terrain. He held my knapsack steady as the contents clanked around.

"I think it'd be a misdemeanor," I whispered back through the cold night air. "It's Missoula. It's not like we'd get anything more than a slap on the wrists. I think a lot of people would come to our defense, even. Can you imagine, we'd be folk heroes?!"

Mike shook his can of navy blue spray paint and popped the plastic cap off. "My dad was in the Navy, remember? He'd kick my ass for this, Mona Lisa," Mike whispered. "You know I'm only doing this 'cause I feel bad about breaking your tea cup. We were right to go to war with Iraq."

We crouched down to hide ourselves, and searched for a good clean stretch of mountainside that would be seen by the entire town. I whispered, "The war's over, you idiot. Besides, if you're so gung ho on America, you should support people expressing a political view."

"I hate to break this to you, Mona Lisa." Mike contained a snort of a laugh. "This is vandalism, and it's not like this kind of shit changes people's minds anyway." I turned my kneeling body toward him and placed my hand on my hip, mocking a stature of reprimand. "It doesn't!" Mike defended.

"Maybe some pro-war nut like your father won't look at our peace sign painted on the side of the mountain and change his mind, but a lot of people who oppose Bush's attack on Iraq—or North Korea or Sudan, Pakistan or wherever his crusade leads him next—will see this and know they're not alone. They'll see a very public demonstration that there are likeminded people out there and that their own activism is not occurring in a vacuum. That's how people go on, Mike. That's what makes for a fulfilling life, knowing that you're not alone and that you're actually making a difference in the world."

He shook the can and sprayed. The cold gray mountain enlivened with its first blue arc that grew into a circle, then was filled by Mike, with peace.

The next morning, as we drove to the airport, Mike made fun of our creation, but I could tell he took pride in his act of rebellion. He made an exaggerated sigh and wiped an imaginary tear from his eye upon seeing our gift to Francesca. "And once again, there was peace in Missoula." He turned to me as I sat in the passenger seat. He held out his hand for me to slap, which I did. My hand fell exhausted into his with the clap, and his fingers curled around it.

We arrived back in San Diego a little after noon and Mike insisted on walking me back to my car in the airport parking lot. "I'm totally safe." I laughed.

"I'll carry your bag," he offered.

"It's on rollers, Mike." I smirked, hoping he would just admit that he wanted to extend our visit a bit. I wanted him to bring up the whole high-five turned hand-holding incident back in Missoula. I wanted him to say something—anything—about our week together, but instead he just said he had something to give me. "What?" I smiled.

"It's a surprise," Mike said. He placed my suitcase in the trunk of my car and asked if he left his jacket in my backseat.

"Mike, you haven't been in my car in four weeks," I reminded him.

"That's right around when I lost it. Can you take a look?"

*Can I take a look for his jacket?*

Honestly, I don't know why I even hope for anything deeper than a superficial friendship with Mike. After I dug around the backseat of my car, looking for the jacket, Mike forgot all about any surprise for me. It was probably that he could belch my name or something equally touching.

As I left the airport, I called home to see if Vicki was there. She said she would try to finish the house while Mike and I were away. After four rings I heard my own voice asking me to leave a message for myself, and hung up.

I dialed Greta's office, which automatically rolled over into voice mail. "Your call is very important to me and I *do* want to speak with you so leave a message and I *will* call you back just as soon as I am able." Greta's coddling formality seemed even more pronounced after not having heard it for a week. Her message sounded overly concerned with the caller's fragile mental state.

I dialed the phone again and the honker put my call right through to Adam. "Mona!" he beamed through the telephone. "Gosh, I missed you. How come you didn't call?" Why doctors have never attempted a personality transplant

was beyond me. Imagine taking all of the sweet words and
kind thoughts from guys who weren't compelling and giv
ing them to the sexy ones who couldn't string together two
decent thoughts? Now that would be a surgical break-
through.

"I'm sorry. I was just so busy in Missoula, I didn't have
a moment to call," I explained.

> *What women need to realize is that when guys
> say they're too busy to call, what they mean is
> they're too busy to call you. Hate to be harsh,
> but how long does a phone call take? If I want
> to call a chick, I do. Period. I can always make
> time to talk to someone I want to. It takes thirty
> seconds and if I'm really that busy, I can just
> multitask, call her on the crapper and hit mute
> while she yaps about her day. I've made my "keep
> the relationship alive" phone call without spend-
> ing any real time on it. Think about all the un-
> scheduled things you can squeeze into your day
> if you want. I'm on deadline for this article and
> yet I managed to trim my nose hairs, take a
> leisurely shit, and change the Odor-Eaters in my
> shoes. Ladies, if a guy says he's too busy to call,
> what he's saying is that these tasks are more ap-
> pealing than talking to you.*
> —The Dog House, June

Adam was undeterred. "That's okay. I'm glad you had a
safe journey home. When can I see you?"

"We have a date this weekend," I reminded him. "Remember Greta's karaoke night?" I tried to be nonchalant
as though the whole thing weren't my idea, and I hadn't
been practicing with Ollie for weeks. The plan was that

Ollie would pose as a stranger in the bar who would approach our table and ask if any of the ladies would sing a duet with him. I, of course, would not volunteer, but Vicki would coax and cajole me until I finally, reluctantly, agreed. Then Ollie and I would blow away the audience—Adam in particular—with our well-rehearsed impromptu duet.

A better plan would've been to find a gentle way to break up with Adam. He was such a good guy, it was impossible to just cut him loose without feeling guilty about it. Vicki said I was being ridiculous—that people break up all the time without it being a big drama. But in my world, that hasn't been the case. The only other boyfriend I ever had pledged his love till death did we part. Then he was killed. I didn't think that my ending the relationship with Adam would kill him. I felt cruel rejecting him and yet I knew it was unkind to hang on to him like a security blanket.

"Oh yes, karaoke," he said, not hiding his lack of enthusiasm.

"I thought you loved music," I said.

"Karaoke is a bunch of drunken wannabes crooning off-key. That's not music."

"Oh." I wondered if he would be impressed by Ollie and me. "We could go somewhere else." But I didn't want to go somewhere else. About five minutes into my first singing lesson with Ollie, I realized I wasn't learning how to sing because I thought Adam would like me more. I was doing it because I loved to sing and I always have. I was doing it because the breath coming from deep within me, turning to music and joining with lyrics, was powerful for me. I felt freedom like my evening sky was supposed to give me. It was the same sensation skiers and motorcycle riders describe when they talk about the wind whipping through their hair and feeling as though they might actually take off in flight.

Adam said he was willing to go to Vicki's karaoke night,
but he said he'd like to spend time without the group, too.
I retorted that he didn't see this as an opportunity to meet
my friends and win them over. If I was still interested in
him and he invited me to meet his buddies, believe me I'd
be scrambling to make sure they gave me the guys' seal of
approval. Meeting the friends is really the prerequisite to
meeting the parents. And in my case, meeting the friends
was doubly important. Why Adam seemed indifferent to
the idea was irritating. I wondered if I might just be looking for an excuse to be annoyed with him so I could justify
breaking up.

"Listen, if you really don't want to go—" I said.

"I want to go. I want to meet your friends, but I also
want to spend some time with you. It's been awhile.
There's something we need to talk about."

*He wants to have sex.*

*He wants to break up.*

*He wants me to meet his friends.*

*He wants me to come to Jesus.*

*He wants to discuss my tax liability.*

"Okay. Why don't we have brunch at the Big Kitchen
on Sunday morning?" I asked as I silently calculated the
caloric intake of Judy's biscuits and gravy. If I ran about
eight extra miles I could work off about half a portion.
Worth it, I decided.

"Okay, sounds good to me. I've got a two o'clock I still
need to prepare for, so I'm going to run. Call me later, or
I'll call you," he said sweetly, though it sounded like a threat.

As I turned on Alameda, I saw the navy guys waving in
the car ahead of me. Then I realized there was no car
ahead of me. I looked to my right and there were no cars
there either. My car sat motionless, purring at the stop
sign, ready to head straight toward home, but curious why

the navy guys were waving me toward their gated entrance. They waved again and laughed a bit at my hesitation. I pointed at myself and mouthed *Me?* One guy looked like he was losing patience and started waving as though he was saying *Come in or don't, but stop pissing around at the intersection.*

Then it jumped out at me. A small navy decal was placed on the lower right corner of my windshield, and the guys thought I was one of them. Or at least had the right to be there.

I saluted and drove into the base. "He got me in," I said aloud to no one, smiling uncontrollably. "What do you know, the Dog got me in."

# Chapter 40

As I opened the front door, the theme from *Gone With the Wind* assaulted me. Vicki was dressed in full Southern belle garden party regalia, somewhat updated to suit her personal style. Surely, the proper ladies of Tara would have fainted to see her cropped frilly tank top just north of a full-length hoop skirt—a territory divided by a Confederate flag navel ring in front and a yin-and-yang tattoo on the small of her back.

The first things I noticed were the deep burgundy plush carpeting on the floor in the living room contrasting with the marble foyer floor. Textured parchment color was thickly sponged onto the living room walls. In the center of the wall facing the garden, Vicki installed the funky Southern window we had found after the Kickin' Chicks soccer game. On each dark wood end table sat pink painted parlor lamps, the kind that look like double-blossomed mums. She replaced the mantle and dining room table with the same gray marble as the foyer. In the corner was a mannequin wearing a full-length gown in the exact same pattern as the curtains.

Vicki extended her white glove to me and curtseyed. "Tell me you love it. Say something, 'cause frankly my dear, I do give a damn."

"I love it," I said. And I did.

She shrieked and clapped for herself. "Let me show you the kissing parlor," she said, skipping out of the room.

"The kissing parlor?" I asked. Upon seeing my small library—or what used to be the library—I needed no further explanation.

"I hope you don't mind, but I saw this totally cute little sofa and the rest just kind of happened," Vicki said, gesturing to a pink velvet love seat in the shape of a set of women's lips. Crowding the walls were pink-framed movie posters featuring famous kisses. *Casablanca. Roman Holiday. Niagra. Transglobe.* And of course *Gone With the Wind* and *It's a Wonderful Life.* In front of the lips sofa was a glass top coffee table resting on the brushed stainless steel letters X and O. A red glass candy dish held chocolate kisses, but my favorite touches to the little-needed kissing parlor were the Blarney Stone replica in the corner and the Jimi Hendrix dummy scaling the wall to kiss the sky.

"Oh my God." I stared in awe at the transformation of a hundred-square-foot nook.

"Do you like the bottle?" Vicki asked. I hadn't seen that she'd mounted a lain wine bottle onto a wooden base with the words "Peck," "Smooch," "Smack," and "Make Out" hand painted in each quarter. "It's on a spinner, so we're always ready for a party." Vicki beamed. "I thought of that myself. No one else has their own spin-the-bottle game. Let me show you the rest." She led me by the hand to another room. "Now this is a little different than what we talked about," she warned as we stood outside the door. "But you said you find rainstorms soothing, so—" she opened the door dramatically.

I can only describe my new spare bedroom as a dry, indoor rainstorm. The walls were painted a deep bluish purple with windows tinted the same color. The ceiling was covered with umbrella tops in solid colors with metallic undersides. Hanging over the windows were sheer white curtains. The bed was covered with a deep blue comforter, which was possibly the fluffiest bedding I'd ever seen. "Triple down," Vicki said with pride, explaining that each of the eight pillows were just as luxurious. "Now watch this." Vicki flipped the switch to what I thought would be the lights, but set off a storm soundtrack. The sound of pouring rain against a tin roof filled the room and suddenly a bolt of lightning appeared from the window, which I could now see was rigged. A flash of light illuminated the umbrellas on the ceiling and curtains were breezed subtly by low fans set into the windowpanes. I was about to comment on its beauty when a crash of thunder filled the room.

"This is fantastic!" I shouted. "How clever of you to pick the guest room with the fireplace!"

"Do you love it?" she asked, already knowing I did.

We toured the rest of the house as Vicki told me about where she purchased each item and how every room evolved. She regaled me with stories of movers and contractors and how she did the impossible job of turning the house into my home in just over a week. She said that Captain John came by as she was finishing the rain room, and hired her to do some sort of nautical theme for his family room. "Do you think we could have a housewarming party and invite your friends so they can see what I've done with the place, and maybe hire me if they need?" she asked. "That's why I made you the curtain dress." She giggled. "Remember that scene? I'm your mammy!"

"You *made* the dress?"

She nodded. "Do you like it?"

"Like it? I love it!"

"Good. I want to show you one more thing," Vicki said,

reaching into her purse. She pulled out a business card with her name on it as an interior designer.

"No more stripping?" I asked.

"Hey, it was fun while it lasted, but they fired me for being late again." she grinned sheepishly. "And the bruises, you know. Not sexy."

"Not sexy?!" I gasped like Scarlet O'Hara. "Clearly these men are crazy."

Vicki was probably the sexiest woman I'd ever known. That weekend she proved it by keeping the patrons of the Lamplighter Bar roused with her absolutely horrid rendition of "Brick House." It just goes to show you that in karaoke—and in much of life—attitude is more important than talent. When I say Vicki cannot sing, I don't mean she's mediocre. She butchers a song. The notes are so flat they hurt to listen to, but boy could she pull it off anyway. She danced on the speaker, walked into the audience and sat on some old Sinatra impersonator's lap, and just looked like she was having the time of her life onstage. After the initial thirty seconds of shock that someone so beautiful could emit such cacophony, people got into her over-the-top horrible act. They sang the chorus along with Vicki, partly because they were into it, and partly to drown out her voice. When the song ended, everyone rose to their feet and cheered. A smidge tipsy, Greta missed Mike's hands for the high-five attempt. Everyone was in a drunken state of giddiness. Everyone except Adam, who suggested we call it an early night.

"And next we have Mike," said the hefty karaoke disc jockey. "Ready Mike?" Mike filled a thick gray cotton Naval Academy T-shirt and Levi's that were so well-worn, the knee was beginning to guitar-string.

"That's you." Vicki shoved her brother.

"I didn't sign up to sing." He shrugged. "Must be a different Mike."

"Mike? Is there a Mike in the house?" the man announced again.

"I signed you up," Vicki shouted him again as the music began. The words " 'Just the Way You Are' by Billy Joel" unfolded in red lettering on a large screen and piano music began.

"Come on, Mike, stop being a weeny and get up and sing," blared through a microphone. Everyone in the bar started cheering, chanting his name like the final football game in *Rudy*. He held his hands up in surrender and stumbled onto the stage just in time for the second verse. " 'And don't imagine, you're too familiar and I don't see you anymore,' " he sang a beat behind the music. His voice was uncomfortable, like he was speaking, trembling slightly. Good God, Mike was actually nervous. I loathe to confess, it was thrilling to watch. It was like seeing a glimpse of myself in a self-assured, often arrogant, guy. I snuck a peek at Adam and had the slightest tinge of guilt over the fact that I was hoping Mike was thinking of me as he sang about loving a woman just the way she is.

I would have felt thoroughly awful if Adam wasn't acting like a petulant brat that night. His arms were folded and he sulked as singers got up and worked their hardest to entertain us. I remember Vicki telling me once that, just as our teacher Tabitha promised, for every lap dance she hustled, she was rejected five times, and that it was a real ego drain. I couldn't imagine how beautiful vivacious women like Vicki could even bank a nickel of their self-worth on what a bunch of average Joes thought of them, but when I saw her get up onstage and work the crowd so hard, I saw a well-concealed hunger, an aching for adoration. Sure, Vicki was in the game for the money, but there was a natural fallout from being rejected forty times a night. I felt like Adam, with his sour puss, and disengaged body language, was rejecting Vicki and Mike. And soon it was my turn.

"Excuse me, but could one of you ladies accompany me in a duet," Ollie asked, approaching our table.

"Darlin' I'm about to take these boots out a walkin' if y'know what I mean, but maybe my friend here can help y'out?" Greta gestured toward me. Finally, she was a fully enlisted partner in crime.

"Oh no, I couldn't," I said, glancing at Adam to see if he'd encourage me.

"Go ahead, Mona," Vicki said. "This is a very nice crowd."

When you look like Vicki, every crowd is a nice one. Though this was planned and Ollie and I had been rehearsing for months, I was apprehensive. Terrified. Vicki was truly the worst singer I'd ever heard in my life. Mike was a little better. Greta—who was sizing up the width of the bar to see whether she could prance across it with her boots that were made for walkin'—has a mediocre voice. Yet I was the one who was light-headed with terror because I actually cared. There was a part of me that was dying to get up on stage and have all eyes on me. Another part was frightened not just of what I wanted, but because I wanted it. I had always been quite satisfied being life's wallpaper. That night, I wanted something more.

We waited another five songs, including Greta's shameless version of Nancy Sinatra's hit, complete with dance moves from the Vicki school of gyration. "Are y'ready boots?" she asked. "Start walking."

Ollie and I had no dance moves. I shook with fear as they called our names for our duet. We sang "Cruisin'" like Gwyneth Paltrow and Huey Lewis in *Duets*. Ollie harmonized perfectly and I made it through the tough parts I'd practiced no less than a hundred times in the shower as the audience sat silently watching us. I thought we are either bombing or rocking, but in the glare of the stage lights, I couldn't see a single face in the audience.

When we finished, the audience clapped politely, but no wild cheering like they did for the theatrics of Vicki and Greta. I returned to the table and Adam looked downright angry, but before I could ask what was bothering him, the old Sinatra guy approached our table and asked if I could sing another song for him. "Can you do something contemporary, something more urban?" he asked.

Mike winked at me, and I realized he must've set this up for me to look cool in front of Adam, like I had fans. Even though I knew it was staged, it was thrilling to have someone asking me to sing again. Or maybe it was just the prospect of singing again that was titillating. Six months ago, I would've picked Nelly Furtado's "I'm Like a Bird" because when I heard her sing that she doesn't know where her home is, or her soul is, I knew exactly what she meant. This night, I tried something different.

"Do you mind?" I asked Adam.

"Knock yourself out," he said, letting me know he wasn't at all pleased with me. It sounded like something he might say before my first boxing match.

I had another two glasses of red wine before it was my turn to go on stage. By then, all inhibitions vanished.

I winked at Vicki, who recognized the humming intro to Christina Aguilera's "Beautiful." We smiled, remembering Tabitha the stripping teacher telling us about how she sang this into the dressing room mirror before she started her shift. Before I could wonder how the rest of them were doing—how Betty Paige's wedding went, if the Viagra prescription was filled, how the coffee table pole dancing was going—it was my turn. " 'Every day is so wonderful,' " I began.

Being on stage alone is possibly the most naked and vulnerable feeling I'd ever experienced. Still, naked and vulnerable had its advantages. There was a potential payoff from naked vulnerability that cloistered anonymity just did not offer. I squinted to see Mike, who gave me a thumbs-up. I don't even remember singing the song. I just remember that when I finished, my group howled applause and the rest of the bar seemed to join in. Sinatra came back and handed me his card. "You got a great sound," he said. "You working with anybody?" *Shit, now I'm going to have to reveal that I have been taking voice lessons.*

"You mean, like a voice teacher?"

He laughed. "I mean an agent."

Mike winked again, and I realized that I'd recruited a true believer in the art of public relations. How sweet of him to stage this for me. I grinned and winked back.

"No. I just sing in the shower," I told Sinatra.

"That's a waste. Give me a call this week. We're looking for a cute young thing with your kind of sound to front a new girl band we're putting together. You may be a good fit. No promises, but who knows."

*Classic!*

"Oh, okay." I winked at Sinatra.

As we all walked toward our cars, I sidled up to Mike and whispered "thank you" in his ear.

"For what?"

"For that. Back at the bar."

"For singing?"

"No, stupid! For Sinatra. He was perfect. I don't think Adam was too impressed by it, but it was sweet of you to set up."

"Mona Lisa, you're drunk."

"This is true, but it's also true that you're a total sweetheart."

"Don't get me wrong, I'm into the sweet talk, and if you dink Grumpy over there, I'll give you something to really thank me for, but I don't know what you're talking about."

"That Sinatra guy!" I reminded him by drawing out the sentence. "The way he came over and asked me to sing, then gave me his card for his chick band. That was your doing." Mike stared blankly. "Wasn't it?" He said nothing. "Wasn't it?!"

"Mona Lisa, I don't know what you're talking about."

"I am so on to you, Mr. Navy sticker putter-oner," I slurred.

"Mona, listen to me. I put the sticker on your car. I didn't put that guy up to approaching you."

*Really? Someone really and truly thought I might be good enough to sing in a band? Ahhhhhhh!* I silently screamed with elation. *Ahhhhhhhhh!*

"Oh." I smiled. "That could be fun."

# Chapter 41

As it turned out, Adam had no particular affinity for music. Every article I'd found in my Google search which quoted him loving opera and theatre, and contributing to the chamber orchestra, was actually written about his father—Adam P. Ziegler. Further, Adam explained on the drive home that evening, he didn't like seeing me sing with another man.

"First of all, you were pouting waaaaay before I sang, and secondly I was just singing. It wasn't like, like we were . . . I can't even believe I'm explaining this to you! Who cares if I sang with someone else?"

"I care!" he shouted. "And if you cared about me, you'd care, too. Mona, I am starting to have very real feelings for you, and it seems as though I'm in this alone!"

And suddenly all of my righteous indignation evaporated. Adam was right. I had been using him to fill a void all along, and it was patently unfair to him. He wasn't the E ticket to the wonderful life I'd hoped for, but he was a kind and decent person who deserved better than what he was getting from me. That night I vowed, I would absolutely, positively put an end to this scam of a relationship. And yet, when he dropped me off, I told him I'd see him soon.

\* \* \*

For the next few days, I avoided calling Adam and screened my answering machine messages, picking up only for Greta and Mike. Finally, Friday night I heard his voice on the answering machine and realized my cowardice was bordering on cruelty.

"Hi, Adam." I picked up the phone breathless, hoping he'd think I just walked in the door.

"Hi, Mona." Awkward silence. "I want to apologize for the other night."

*Nooooooo! Please don't apologize to me.*

He continued. "I was out of line being jealous over your singing with another guy. You were fantastic, by the way. I wouldn't be at all surprised if that band wanted you to be its lead singer."

"Oh, um, thanks, Adam. You really shouldn't be the one apologizing, though. I could see you were having a bad time and I should've suggested we leave."

"No, you shouldn't have. I should have snapped out of my mood. People in relationships need to focus on their partner's needs before their own. That's what I believe. Anyway, I was hoping we could get together Saturday night."

"Oh, thanks," I hesitated. "I'm going to the theatre with Vicki, Greta, Mike, and two women from the Kickin' Chicks. How 'bout midweek?"

"What are you guys seeing?" Adam asked.

"I'm not sure. Vicki's going to pick up tickets at the half-price kiosk downtown tomorrow. Whatever they have six tickets for that night is what we'll end up seeing."

"Oh, in that case, do you mind if I come along?"

*Adam, we need to talk.*

*Adam, it's not you, it's me.*

*This relationship has run its course.*

"Okay!" I said with too much enthusiasm. I sounded like the head cheerleader getting the squad ready for the halftime show.

At dinner Saturday night, I gasped with horror that I'd forgotten to tell Adam where to meet us for the play. Vicki held up her hand as she finished chewing her grilled salmon. "Mmmmm, not a problem," she said. "He called this morning while you were at the gym, and I gave him the details. He'll meet us there. I told him to look for Mike and Greta if we weren't there right at seven-thirty."

"What are we seeing anyway?" I asked Vicki.

"Oh, you'll love it. It's a musical adaptation of *It's a Wonderful Life*. One of the girls from the team saw it last weekend and said it was wild. One of those 'different' theatre companies, you know."

"*It's a Wonderful Life* in June? Hmmm, weird."

"Very weird," she said. "It got written up by the *San Diego Reader* as the most bizarre production to come out of San Diego since Sledgehammer did *Faust on Ice* in 1992."

I wish I could report whether or not the musical adaptation of *It's a Wonderful Life* was weird, but I only saw the first ten minutes of the play. Adam sat on my right side wearing a fresh pressed canary yellow oxford shirt and khaki pants, fidgeting with his program. Mike was seated to my immediate left with a denim shirt and jeans staring straight at the closed velvet curtain. "How's it going?" I tapped him on the knee.

"It's going." He shrugged. The lights dimmed. I heard the familiar opening of Billy Joel's "Allentown." A chorus of townspeople marched on the stage with Christmas ornaments in hand and began singing, *"Well we're living here in Bedford Falls, and George Bailey thinks the time just crawls. And his life has made no difference, but he is*

*wrong, shows angel Clarence. And it's really been a won*
*derful life. And George Bailey's got a wonderful wife. And*
*his kids are happy kids then died, if he jumped off that*
*bridge they'd be so sad. And so would all the folks of*
*Bedford Falls."*

Mike looked at me in terror as if to say he couldn't bear
another hour and a half of such shameless corniness. The
scene changed to the Bailey living room where George en-
ters after he learns his uncle misplaced eight thousand dollars.

Adam whispered as George Bailey appeared on stage,
"He looks exactly like your ex-boyfriend, Poison."

*Shiiiiit!*

Bailey's adoring wife wraps her black-and-white dress
sleeves around his waist. "Oh honey, it's Christmas Eve,
try not to think about that mean old Potter anymore."

Adam squinted at the actress. "Is that the lady who
passed out at the zoo?"

*Oh my God! Soon he's going to see Potter, who—*

Knock, knock, knock on the set door. Julie opened the
door and held her hand to her head. "Potter!" she yelped.
"Can't you leave us alone on Christmas Eve, you mean
and greedy old man?!"

"What the—" Adam said louder than he should've in a
theatre.

"Shhh," I rested my hand on his leg. "I'll explain later."

"That's the guy you sang with last week at the bar!" Adam
shouted and stood. "What the hell is going on here?" The
actors were startled into silence by the irate audience
member, but soon continued with the show.

"Sit down, Adam," I whispered. "I'll explain this all to
you later."

"You will explain it to me now!" he shouted and stood.
I looked up at the stage to apologize, but caught Ollie di-

recting his lighting crew to turn the spot on Adam. The rest stood agape, completely out of character and engrossed in what I would say or do to explain myself. I expected someone in the audience to speak up and urge Adam to sit down, but all eyes were on him—and me. Suddenly, I was in the spotlight, too, and everyone was waiting for an answer. "Who are these people?" Adam demanded.

"They're actors, Adam," I said, hushing him.

"But George Bailey is your ex-boyfriend from a heavy metal band!" Adam snapped. The audience looked as though they were watching a tennis match. Every head simultaneously turned to me for the answer, though they were all thoroughly confused by the question.

"Adam, can we talk about this later?" I begged.

"Why were you singing karaoke with Potter at a bar last weekend?" Adam shouted.

I heard a woman three rows back whisper, "This is such an original production." I realized about half of the people in the audience probably assumed that Adam's outburst was part of the show because of the spotlight on us. At that point, Toby peeked his head out from behind the curtain. "Mona, you were mugged by that angel!" Adam shouted when he saw Toby in his Clarence regalia. "And isn't that woman in the feathered hat your former lesbian lover?! I absolutely demand to know what's going on here!"

This time the actors stopped dead and turned to me. All eyes in the audience were on me. Everyone wanted to know what Adam was talking about.

"I was . . . I tried . . . Adam, it's not how it seems," I stammered.

"I loved you!" he shouted. "I was going to ask you to marry me. I don't even know who the hell you are. What kind of nut are you?!"

"Okay, buddy, you're gonna have to back off now." Mike finally stood up to defend me. Suddenly, a spot light shone on him. "Fuck," he said, resigned, as if he saw that coming. Then he went on. "Ease up on Mona, man. She was doing all this 'cause she wanted you to like her."

"*What* was she doing?!" Adam shouted at Mike.

"Settle down, buddy."

"Why don't you make me settle down, *buddy*?" Adam challenged.

The woman three rows back whispered, "I've got to tell Louise about this show."

Mike ignored the challenge to a fight and turned to me sitting in the seat between them. I had momentarily shrunk back into obscurity, but Mike grabbed my hand and I was in the spotlight again. Softly he said, "Look, Mona, I know this isn't the best timing, but I gotta tell you, I love you, too. My whole . . . the way I . . . I don't know, I just love you, Mona Lisa. When you first hired me, I thought you had a screw loose, but man, the more I got to know you, the more I felt completely and totally at home with you. You're the first woman I've been able to really be myself with. Not even myself, better than myself. Like the me I didn't know I could be. I don't know, maybe it's because you weren't even on the radar as a possible girlfriend; there wasn't any need to impress you or pull my usual bullshit. It was like since there was no possibility of us getting together, we could hang out and I could, I don't know, just be me and just being me made me better than me, does that make any sense at all? Don't answer that, I know it doesn't, but I don't care. I love you, Mona. I'm like crazy, freakin' in love, wanna be your pussy-whipped husband in love with you, Mona. And you know I never get sappy like this, but I can't stand watching you try to impress this clown anymore when you and I both know that it's you and me who belong together."

The group of audience members surrounding us let out a big "Ahhhhh!"

Someone from the back shouted, "What'd he say?!"

"He said he loves her. Shush," Vicki returned.

Greta closed her eyes, looking as though she was mortified at the public display. But then she rose from her seat and right on cue, she was at the center of a bright circle of light. "Mona, I've been giving you a hard time for months over these public relations stunts you've been pulling to lure in Adam."

Her preamble was interrupted by Adam. "Okay, finally I'm getting a little insight into what the hell is going on here."

"Shut up!" three people in the audience snapped at Adam. "Somebody else is talking, Mr. Big Mouth," one said.

Greta looked toward the ground then shot her head up like she was about to lead the troops into battle. "Anyway, it's me who's been the fraud here. At least you were honest about what you want. I haven't even had the guts to tell you who I really am, and that, that . . . Good Lord, help me, but Terry back in Texas is a woman, and I left her because she wanted more of a commitment from me, but I couldn't do it. I couldn't stay with her any longer because I love *you*, Mona."

"Hot diggity dog," a guy in the audience said as he rubbed his hands together in delight.

From onstage, Ollie shouted, "Enough!" And finally, the show returned to its rightful venue. At last, Ollie had decided to put an end to this spectacle and resume his production. "Mona, I love you, too," he declared.

*Ollie?*

"Ever since you walked into my theatre that day I was

smitten. No one questions the director, but here came this little pistol telling me that my choices are all wrong, and that I wasn't being true to the script." He sighed audibly. "And then when we sang together, that was it. That voice. It's intoxicating and I am utterly intoxicated by you, Mona Warren."

"Isn't she great?" Vicki shouted to Ollie. "That guy at the bar turned out to be legit and Mona may front a new chick band." This hardly seemed the time for a chat, but people in the audience began muttering that they were impressed. The woman three rows back even wished me luck, so all things considered, Vicki's update wasn't too out of line.

From the back row, a guy I'd never seen before stood up and declared his love for me, too. Even with the spotlight on him, I had no idea who he was.

"Do I know you?" I asked.

"No, baby, but three guys and a lesbian can't be wrong. You must be one hot number."

"I like the second boy," said a yenta in the front row. "That other one—shouting, shouting, shouting. Not very nice. Mona needs a sensitive boy like number two."

From onstage, Julie offered, "Ollie is very nice, too."

The yenta replied, "Eh, she could do worse, but my money's on number two."

"His name is Mike," Vicki corrected.

"Well, then I like Mike." She smiled at Vicki, who returned the gesture.

"Take the lesbian!" shouted the same guy who was fired up over Greta's declaration. "Take me *and* the lesbian." Greta rolled her eyes.

Soon, nearly everyone from the audience and cast was shouting their suggestions at me. Most were rooting for Mike. Many of the men wanted Greta, though their motives were questionable. And a handful thought I should give Ollie a shot. No one lobbied for Adam, least of all Adam.

"Take Mike!"

"Go with the chick!"

"Ollie's a good guy."

"Shut up!" I shouted at the top of my lungs. "This is *not* elimiDATE," I said more calmly. "These are people with feelings and you're treating them like they're each a disposable commodity. Please, please, be quiet for just a moment." I inhaled deeply at the annoyance of being yet again in the bright heat of the spotlight. "Adam, I'm so sorry. I fell in love with you seven years ago from afar and thought so little of myself that I orchestrated all of these scenarios because I thought I couldn't win you over on my own. I figured you'd find me more interesting if I dated rock stars or saved lives, but everything I tried failed miserably, and frankly I can't believe you fell in love with me in spite of everything. I mean, I looked like a total loser and you still loved me. You can't possibly know what a gift that is to me, Adam. I swear, I love you for that, Adam. I do love you as a person and for what you've given me, but I'm not in love *with* you, and that's the first thing I've ever told you that is completely honest. That, and I'm so sorry that I hurt you."

Adam said nothing.

"Greta, you are my best friend in the world. You were a friend to me when no one else was, and these last few months that you've been back in San Diego have been wonderful. I love you dearly, but I'm just not a lesbian. I'm glad you are, though. I mean, I'm glad that if that's who you are, you finally told me. And again, I can't believe that knowing what you know about me, you still developed feelings, but just like you can't change who you are, I can't

change, who I am." Greta smiled. I honestly don't think
she was ever truly in love with me as much as she loved me
as a friend as a teen, the same time she was coming to
terms with her sexuality. "And Ollie, I don't know what to
say. I've enjoyed singing with you, but we hardly know each
other. I think you're a sweetheart and maybe we could've
had a shot at something had you not directed your lighting
crew to spot everyone for our little sideshow here." I
laughed. "Ollie, you're the first man who's ever said I was
a bossy pain in the ass. You're the first person who's ever
characterized me this way, and knowing that I can be accepted and even loved this way is invaluable to me."

"What about me?" the guy in the back shouted.

"Sir, I don't even know you."

"Strangers need love, too."

"Mike." My voice quivered. "I'll be honest, though it's
fairly new territory for me. You scare me. I was about two
inches from falling in love with you the moment we met.
There's something so unbelievably compelling about you,
but you can be so detached. There are times when you are
so completely disengaged from the real you, I can't tell
which is the persona and which is the real Mike—the column or the guy who glued my mug back together. I would
love to throw myself into your arms and end this show
with the big Hollywood kiss, but you scare me. Once I let
myself fall in love with you, I'm not sure I can fall out. But
you might, and Mike," my eyes filled with tears, "I can't
risk losing another person I love, so I'm going to just hold
off on this one with you. If you really love me, you'll wait.
And I know this sounds odd, but I kind of need to see that
you'll wait."

I realized that the entire theatre was silent, disappointed
that I didn't give them the ending they'd hoped for. Shockingly, our whole group—even Adam—was still seated, and

seemingly ready to watch the rest of *It's a Wonderful Life, The Musical.*

Ollie waited to see that I'd finished. "Okay, then, as they say, the show must go on."

*"Well we're living here in Bedford Falls,"* a group began to sing as I rushed from the theatre and caught a taxi back to my quiet home.

# Chapter 42

---

Six months after the staged Christmas at the Bailey home, I finally got my old-fashioned family holiday. It was quite different looking than the one I fantasized about in Larry Fontaine's office last year. Twenty of us were scattered across the house. Greta and Vicki helped me in the kitchen while Mike set the dining room table. Christmas music filled the living room and sun poured into Tara. There was a feeling that while tomorrow may be another day, life was pretty wonderful today.

Vicki brought a cup of eggnog to her new husband, Captain John, which I must confess took a little getting used to. Somewhere between redecorating his family room and the bedrooms, something sparked between them. When she finished the job she asked what he thought of the house, and he replied, "It could look a lot better with you as a permanent fixture," and presented her with a rock that rivals any self-respecting doorknob. Mike had a hard time with it at first and kept calling the captain the "Quaker Oats guy." When the word got out that Vicki was a stripper, everyone on the island started buzzing that she was our hometown Anna Nicole Smith, but two weeks later, one of the most successful real estate brokers' sons drove his father's Porsche into the family room of a three-million dollar beachfront listing, and all gossip was refocused on the O'Connor boy's DUI.

Greta and Brooke got together after the Kickin' Chicks season opener. They are two of the most fierce and intense athletes I've ever seen play soccer. I shudder to think of the sex they have. Then, I just stop thinking about it. What I love most about Brooke is how she calls Greta on her need to psychoanalyze the other teammates. I laughed at the thought that in my makeshift family, a lesbian mid-fielder was my new sister-in-law. My eighty-year-old brother-in-law was my grandmother's former illicit lover who married a stripper-gone-decorator. My, how Coronado had changed. And all under one roof.

Sitting at the piano, Ollie asked if anyone had another request and Julie said she'd like to hear "Auld Lang Syne." "After dinner, Ollie," she said. "Everyone's starving."

"Shall we say grace?" asked Francesca. She moved in about two weeks after Thanksgiving when I called to tell her I was pregnant. She said that while she's enjoyed her life in Missoula, she was ready to be surrounded by family again. With that, I felt a marble in my throat and invited her to come and live with Mike and me. God knows, neither of us has a clue how to take care of a baby. She was the house grandmother we desperately needed. An ordained minister, she plans to marry us next week.

Mike's contract with *Maximum for Him* was not renewed after Mike dared to suggest that uncomplicated love with a woman was possible and even probable if both sexes stopped thinking of themselves as inhabitants of different planets. Of course, a great deal of Mike's identity was as The Dog, so he went through a bit of depression when he got kicked out of the Dog House. A week later, he got a call from *Glamour* asking Mike to take over as the new

"Jake," the columnist who offers women the inside scoop on how men think. And he got an enormous advance to work on a new book on male-female relationships. Working title: *Who Let the Dog Out?* Proudly, I smiled upon hearing the title. I did, I thought. Mona Lisa did.

As for me, I made the cut for the chick band, which ultimately named itself Total Fraud (my suggestion). We sing everything from AC/DC to Norah Jones to hip-hop and play local dive bars on the weekends. Our first CD will be released this spring. No one seems to mind that I'll be visibly pregnant by then, and as long as California bars remain smoke-free, I have no issues going on stage as big as a house. I also had my first real boxing match in September and was treated to a serious ass-kicking. I was knocked out in the second round. Tio thought I could've done better, but when I came to, and they told me what had happened, I said "It took her two whole rounds to knock me out, that's pretty damned good." I was most proud of the fact that I got up and walked out of the ring on my own. My next fight, I lost by judge's decision. Three rounds totally conscious. I am a champion. Of course, my *Rocky* days are over, at least until the baby arrives.

The only one who was missing from our night at the theatre was Adam. I called his office in September to ask him a question about my filings and the honker said he'd left the family business. "Yeah, one day last summer he came in, said to hell with his obligation to the family business, that Southern California was full of nut cases and he took off for Oklahoma. Can you believe it?" I did. And I was happy for him.

As we sat down to eat, Mike squeezed my knee under the table. "Hey, happy birthday, Mona Lisa."

"Yes," I said, smiling at him.

The doorbell rang just as Captain John began carving

the turkey. I looked at Mike, who was sitting closest to the door. Vicki looked at him, too, as if he were a clod for not getting up to answer the door.

"Remember the first time you rang that doorbell?" I asked him.

He grinned as the doorbell rang a second time. Who was at the door? I wondered. All of our friends and family were already at the dinner table.

"Do you know what that means?" I dreamily asked Mike.

"An angel got his wings?" he offered.

Vicki shot, "It means there's someone at the door, you spaced-out lovebirds. Listen, if neither of you is going to answer it, I will."

"Atta girl, Vicki," Mike winked at me.

"Atta girl," we finished together.